W9-AEK-158

BOYS "DON'T" KNIT

(In public)

T. S. EASTON

FEIWEL AND FRIENDS · NEW YORK

SQUARE
FISH

An Imprint of Macmillan
175 Fifth Avenue
New York, NY 10010
fiercereads.com

BOYS DON'T KNIT. Copyright © 2015 by T. S. Easton.
All rights reserved. Printed in the United States of America by
LSC Communications, Harrisonburg, Virginia.

Square Fish and the Square Fish logo are trademarks of Macmillan and
are used by Feiwel and Friends under license from Macmillan.

Our books may be purchased in bulk for promotional, educational, or business
use. Please contact your local bookseller or the Macmillan Corporate and
Premium Sales Department at (800) 221-7945 ext. 5442 or by e-mail
at MacmillanSpecialMarkets@macmillan.com

Library of Congress Cataloging-in-Publication Data
Easton, Tom (Children's fiction writer)
Boys don't knit / T. S. Easton.
pages cm
Summary: After a brush with the law, Ben, a dyed-in-the-wool worrier, must take
up a new hobby and chooses knitting, an activity at which he excels but must
try to keep secret from his friends, enemies, and sports-obsessed father.
ISBN 978-1-250-07354-9 (paperback)   ISBN 978-1-250-06655-8 (ebook)
[1. Knitting—Fiction.   2. Conduct of life—Fiction.   3. Family life—
England—Fiction.   4. England—Fiction.   5. Humorous stories.]
I. Title.   II. Title: Boys do not knit.
PZ7.E13159Boy 2015
[Fic]—dc23
2014042419

Originally published in the United States by Feiwel and Friends
First Square Fish Edition: 2016
Book designed by April Ward
Square Fish logo designed by Filomena Tuosto

10 9 8 7 6 5 4 3 2

AR: 10.0 / LEXILE: HL720L

JULY 1ST

Mum and Dad are at it again. They're doing that thing where they make food-based double entendres all the time, thinking it goes over our heads. It goes over Molly's head; she's only six and she never listens to Mum or Dad anyway. I guess it used to go over my head too, when I was little. But I'm older now, and more sophisticated. I know what they're up to and it makes me want to vomit.

On Friday night, we had chicken and baked potatoes. As she was serving, Mum said, "Dave, could you get the spuds out?"

And Dad said, "I'm always happy to get my spuds out for you."

This is what passes for humor in our house. Though that wasn't quite as sick-making as today when we had a BBQ down in the park. Mum was carrying too much from the car and nearly dropped a pack of burger buns.

"Let me take hold of your buns, Susan," Dad said.

"Don't squeeze them too hard," Mum replied, giggling.

How can I make them stop?! Surely they know I understand the concept of the double entendre, even if Molly is too young to get it. In fact, I know they know, because Dad winked at me as he made the bun comment, trying to include me in the "joke." They've both been trying to be more inclusive and chummy with me lately, ever since the lollipop lady incident. It's like they've talked it over and decided it must have been their fault and that I need more support or something. I liked it better the way it was when they'd just ignore me and offer no support whatsoever.

Mum and Dad never really got angry with me about the lollipop lady, even when that policewoman told Dad he might be made to attend an Effective Parenting Course. Even when I had to go to the magistrates' court. Even when I got probation for twelve months. It's the first time I've ever been in any real trouble. To be quite honest, I think a part of Dad was pleased I'd finally done something "cunning," as he put it. He's always telling me stories about the scrapes he used to get into with his friends.

Anyway, Bun-gate wasn't the only embarrassing thing that happened at the BBQ today. Dad insisted on bringing his big iron bucket barbecue, which is about the size of the Olympic cauldron. We'd had to come in his work truck as it wouldn't have fit in the back of Mum's car. Dad had filled it with equal thirds of wood, briquettes, and fire starters. Thankfully Molly had disappeared into the woods down near the river, looking for animals.

"Are you sure you're allowed to light that thing here?" I asked uncertainly.

"The sign says you're allowed barbecues as long as they're raised off the grass," Mum said. She was sitting on a bench, twisting her long fingers, practicing her magic by making boiled eggs disappear, one by one.

"I think, though," I said, "that they mean those little disposable jobs you get from the hardware store, rather than the nuclear fission–fueled thing we've got. We only have one pack of sausages and some chicken drumsticks to cook. We're not burning a Viking chief."

Dad ignored me, as he usually did when he thought I was fussing. That's what they think I'm doing. Fussing. But it's not fussing, it's worrying, and with good reason, because people around me like to do stupid things.

It was then that I noticed Megan Hooper with her family. They were at a picnic table about a hundred yards away. There she was, sweet Megan Hooper with her ample chest, sitting next to her weirdly hot mother and opposite her normal-looking dad and her quiet little brother with the enormous Bambi eyes. They had a little supermarket barbecue and were laughing and eating posh crisps one by one and they just looked so neat and organized and I found myself wishing I were part of their family.

"Seriously though, Dad," I said haltingly, as he squirted flammable liquid over the critical mass. "Maybe you should take out some of the fire starters?"

"Nah, it'll be fine, Ben," he replied. "You need heat when you're cooking on a barbecue. You've got to make sure it's hot enough to cook the meat all the way through, do you see?"

I could see all too well. So I stepped back, and he stepped forward and dropped in a match.

The ensuing fireball must have been visible from space.

It was okay, though, because Mum's since drawn his eyebrows back on with eyeliner. We had to wait forty-five minutes before the barbecue had cooled enough to cook on and then it only took about twenty-six seconds to burn the chicken. But just when I noticed that the sausages were looking comparatively good, Dad took away my appetite.

"Give that one there to your mum, she likes a nice, long sausage."

I couldn't bring myself to look over at the Hoopers while all this was going on, but I could feel them looking back at my messy family standing around Mt. Vesuvius, their eyes on my back hotter than the barbecue itself.

Why does no one ever listen to me? This is how I got into trouble in the first place, because no one would listen to me.

JULY 3RD

Today I received a letter from Claudia Gunter at West Meon Probation Services. The letter was reminding me that under the terms of my probation I need to keep a "journal."

She sent a template for me to follow, as though I were some illiterate.

This annoys me. I've been keeping a diary for more than half my life. It's true that some of the earlier entries were a little rough. I read back through them last month and it was mostly self-pitying rants about not being allowed to watch *Antiques Roadshow* (why did I even ever want to?) or having to go to bed before I'd finished sorting out my stamp collection. I'm aware that keeping a diary is considered part of the female domain, but in my life, with the family and friends I'm stuck with, it is the only reason I haven't run away and gone to live in the woods.

Anyway, I clearly remember telling Ms. Gunter about my diary during our interview after the court appearance, so I assumed there'd been some sort of mistake. I phoned her on the number at the bottom of the letter. It took an age for her to come to the phone and she seemed a little distracted when I explained who it was.

"Who? Fletcher? Oh, hello, Ben, how are you doing?"

"I'm well, thanks, but I think there's been some confusion with the letter."

"What letter?" she asked.

"The letter I received today asking me to keep a diary."

"Oh, okay," she said. "The computer sends those. It's just a reminder."

"I told you in our meeting of the seventh of June that I already keep a diary."

There was a slight pause. Did I detect a sigh?

"Well, that's fine then, isn't it?" she said. "Just keep going with your normal diary."

"But there's a template attached to the letter. And the letter says I need to hand it in at the end of the probationary period."

"Okay," she said slowly. "What's the problem exactly, Ben?"

Claudia Gunter is clearly a busy woman, which perhaps explains why she was being a little slow. I pointed out that I couldn't very well keep going in my usual diary if I had to hand it in. It's leather-bound.

"Should I stop writing in my usual diary," I went on, "and switch to the template?"

"You can't do both?" she asked, sounding tired.

"I write a lot and won't have time to do both. I'm doing AS levels this year."

"So use the template," she said.

"But then I'll need to hand it in," I told her. "And I won't have it anymore."

"Can't you photocopy it?" she spluttered. "Look, Ben. You're a bright kid, if slightly . . . unusual. I'm not really that worried about you, to be honest; I have a hundred and four other clients, most of whom don't speak English, some of whom have murdered people. One of them killed an ice-cream vendor and ate his kidneys out of a waffle cone. Just sort it out, okay?"

I told her I would and hung up.

Ben Fletcher
3 Standish Place
Hampton
United Kingdom

June 28th

Dear Ben,

As part of your Fresh Paths Social Contract Probation Journey, you have been asked to complete a personal journal, giving as full an account as possible of the events of each day and recording, in detail, your thoughts, concerns and feelings. You are expected to complete at least two entries a week for the full term of your Probation Journey (twelve months). At the end of this period you will be asked to hand the journal to your probation officer. Please be assured the contents of the journal will be strictly confidential. Whilst the Home Office may use the information therein for statistical or research purposes, your name will not be attached to the document. You should therefore feel free to write whatever you like about your life, your family, your school and your circle of friends.

Research shows that only a small minority of teenage boys keep diaries and we realize this may be a daunting prospect. We have attached a series of simple guidelines to help with your initial entries. Feel free to adapt or ignore these template suggestions if you feel confident to write the journal in your own style; remember, this is a private dialogue between you and your diary. As long as the writing is legible, it's up to you how you control the format.

I wish you success in your endeavor.

Yours,

Claudia Gunter

West Meon Probation Services

JULY 4TH

Introduce yourself to your journal—remember, your journal does not know who you are, it can't see you and it only knows what you choose to write in it.

My diary knows very well who I am, thank you. But for the purposes of the exercise, I'll go along with this for now. I'm all over the template idea, believe me. Call me Mr. Template. Otherwise known as Ben Fletcher. My friends sometimes call me Bellend Ben, which I'm not so keen on. I didn't even know what a bellend was when Gex first called me that. In case someone at West Meon Probation Services is as confused as I was, a bellend is the tip of the male reproductive organ. So named because it looks like a bell—sort of.

I am small and thin with black hair and brown eyes. I don't like sports, though my mum thinks I like soccer. I don't like cars, though my dad thinks I like Jeremy Clarkson, the loudmouthed, conservative presenter of popular motoring program *Top Gear*. I don't like fighting, though Lloyd Manning from school thinks I like being punched in the back of the head. What do I like? I like writing and reading and math and organizing things. I sort of like spending time with my friends, though I'm constantly worried about what new trouble they're going to get me into.

Why have you chosen to keep a journal?

Again, and without wishing to belabor the point, I've been keeping a DIARY for years. Now here comes West Meon Probation Services with their fancy template arrangement. The reason I chose to keep a DIARY was because sometimes my head is so full of thoughts and worries and confusion that the only way I can make sense of it all is to write it down on a clean, lined sheet of paper. Once it's written down, it's sort of locked into place and I can stop worrying about it for a bit. I suppose that at the heart of it, I keep a diary to try and bring a bit of order into my mad world.

JULY 5TH

What were the circumstances surrounding the events that led to you being placed on probation?

The problem with my friends is that they don't really think things through. Not like me. My role is always to be the one who points out how mad/dangerous/illegal their escapades are. They're not bad people. They're just stupid people. And needless to say, they never listen to me. Somehow though, I'm always the one who ends up paying for it.

So this is what happened, the whole truth.

It was a Thursday. We were hanging out in my yard because I had to look after my sister while Mum and Dad were both out. Molly was in the overgrown hedge at the bottom of the garden stalking young blackbirds with a fishing net.

My friends and I were discussing the fact that Anaya Anabussi was having an end-of-term party on the Friday, which none of us had been invited to, but Gex reckoned he could get us in because Anaya's sister, Seneira, fancied him.

"I don't really want to go," I said. "I don't like parties."

Too much noise, too many people. I get anxious. And, since I'd just end up hanging out with Joz, Gex and Freddie anyway, why did we have to go to someone else's house to do it?

"They won't let us in without a bottle of liquor each," Freddie said.

"Well, that settles it," I said, relieved. "None of us has any money. Let's just hang around here."

But Gex had other thoughts. There's a side of him that makes me uneasy. He thought we should go and shoplift some booze from Waitrose in town. Waitrose, being such a high-end supermarket, isn't so security conscious as the more down-market Lidl, where they employ Rod Hogan as the security guard, who used to be the bouncer at Wicked nightclub before he got fired for snotting on the deejay.

"Why is shoplifting always the answer?" I asked.

"What do you suggest, Hermione?" Freddie asked. He lay sprawled on the creaky deck chair hidden behind retro sunglasses. He was starting to go pink. "Maybe we could raise money by selling fairy cakes at the farmer's market?"

Joz laughed. I gave him a look. Why wasn't he backing me up? I knew he didn't like breaking the law any more than I did.

"I'm just trying to be, you know, moral about it," I said.

"Shoplifting is stealing. There must be ways of raising money honestly."

"Yeah," Joz said. Finally he was speaking up. "Freddie, can't you sell the dope I gave you last week?"

"Nah, smoked it," Freddie said as I buried my face into my palms.

"Oh cripes," I moaned. "I really don't think this is a good idea."

"Just chill, my man," Gex said, taking charge. "Since you're a wuss, you can be lookout."

I sighed. Gex had totally missed the point again. I'm not cut out for stealing. I like things to be done fair and square. I'm racked with guilt if I help myself to more ice cream than anyone else at dinner. I once found a wallet on the street with twenty-five pounds in it and handed it in to the police station. I'm a good guy. I'm a civilian.

"I especially don't like the idea of stealing from Waitrose," I said, trying to make a joke out of it. "It doesn't matter so much if you nick from the ninety-nine-p shop on Argyll Street, you're doing them a favor helping to clear the stock, but Waitrose? It just feels wrong."

"They don't sell alcohol in the ninety-nine-p shop," Freddie pointed out, even further adrift from the point than Gex had been. Freddie's not the brightest, as we discovered in French last year when he admitted he thought "conjugate" was a scandal involving a stage magician.

"Why do you want to go to this party anyway?" I asked Gex, trying a different tack. "You don't fancy Seneira; you said her new haircut makes her look like Professor Snape."

"Crumpet is crumpet," Joz contributed unhelpfully.

"You don't look at the mantelpiece when you're poking the fire," Freddie agreed.

"True dat," said Gex. "And if I make myself available, it gets you guys into the party, you feel?"

"Oh, right," I said. "You're doing it for us."

"Taking a hit for the crew," he said.

Anyway, so after my parents came back, we biked up the hill into town and there I was sitting on the bench behind the checkout at Waitrose, heart pounding, pretending to text but really watching out for the guard. If he turned up I was supposed to send a warning group text to everyone's phones, which were on vibrate. The plan was that Freddie and Joz would grab a couple of bottles each, fill up a cart with loads of other crap, then when no one was looking they'd slip a bottle under the front wheel of the trolley and push it toward the checkout, rolling the bottle as they went. If anyone saw, they'd just act all surprised, like "How did that get there?" As the trolley got close to the lanes, they'd stop suddenly and the bottle would keep rolling, right through the checkout aisle and under the seat where Gex was sitting. He'd shove the bottles into a bag and walk right out. Then Freddie and Joz could just abandon the trolleys and go out the other door.

I still wasn't happy about the criminal aspect, but I was starting to feel it might actually work. That is, until I heard a voice.

"Hey, Ben. Don't usually see you in here."

It was Megan Hooper—or Hooters, as Joz calls her for reasons which I probably don't need to spell out. She was sitting behind the till on aisle nine, waiting for the next customer. Megan's all right. Probably not the most attractive girl at school. And considering how hot her mum is, probably not even the most attractive girl in her own family, but that's a good thing because pretty girls scare me.

The best thing about Megan is that she doesn't call me Bellend.

"Just, er. Just picking up some things for Anaya's party tomorrow," I said, trying not to look guiltily at Freddie and Joz, who were, in turn, trying not to look guiltily at the security cameras as they ran a trolley down the cheese aisle like they were auditioning for *Jackass*.

"Oh, you going to that?" she said. "I was invited but I wasn't sure if I should go."

"Uh-huh . . ." I mumbled, only half listening as I watched the boys come to a sudden stop. All the random food they'd put in their trolley crashed forward and I winced as loads of shoppers turned to look. But it actually worked out well as everyone was too busy tutting at the hoodies to notice the bottle of Bell's whiskey rolling cheerily between checkouts seven and eight and into Gex's rucksack as he sat casually reading a recipe card for zucchini pasta bake.

"So should I go, do you think?" Megan was asking. I turned back to her. She was smiling at me. That doesn't usually happen. I normally get this look from girls like I've got a small piece of dog poo stuck on the end of my nose.

"Yeah, sure, it might be fun," I replied.

"See you there, then," she said.

"See you there, then," I repeated, like an idiot.

Then she had a customer and I went and sat at another bench, watching her work, smiling at the customer. Soon there was another crash in the aisles and a few seconds later a second bottle rolled gently into Gex's bag.

The situation wasn't ideal, but maybe it wouldn't be such a bad day after all, I thought to myself as the third bottle rolled cheerily between the checkouts. The Great Trolley Robbery was proceeding, and I had a sort of date with a real live girl who was in a narrow bracket, being both pretty datable and also in my league.

That is, it was going great until Freddie grabbed a bottle of gin. Nothing wrong with gin, except this particular bottle wasn't round, it was semicircular. I watched him in alarm, frantically texting as Freddie shoved the misshapen bottle under the wheels, got a good long run up toward the checkouts and stopped suddenly. Of course, this bottle didn't roll, but instead slid noisily across the floor, stopping right behind a customer at the checkout, who stepped back and tripped over it. The bottle shot forward and shattered against a stack of shopping baskets and they had to get a cleaner and the store manager came over to look after the customer and the security guard started sniffing around and a baby started crying and everyone had to have counseling and take legal advice. Freddie and Joz had disappeared and Gex only had three bottles.

"You better do it, man," he said, nodding toward the booze section. "We need one more bottle."

"No way," I said. "I'm no thief."

"If you don't go in, Bellend, then you can't come to the party," he hissed.

"Why do I have to miss out?" I hissed back, forgetting for the moment that I didn't even want to go to the party. "I didn't panic and run at the first sign of trouble."

"They went in and got the bottles, you didn't do nothing," he said.

I was going to just walk, but then I remembered Megan. I had sort of promised. She was only going because of me. I couldn't let her down. And do you know something else? Just at that moment I felt something unusual. Something I never feel. I felt confident. I felt strong. I felt that everything was going my way, nothing could go wrong. Everything suddenly seemed clear, and neat, and . . . and just right. I don't get that feeling very often.

So I went in. How hard could it be?

I steeled myself and walked right to the back of the store. I took the cart Freddie and Joz had abandoned and casually walked past the alcohol section.

But just as I reached out my hand to grab a bottle, an employee walked round a corner and gave me a funny look and I think I might have panicked a bit, so after he'd gone I grabbed the first bottle that came to hand and went back to the cheese aisle.

When no one was looking, I slipped the bottle under the front wheels and started pushing toward the checkouts. I could see Gex pretending not to watch as I worked up a good head of steam until I was nearly running. It was going to work!

But then disaster! A lady with a stroller appeared from nowhere and I had to stop, but I was too far away from the checkouts and the trolley was slightly off-center. The bottle rolled away, clipped a display unit full of pork pies and went off at the wrong angle, toward aisle nine, bumping into Megan's foot. Megan, who had her back to me, looked down at the bottle. Then she looked up, saw me and raised an eyebrow.

"Is that bottle yours?" she asked.

I should have just denied it, but for some reason I couldn't bring myself to lie to her. I nodded, eyes down. I was all too conscious of the store manager and security guard just a few checkouts away.

"Do you like Martini Rosso, then?" she asked.

I shrugged. "I don't know. I've never had it."

"Me neither," she said, and laughed. "Save some for me, will you? We can try it together." And she kicked the bottle over to where Gex was sitting, still staring straight ahead. Gex quickly shoved the bottle into his rucksack and walked out, hoodie up, head down.

"You didn't have to do that," I said. "But thanks."

"You owe me," she said, grinning. "See you tomorrow night."

"See you tomorrow," I said, grinning back. Then I bolted.

I caught up with Gex again down the street.

"You're such a Bellend," he told me, shaking his head.

I'm tired, my hand aches and I haven't even got to the lollipop lady yet. Tonight I need to finish rating all my iTunes songs. I've only done half of them and it's been preying on my mind.

I'll finish the rest of this tomorrow.

JULY 7TH

So, the lollipop lady.

We met back up with Joz and Freddie after the Great Martini Heist.

"Well, look who it is," I said as they sauntered up. "Top Olympian runners Usain Bolt and Jessica Ennis."

"Did you get busted?" Joz asked.

Gex showed them the bottles and we all grinned. Despite my misgivings, I have to admit I was enjoying this. I had the theme song to *The Sopranos* in my head.

"Shh," Freddie said, not at all suspiciously. We stopped talking as two fairly attractive girls walked past wearing crop tops, showing off their belly buttons. Joz ogled them unselfconsciously, turning to watch them go by.

"Joz," I sighed. "Try to be less obvious."

"I'm just being polite," he protested. "Girls dress like that because they want to be looked at."

"Not by you," Freddie said.

"You take these," Gex said to me, holding out the clinking bag of bottles.

"Why should I take them?"

"Cuz you got the bags on your bike," he said.

This was true. The others all have BMX bikes with no seats or gears, let alone racks. I, on the other hand, have a twelve-speed hybrid with rear panniers. I take my bicycling seriously.

I jammed the bag into one and we set off back down the hill.

Repton Street runs off the High Street right down the hill to the river. My house is at the bottom. Halfway down there's a pedestrian crossing next to the Infant School where Molly goes. Freddie, Joz and Gex shot off down the slope, for once able to show some speed. I'm usually miles ahead of them, trying not to go too fast as they pedal furiously on their tiny little bikes. This time all three were ahead. I took it easy; the incline is substantial and it's easy to go too fast.

I could see there was going to be trouble as they approached the pedestrian crossing. An old man was moving across slowly on a mobility scooter and Mrs. Frensham was standing, holding up the traffic. I should explain that Mrs. Frensham is the crazy lady with the giant lollipop-shaped stop sign whose job it is to make sure traffic stops for children before and after school. Anyway, there were two cars on our side of the road and one coming the other way. Mrs. Frensham takes her job very seriously. Arguably too seriously. Mrs. Frensham hates cars, and she hates cyclists even more than she hates cars. She's got mad hair and looks really tall because of the lollipop thing. She stands there on her crosswalk like a warrior queen holding a huge spear except with a large circle on the end. She glares at the drivers as though they're Roman legionnaires, daring them to move, keeping them waiting for ages.

The problem was that my idiot friends didn't look like they were going to stop at all. They didn't want to get stuck waiting for Mrs. Frensham. A dozen yards from the crossing, Joz, who was in the lead, bunny-hopped up onto the pavement, followed by the other two. It was clear they'd have time to whiz along the pavement and get by before the old codger in the scooter reached their side of the road.

I had a choice. I could have done the right thing, which was to slow and stop behind the cars, wait for Mrs. Frensham to move aside, then proceed carefully. Or I could have followed my friends up onto the pavement and carried on, illegally, but perfectly safely, as it was clear there was no risk to pedestrians.

I got it wrong. I was still feeling reckless. I thought I could do anything, break any rule and get away with it. So I did something I've never done before: I biked on the pavement.

There. I've said it.

Unfortunately, Mrs. Frensham had seen the others shoot past.

"Hooligans!" she yelled and ran toward that pavement. She was too late to catch them but then I came hurtling by, already starting to regret what I'd done. With a roar she swung the lollipop like it was a poleax and smacked me on the head. I was wearing a helmet of course, but the blow stunned me nonetheless and I clipped the fence to my left. I ricocheted off at an angle that took me back onto the road, right across to the far side and into the path of a Porsche Cayenne. The Porsche had to swerve, and it hit another car with a sickening crunch. I swerved too, came back in a big, uncontrolled loop and slammed into Mrs. Frensham, who'd come charging after me. We went down together in a tangle of spokes, limbs and lollipops and I heard the crunch of breaking glass under me.

I lay there for a few seconds, dazed and confused, and when I finally managed to sit up, my heart leaped into my throat as I saw blood everywhere. All over my bike, all over the road, all over the lollipop and all over Mrs. Frensham.

Oh my God. For one surreal and horrifying moment, I thought I'd killed a lollipop lady. Which is serious. It's worse than killing a cop, almost.

But then she groaned and lifted her head. I sighed with relief.

"Are you all right?" I asked nervously.

She looked at me, puzzled, then licked her bloodied lips.

"Martini Rosso?" she said, then slumped back down, unconscious.

It all went even more mental after that. The police figured out where the bottles had come from when they searched the bag they were in and found a Waitrose recipe card for zucchini pasta bake. They checked the security footage. Joz, Freddie and Gex got away with cautions but because I'd caused about thirteen thousand pounds' worth of damage to the Porsche and the other car and the lollipop, I got probation.

I'm obviously not cut out for organized crime. I'm straight as an arrow now. Never again.

JULY 8TH

I t's 6:37 a.m. and I've just woken up. I've had that dream again about Chelsea midfielder Frank Lampard and thought I'd better scribble it down before I forget it all. He's living in our loft (in the dream), and is clearly on the run from something or someone. I can hear the spikes on his soccer cleats tapping around up there as he slowly paces.

I wonder if I could discover what it is he's running from, whether it might make things clearer. This dream interpretation thing is really interesting. I downloaded a free ebook about it yesterday. I've noticed my dreams have been vivid and a bit weird since the incident with the lollipop lady and the book says that it's quite common for stressful or life-changing events to trigger a period of intense dreaming as your brain tries to make sense of it all. Everything can be interpreted somehow and it's never straightforward. Apparently, everything's an allegory or a metaphor or a symbol of something else, though I'm not convinced there could be many alternative interpretations of my recurring dream about Jennifer Lawrence. Perhaps the massage oil isn't really massage oil?

JULY 9TH

Describe the members of your immediate family. Explain what they're like physically and also how you see their characters. How would you categorize your

relationship with each person: Very Good, Good, Okay,
Poor, Very Poor.

Family Member 1—Dad
Relationship—Okay

Dad has no eyebrows. He is a bit taller than me, but not much taller, which makes me worry that I'm not going to grow any more. Joz told me he read that you always end up halfway between the heights of your parents, which doesn't seem right to me.

"Your dad is shorter than you," I pointed out.

"I know," he said. "Which is why I think he's not my real dad."

"I see your thinking," I said, "but it's not a lot to go on. I wouldn't go making any dramatic accusations in front of the whole family at Christmas on the strength of that evidence."

Joz didn't say anything, which makes me wonder if he is going to make a dramatic accusation. I wouldn't put it past him, and he might even be right. It's like the worst kind of soap opera around his place, always some big drama. He's got three older sisters and everyone's always sleeping with each other's boyfriend or, even worse, borrowing each other's clothes without asking and generally having hissy fits and storming out of rooms, slamming doors.

Dad is dark-haired like me but is going gray because he's old. We have a Good relationship mainly, except for that time he took me to a soccer match and then abandoned me in a pub as a fight kicked off, and I got a broken nose. My relationship with my dad on that day was Very Poor.

He loves soccer, and is a huge fan of Frank Lampard, which I don't get at all. Seriously, what's the big deal about

Frank Lampard? I've never seen him score. He just boots it up into the top row of the grandstand then holds his head like he's missed by an inch.

He's a mechanic (Dad, I mean, not Frank Lampard), but he doesn't work full-time, which he likes, because he's quite lazy. He does three days a week at Hutch's Auto Repairs and does a few private jobs for friends, which means we usually have some random car in the garage or the driveway up on bricks, leaking oil all over the pavement. What with our old van out the back, our house sometimes looks like a council-approved traveler's site. And that's ironic because Dad's always complaining about travelers.

"I don't like all them mechanical gypsies on the Common," he said the other week.

"*Ro*-manical," I corrected him.

"They don't look very Romanic to me," he said. "They've been there a month."

"Our camper van hasn't moved since July 2009," Mum pointed out.

"I'm just saying," he grumbled.

Dad "just says" things quite a lot. Mum says he's "largely unreconstructed." Like Corfe Castle.

Dad sometimes gets me to help him with his work on the weekends, which, owing to my ham-fistedness, usually means me just sitting in the car turning the ignition on and off again according to his instructions. Sometimes afterward he takes me to watch soccer with him. He's crazy about Chelsea, but he can't afford Premier League prices, so we go to watch local team Hampton FC, who aren't as bad as they sound. This season they have Joe Boyle playing for them, who used to play for Portsmouth before he got injured, and he's a minor celebrity around here. He also happens to be going out with my English teacher, the amazingly beautiful Miss Swallow. So double props to him.

I suppose he's all right, my dad, except he just talks about nothing but soccer and *Top Gear*. Oh, and the Second World War. He has an entire bookshelf of books and box sets about the Second World War (along with Frank Lampard's autobiography, which I haven't yet read).

"There were other world wars, you know, Dad," I told him.

"There was one other world war," he corrected. "And it wasn't as good."

"What was wrong with it?" I asked. "Not enough people died?"

He shrugged. "It doesn't really interest me. They just sat in holes most of the time then ran out into machine-gun fire."

The real reason, of course, is the Nazis. When men get to a certain age they become obsessed by the Nazis and watch endless programs on the History Channel called *Hitler's Dogs* or *Brides of Belsen* or *Extreme Nazi Hunters*. Joz says men start watching programs about the Nazis when they get too old for video games.

I may have mentioned this before, but I don't really like soccer. Or cars. Or the Second World War. If Dad found that out I think he'd be really disappointed and probably start thinking I'm gay. (I'm not.) So I pretend to know what he means about Christmas tree formations and differentials and universal joint offside traps. And I watched *Band of Brothers* all the way through even though I felt a bit queasy, and that mournful trumpet music made me want to slit my wrists.

Dad wants me to watch the new *Top Gear* season with him tonight. "Clarkson's going to reveal the new Stig!" he told me, giddy with excitement.

"Sounds great," I said weakly, giving him the thumbs-up. "Though if you believe the tabloids, there are a few BBC interns who've already had a good look at Clarkson's Stig," he went on.

Is the double entendre really the only form of humor he recognizes?

Dad is EXTREMELY untidy.

Family Member 2—Mum
Relationship—Good

Mum's a bit odd. She's a stage magician, which sounds quite cool but it's not really, because it isn't like David Copperfield with a huge stage and special effects. It's just little clubs and pubs with dodgy sound systems, unappreciative audiences and nowhere she can keep her white doves. She's always off "on the circuit." My relationship with my mum is Okay, when she's around. On the one hand she never cooks or cleans or does any of the stuff mums are supposed to do; on the other hand she can make Pringles come out of my ear.

Physical description? Mum is tall and thin, wears glasses and has dark curly hair. She wears jeans a lot. What else is there to say?

Oh yes, Mum is EXTREMELY untidy.

Mum and Dad get on well most of the time, except for the occasional random blazing argument, after which Dad goes away for a bit. Just a night here and there. Not like when I was little and he left for a year. Frankly, I don't understand how they ever ended up together in the first place. Mum went to college but it took Dad eight years to finish his apprenticeship because he kept failing his NVCs (National

Vocational Certificate). He says he has dyslexia so bad he thought he was doing QVC and stayed up all night watching shopping channels. I told you he was unreconstructed.

Mum reads a lot, like me. She introduced me to *The Hobbit* and *The Hunger Games* and bought me a Kindle Fire. If it had been up to Dad, he would have introduced me to a 1972 Ford Capri owner's manual and bought me a blowtorch.

Mum's at home at the moment, after a minitour in Scotland. She has a small cut on her nose from where someone threw a bottle at the stage in Glasgow. Her glasses got broken, so now she keeps walking into things and therefore has a genuine excuse for not tidying. Mum's eyesight is Very Poor. Her prescription is −8, which on the blindness chart is about the same as those fish that live in totally dark caves. Mum now somehow believes that means she is allowed to park anywhere she wants at Tesco supermarket, even the disabled spaces, if she can find them.

Family Member 3—Molly
Relationship—Okay

Molly is my little sister. She's six. She's totally crazy. She's not unlike Lola from the kids' cartoon show *Charlie and Lola*. If you haven't seen it, at the start of every show Charlie says, "This is my little sister, Lola. She's small and very funny." Except with us I'd say, "This is my little sister, Molly. She's small and completely nuts." For example, she painted her teeth in the colors of a rainbow once. She sat for ages with her mouth open "to dry them out," then painted them in acrylics in the mirror. She was furious when she realized she'd done them back to front. She had to go to the hospital with blood poisoning. Also, once she ate a toad. Well, she ate a tadpole that had started to grow back legs. She said she wanted to see how it felt as it slipped down. She's bonkers.

Molly thinks of herself as some kind of animal rescue service, but as I tried to point out to her the other day, you're supposed to rescue animals that have already been orphaned, not go around taking baby animals while their mothers are collecting food. It's the animal equivalent of snatching a toddler from outside Tesco. Our house is always full of baby hedgehogs or stray cats (which usually eat the baby hedgehogs), and once she came back with an owl.

Molly is EXTREMELY untidy, and Mum and Dad just don't care. I'm the one who tidies her room. Me.

Friend 1—Gex
Relationship—Okay to Poor

Gex thinks he's black, but in fact he's more Kid Rock than Chris Rock. Gex only came to our school last year after he was expelled from Hollingdale and he didn't have any friends and he sort of attached himself to me—as I didn't have any friends either—so we could get bullied together rather than separately. You know, to make things easier for the bullies. But the thing was that eventually people got used to Gex pretending to be black and he stopped being bullied and he kind of became popular, and by association, so did I. So however much trouble he gets me into, I owe him. And he does get into a lot of trouble. He's been suspended three times since he started at our school. He's been known to avoid double English on a Monday morning by telling his parents he's suspended.

Gex is tall (though everyone is, compared to me) and

blond, with sort of translucent skin and pale, watery eyes. He's not much to look at but quite successful with girls for some reason. I think it's because he gives off such an air of confidence they're fooled into thinking he knows what he's doing. Which he doesn't at all if Kirsten Hatton is to be believed. Apparently, she spent an uncomfortable half hour in an alley beside the O2 cell phone shop on the high street trying to explain the difference between snogging and chewing to the confused Gex. At least he got her to the O2 shop in the first place. I've never gotten a girl past Vodafone.

Friend 2—Joz
Relationship—Good

Let's start with the physical description. Hoodie, jeans around his ankles, can of spray paint in his pocket. Got a mental image? Now add big bags under his eyes because he never sleeps, like Edward from *Twilight* only with dark, lank hair and acne. He lives with his mum and sisters on the local estate and I've never seen him eat anything but prawn cocktail chips.

Joz doesn't say much. And what he does say is usually incredibly offensive. Let's just say he has a disrespectful attitude toward women. And men. People in general. He says graffiti is his means of expression, but all he ever does is his own tag, which you can't read. He's good at drawing; I've seen what he does on paper. But he never paints anything on walls. He was another one who never had any friends until Gex turned up. Joz just kind of joined the group one day and now follows us around everywhere. Despite his lack of social skills, I actually get on quite well with Joz, probably better than with Gex.

Friend 3—Freddie
Relationship—Okay

(Though now I feel bad that I've given Joz a higher relationship rating than either Freddie or Gex. Not so bad that I'm going to change them, but it does all seem a bit disloyal.)

If Freddie was a Hollywood film actor, he'd forever be cast as a lovable slacker who triumphs against the odds and gets the girl. Except with Freddie he's not that lovable, he finds it difficult to triumph over the challenge of tying his shoelaces and as far as I'm aware he's never got any girl, let alone the girl.

Sometimes he can seem really slow on the uptake, but then he'll come out with stuff that's actually quite thought-provoking. He makes totally random statements that are almost clever, but at the same time really stupid. Like the other day in English Lit he asked if there was another word for "homonym." And then he complained to Miss Swallow that phonetics should be spelled "fonetics." "That's if they're serious about it," he said.

Maybe Fred's a bit autistic, but with words instead of numbers. I think the perfect job for him would be as the guy who thinks up all those weird two-word phrases you get on social media to verify you're not a spam-bot. Beveled Sunday. Flannel Growler. Clough Tangent.

Now, to be fair, Freddie was sort of my friend before Gex arrived. His dad and mine are friends and we used to hang out together a lot, usually freezing our backsides off in the uncovered stand at Hampton FC. He's one of those friends you just end up with rather than one you'd choose. Freddie happens to be the cousin of local soccer hero Joe Boyle, which gets him a small amount of respect at school;

an even smaller amount of that respect rubs off on me, as his friend.

Just read all of this back to myself. To be honest, if I were Ms. Gunter I might put a red flag on my case notes at this point. My family and friends all sound like sociopaths.

JULY 10TH

Dear Mr. Fletcher,

One of the Waypoints on your Probation Journey is involvement in some suitable extracurricular activity, midweek. Research shows that if young men are occupied after school they are far less likely to offend. You indicated to me at your interview that you're not interested in sports or games and so it has been decided that you should attend a regular, suitable class on Thursday evenings. Though most courses are fully subscribed, Hampton Community College has been kind enough to make a space available for you in one of the following courses, beginning July 26th. Please email your choice to me and I will complete the enrollment process on your behalf.

7:00 p.m.–7:55 p.m. Car Maintenance—David Fletcher
7:00 p.m.–7:55 p.m. Knitting—Jessica Swallow
7:00 p.m.–7:55 p.m. Pottery—Naomi Hooper
6:00 p.m.–6:55 p.m. Microsoft Office (Beginners)—Frank Gavin

Yours,
Claudia Gunter
West Meon Probation Services

What a dazzling array of tempting choices! Can't I do all of them?

Let's see: Car maintenance with David Fletcher? That would be fixing cars, with my dad! Something I hate and which he makes me do on the weekends anyway.

Knitting? Knitting?! A suitable class for me is knitting? What's Ms. Gunter trying to say about me? Should dangerous criminals be allowed near knitting needles? Would they give a crochet hook to the man who ate the ice-cream vendor's kidneys? I think not. Having said that, the class is being taught by Miss Swallow, my English teacher. Miss Swallow is hot, as I think I may have mentioned before. I won't repeat what Joz says about her, especially the bit about the whipped cream.

Microsoft Office? I already know how to use Microsoft Office. Everyone knows how to use Microsoft Office. Sarah Palin can use Microsoft Office. That course is for grannies and people who've just arrived in civilization after having been raised by wolves in the Appalachians. I'm not doing fifty-five minutes on how to plug a laptop in.

Then there's pottery. Seems like the best of a bad bunch at first glance. But I already spend three days a week cleaning engine oil out from under my fingernails. The idea of scraping a ton of clay out every other night doesn't exactly thrill me. Also, there's a very good reason I can't choose pottery. The class is being taught by Naomi Hooper, Megan's mum. Not that Mrs. Hooters doesn't have her own appeal, of course, but if I take her class then Megan's certain to find out and I'm not having her smirking at my wobbly flowerpots. It should be the other way around.

All in all, brilliant. Why couldn't there be something cool, like computer game design, or fencing or home butchery? Come to think of it, what I could really do with is bicycle maintenance. There's something not at all right with the front gears on my bike.

JULY 18TH

Jessica Swallow is not the first teacher I've had a crush on. I've had a bit of a crush on most of my teachers. Female ones, I mean. Dad claims that my teachers have become progressively more attractive as I've gone up through the years at school. Mum says they're not becoming more attractive, just younger in comparison to him. There was Mrs. Hunt in fourth grade, who really wasn't all that but she wore thin cotton dresses you could see through. Then there was Ms. Young in the sixth grade, who was not young in real life but was pretty, apart from the goiter. But even then the goiter just made her more accessible.

I think women need at least one imperfection to make them really attractive. In Miss Swallow's case it's her canine teeth, which come out at an odd angle and are slightly discolored. To me those teeth add to her beauty rather than detract from it. But I'd probably still find her attractive if her "flaw" was having a narwhal's horn sticking out of her forehead.

She's so gorgeous. She's small, with big, green eyes. She has ash-blond hair and this smooth pale skin that just seems to glow.

Now I come to read that back, I realize that description makes her sound like an alien. If she is an alien she can abduct me anytime, which brings me to the dream I had last night. When I lie in bed before I go to sleep, I sometimes like to imagine myself being incredibly rich, or really good at sports, or being a famous writer or something. Often, though, my fantasy is that some really gorgeous chick is my girlfriend. It might be Megan, or Holly Osman or the dark-haired girl who goes past our house on her way up to the college every morning. But quite often it's Jessica Swallow. The problem is that I like my fantasies to be consistent. They have to be plausible, if unlikely. They also have to be ethical. Dream Rohypnol is a big no-no for me.

Of course, Miss Swallow isn't going to fall head over heels in love with me just like that. She's twelve years older than me. She has a massively tall, semiprofessional soccer player boyfriend who drives a flashy car. And she's gorgeous. I mean, she's my teacher for heaven's sake! Miss Swallow loves her job. She's probably not going to throw all that out for me.

So, how do I become rich and successful and attractive to older women? Or younger women? Any female over the age of sixteen? Usually I imagine that Mum invents a new magic trick like TV's Jonathan Creek except real and she becomes incredibly famous and goes on TV like David Blaine, except less of a twat. That provides the money for me to attend a top school where they teach me to be a young entrepreneur who launches my billionaire business at seven-teen; one that gives loads of money to charity, and Jessica Swallow is so bowled over by my dynamism and generosity that she falls head over heels for me and leaves her semipro-fessional soccer player, who just can't compete, frankly. He takes it on the chin, though, and eventually he and I become quite good friends as it happens and he teaches me to play soccer and also how to drive in his flashy car. He becomes the older brother I never had.

My fantasies take ages to really get to the good bits and I usually fall asleep well before I get to first base with the girl. Last night, though, I had a dream that cut through all that crap. I was at a knitting class with Miss Swallow and fifteen old ladies. An alien spacecraft came down, beamed us all up and put us in a zoo on their home planet. Miss Swallow had little choice but to turn to me for comfort. We lay together on a bedspread knitted for us by the old ladies. The fantasy cut to black after that. I can't seem to go beyond that point. It's too much. And in any case it would be a bit itchy because of the wool.

Suffice to say, I've taken this as a big sign that I should choose the knitting class.

JULY 19TH

I've emailed Claudia Gunter at West Meon Probation Services and am now having a massive panic that my email was too sarcastic. I meant it to be funny, but reading it back it just looks mocking. Why do I do these things? Here's what I sent.

Dear Ms. Gunter,
Thank you for your email dated July 18th. Thank you so much for this opportunity for self-improvement. All the suggested courses were so tempting it was a really tough decision. However, after careful consideration I feel the most appropriate course for me to take is:

7:00 p.m.–7:55 p.m. Knitting—Jessica Swallow
I should be grateful if you were to enroll me in said course heretoforthwith.
Yours regardingly,
Ben Fletcher

I might have laid it on a bit thick. Oh well, I expect she gets worse emails from the waffle-cone killer.

I haven't told Dad I'm doing the knitting. I lied. I've told him I'm doing pottery instead. That didn't exactly fill him with joy.

"Pottery," he said, staring at me over breakfast. "Pottery . . ."

"Well, there wasn't much choice," I said.

"What's wrong with my course?" he asked. "Could have been an opportunity to spend some time together."

"Conflict of interest," I said wildly.

"What?"

"It's a conflict of interest. Because you're my dad. My probation officer made it clear she'd be looking for atten- dance and behavior reports from the course teacher. You wouldn't be impartial."

"Yes, I bloody would," he said. "If you played up in my class I'd shop you no problem. I'd sing like a canary, I would."

"Thanks, Dad," I said. "I'm sure you would, but my probation officer wouldn't accept it, I'm afraid."

"Shame," he said, sighing.

"Yes, shame," I replied.

"What about computers?" Dad said.

"Too basic."

"And what was the other choice?"

"Knitting."

He barked out a laugh. "No chance of you taking that at least."

"Why?" I asked, bristling slightly.

He laughed again. "It's just . . . well, knitting. It's a bit . . ."

I waited.

"It's a bit . . ."

"Gay?"

"Hey, I didn't say that," he said quickly. He gets in trouble with Mum if he's homophobic around the house. "I meant it's a bit . . ."

"Effeminate?"

"What's that mean?"

"Girly."

"Yep. That. That's the word. Girly."

Eventually he bought the pottery thing though. It must have been the thought of his son getting labeled as teacher's pet that did it. In Dad's book that would have been the height of big girl's blouse.

Mum, on the other hand, had been delighted when I'd told her over the phone. She was in a Travelodge just outside Honiton. She'd had a bad day. One of the doves had died and the other was too depressed to perform. To fill the gap she'd had to reinstate the trick where she saws an audience member in half. The last time she'd tried it there'd been an accident which had nearly doubled her insurance premium.

"Don't use a real saw this time, Mum," I advised.

"I know," she snapped.

"Ask her what she wants for dinner when she's back on Friday," Dad called from the kitchen.

"Dad wants to know what you want for dinner on Friday," I said.

"Ooh," she said. "Tell him I'd like a nice bit of pork."

"I'm not telling him that."

"But that's what I want."

"Don't do this to me, Mum," I whispered.

"Tell him," she insisted.

"Mum says she wants a bit of pork," I called to Dad, bracing myself.

"Okay, but what does she want for dinner?" he replied, in stitches.

"So . . . knitting," Mum said, after she'd calmed down and I'd told her what I was doing this evening. "It's excellent for developing dexterity, for strengthening the fingers and for improving concentration. All useful skills for magicians."

"Also excellent training for that call center job I'm hoping for after school," I said.

"Or for being a fighter pilot?"

"Those are the three options I'm putting on my form for Career Day," I said. "Magician, call center slave or fighter pilot. I'd be happy with any of those."

"Good for you," Mum said. "Look, gotta go, I need to sharpen my swords."

JULY 21ST

I found Gex, Freddie and Joz in the park. They were sitting on a low wall, in a row, staring into the parking lot at the back of the hardware shop.

"What's up?" I asked as I approached. They ignored me.

"What you looking at?" I asked.

"There," Joz said impatiently, pointing.

I looked in the same direction as them but it wasn't immediately obvious.

"What am I looking at?"

"Just wait," Freddie said.

"Are you looking at that girl in the short skirt?" I asked.

"Yes," Freddie said.

"The one with the cast on her leg?"

"Yes."

"And the crutches?"

"Yes."

"The one who's packing her shopping into her car trunk?"

"Yes!"

"Why?"

"Just wait, Bellend," Gex snapped.

I sighed, sat and watched. Then I saw what they were looking at. The poor girl was having difficulty with her crutches. She didn't have a lot of room and her trolley was stuck behind a post, to the side of her car. She had to use her crutches to get to the trolley, then she'd pull a bag out, do a few awkward hops with one crutch back around to the trunk, deposit the bag and go back for the next one. The problem was, she kept dropping her crutch. Each time she did, she had to lean forward to pick it up, doing a sort of balletic swoop and swinging her bad leg up as she did, which afforded the four of us an excellent view up her skirt. She was wearing black knickers.

"You guys are sick," I said, craning my head to the side.

"She's gorgeous," Joz said.

"You're taking advantage of a vulnerable girl with a broken leg," I pointed out. "You should be helping her."

"She doesn't know we're watching. And she's managing just fine," Freddie said. "She dropped it again!"

"Butterfingers," Gex said appreciatively.

"How can she drive with that cast on her leg?" Joz wondered out loud.

"She's amazing," Gex said.

"She is pretty," I admitted. "And really graceful."

And that's pretty much all we did today. Freddie recorded a bit of the show and after the poor girl had driven off we sat around and watched it for a while until his phone ran out of battery.

I really need to find myself some better friends.

JULY 25TH

Here's a different scenario. After a few knitting classes, Miss Swallow realizes I'm struggling. I'm a man, knitting isn't my thing, but I'm determined to carry on. I may be masculine and rough around the edges, but I also have a more sensitive side and I want to fully explore my own creativity. Miss Swallow recognizes these qualities and finds herself drawn to me, despite the age difference.

After class she asks if I can stay behind and help her ravel the yarn, or catalog the knitting needles, or shear the sheep or something. I agree, after quickly glancing at my expensive watch. We get to chatting, laughing at each other's knitting jokes, discussing the recent editorial in *Crochet!* magazine. I hand her a ball of yarn and our fingers touch, our eyes meet and then she looks away shyly.

Okay, it's unlikely, but I like to deal in possibles, not probables. Probables are depressing.

First knitting class tomorrow evening. Feeling a bit

nervous. Freddie asked me if I wanted to come over and watch a new slasher film called *Hovel* after school and I had to think of an excuse. I told him I had liver fluke.

JULY 26TH

Right, that couldn't have gone much worse. I've just got back from the college. It was my first knitting class tonight and it was a bit of a disaster from start to finish. Dad gave me a lift as he needed to be there to teach his class.

Dad and I arrived at the college early, which I was glad about. I was a little worried Megan might be around. I had no particular reason to think she might be there, other than the fact her mum was teaching the pottery class. But I was a little paranoid about it. I really didn't want anyone to find out what I was doing, especially her. I didn't really want to run into her mother either, so once I'd found out what room knitting was in I scuttled along there and ducked in through the door.

"Hello, can I help?" a voice said from the back of the room. I spun to see Mrs. Hooper standing at the open door of a cupboard. She looked as surprised to see me as I was to see her. She's lovely, Megan's mum. She's no Jessica Swallow, but she's not bad looking for an older woman and I get a bit tongue-tied whenever I have to talk to her.

"Oh, sorry," I said. "I thought this was knitting."

As I said this, Mrs. Hooper took from the cupboard a cardboard box teetering with balls of wool. I realized she also had a pair of knitting needles stuck into the bun at the top of her head, and a sheaf of knitting patterns clutched in her right hand.

"This is knitting," she said, looking at me as if I was a total idiot.

"I thought Jess—Miss Swallow was teaching this class."

"No," she said. "Here, hold this."

Mrs. Hooper passed me the cardboard box and began placing a knitting pattern sheet on each desk.

"Jessica Swallow teaches pottery. She couldn't knit a scarf." Mrs. Hooper snorted as she said this. Apparently not being able to knit a scarf is the knitting equivalent of not being able to organize a boozy night in a brewery.

"There was a mix-up on the course list, as usual," Mrs. Hooper said, pausing in her work and smiling at me. "Sorry. Will I do?"

I looked at her, torn. In many ways she would do, but this meant Megan would certainly find out my yarny secrets. Pottery, should have bloody done pottery, I thought. Too late though. I couldn't back out now.

"Let's knit," I said as enthusiastically as I could.

JULY 27TH

I've just reread my journal entry for Thursday and I think maybe I was a bit harsh. The evening wasn't a complete, sheer sad-case disaster. Not once the class got under way at least. See, I was expecting a bunch of old ladies smelling of lavender and mothballs. But I suppose most old ladies already know how to knit. I mean, they were all definitely older than me, it's true, and all women. But most of them were about my mum's age, and a few were about twenty or thirty and nobody smelled of mothballs. Though one of them smelled a bit of Axe body spray, which was strange. Being the only male I was subject to a few whispers and funny looks, but mostly from the twenty-year-olds, I suspect because they fancied me. I could have taken advantage of the lack of competition, but they weren't my type, and they looked a bit like they could swallow me whole for breakfast. Not that they were fat, maybe fuller-figured. Which is what Joz calls fat. But then he's an ignorant twat.

Mrs. Hooper gave us a little talk, to start with, about the origins of knitting. I made a few notes and this is pretty much what she said:

The word knitting comes from the Old English word "cnyttan," to knot.

We know that the Ancient Egyptians used to knit two thousand years ago, using stranded knit color patterns, which are actually quite complex.

Mrs. Hooper looked at me as she said the next bit.

Knitting was originally a male-only occupation.

I smiled at Mrs. Hooper when she said that. It was nice of her to make me feel more comfortable and to make it clear she for one didn't have any doubts about my masculinity, thank you very much.

The first knitting trade guild was started in Paris in 1527. With the invention of knitting machines though, knitting by hand became more of a leisure activity.

Hand-knitting has gone into and out of fashion many times in the last two centuries, and at the turn of the twenty-first century it is enjoying a revival.

These days it's less about the "make do and mend"

attitude of the 1940s and early 50s and more about making a statement about individuality as well as developing an innate sense of community.

After that we looked at the different-sized needles. Quite simple really: big ones make big stitches, small ones make small stitches. Then Mrs. Hooper showed us the difference between a plain stitch and a purl stitch.

"Those two basic stitches are the most important building blocks of knitting," Mrs. Hooper said. "Once you've mastered those, then you're already a long way along the road to being a knitter. There's very little you can't create if you can knit and purl."

So I gave it a try. I stared at the needles and the yarn for a bit, trying to figure out how these two little bits of steel could turn a one-dimensional thread into a two-dimensional sheet of fabric. I ran Mrs. Hooper's words over in my mind again, closed my eyes and tried to visualize. Then I blinked my eyes open again and got to it.

And you know what? I turned out to be quite good at knitting. It took me a few tries before I made my first stitch, but I got it quickly enough and was soon at the end of the first row.

"You've picked this up really quickly," Mrs. Hooper said to me as she showed me how to start the next row down. "You're a natural."

I went red, but that was mostly due to the fact that I think she caught me looking down her top as she leaned over the table.

"It's great to have a male presence in the class," she went on. "It would be wonderful to break the stereotype of knitting as a female-only pursuit."

"Yes, about that," I said, looking up at her as the rest

of the class clicked away with their own needles, someone uttering a curse every now and again. "I'm not sure my friends would necessarily understand about breaking down stereotypes. I was sort of hoping there might be some sort of confidentiality thing going on here." I sensed my face heating up and waved my knitting pattern up and down in front of it.

"You mean like between a parishioner and a priest?" she asked.

"Yes, or a doctor and a patient?" I suggested hopefully.

"Um. No. No, there isn't really," she said.

"Oh," I replied, my heart sinking.

"But if what you're saying is that you'd like me to keep your attendance here under my hat, I'm happy to do that."

"Great. And would you keep your hat on at all times? Even at home?"

Mrs. Hooper blinked at me. Then she got it. "Don't worry, Ben. I won't tell Megan."

If I'd gone red before, I was now puce.

"Of course. I understand," she said, tapping the side of her nose.

I'd thought I was going to totally hate it and screw everything up as usual and possibly accidentally stab one of the full-figured girls in the eye with a needle, but no, I'm a "natural."

I had punctured the mystique of the art of knitting. Uncovered the mechanics behind Stitch and Bitch. And I've gotta say: I totally aced it. It's a bit like finding out what goes on with the Masons (not that I have, but I bet it's boring) and realizing it's all been a bit of a fuss about nothing. But now I think of it, it was a similar thing at Boy Scouts too, with knots. I couldn't light kindling with flint and I capsized a rowing boat four times and I accidentally knocked Daniel Jacobs into the campfire at the jamboree, but I was always a natural at the knots. I could see them in my head, three dimensionally, in HD. It's hard to explain, but I just have that sort of mind, I suppose. A knotty, stitchy sort of mind.

Not going to analyze that too much.

Anyway, once I got into it, knit purl, knit purl, I found I just lost myself in it. I loved the neatness of it, the repetition, the same thing over and over. I could stop thinking about anything else for a while, just the click of the needles, the floating movement of the yarn, the stitches appearing as if Mum had clicked her fingers and created them out of thin air. Except it wasn't Mum, it was me, making something from nothing.

As soon as the class was over though, I started to panic again. I had this dumb idea that Megan was going to be outside, waiting for her mum. I hung about for a bit until the coast was clear, then went down to the workshop where Dad runs his class. He was alone when I came in. The masculine smell of machine oil hung in the air, accentuating by comparison just how effeminate my chosen course was. I felt bad about deceiving Dad; after all, he'd been so supportive of me since the court case. Maybe it was time to come clean.

"How was pottery?" Dad called. He was at the sink, washing oil from his hands.

"Great," I said quickly. "I'd rather be here, but it's a good alternative."

What is wrong with me? Why do I have to lie all the time?

"Want to wash your hands?" he asked, holding up a bar of oily soap.

I looked blank. Wash my hands, why?

He peered at my clean hands quizzically. "Did you wash up in the toilets?"

Oh crap. Clay, he's expecting me to have clay-y hands.

"Oh, yeah, yeah, I did that," I said. "Totally washed my hands already."

"Cleaned under your fingernails, too?" Dad looked suspicious.

"Yes," I said, holding up my hands to show him.

"Right," he said. "Well done. But next week come straight down here and wash up. You shouldn't really be washing clay down the upstairs plumbing."

Crap. I'd have to work that one out next time. It occurred to me, quite rightly, that I was digging my own grave. Or knitting a particularly stiff poncho for my back, possibly. Either way I was an idiot. But I'd gone too far down this stupid road now; I'd have to see it through.

Dad kept quizzing me on the way home, asking if I had anything to show yet. I didn't know what to say. Eventually I told him I'd tried to make a vase but it had collapsed. I hadn't expected Dad to be so interested in my pottery class, to be honest. If he keeps this up, I'm going to need to bring something home. But what? A mug from Robert Dyas? A flowerpot from someone's garden? A forty-eight-piece dinner party set with gravy boat from Ikea?

The house was dark and cold when we got in and suddenly I felt worried about Mum and about the web of lies I was already creating. Up until a few weeks ago I was neither a criminal nor a liar, and now I am both. So maybe that's why I said the evening had gone so badly when I went upstairs to write about it.

But it didn't go that badly. Not really. I'm already looking forward to next week.

JULY 29TH

Had the Jennifer Lawrence dream again. I'm not writing down the details, but she wore her bow and arrows throughout.

AUGUST 1ST

Went to Joz's house today to play on his Xbox. He revealed he's writing a book based loosely on his own sexual exploits and calling it *Fifty Shades of Graham.*

"The title is clever marketing," he told me. "People looking for *Fifty Shades of Grey* might accidentally come across my book."

"As it were," I said.

"Eh?"

"Never mind."

"I'm going to self-publish," he said confidently.

"Really?" I asked. "And turn down all those six-figure book deals?"

"If you self-publish, you get a higher percentage of the profits," he said knowledgeably.

"True. But one hundred percent of nothing is still nothing," I said carefully.

"It's not one hundred percent," he said. "It's more like sixty-five percent."

"Oh, well in that case . . ." I replied, nodding encouragingly. "Am I allowed to have a look at what you've written so far?"

He eyed me suspiciously.

"You know, like a second opinion. . . ."

"Okay," he agreed, after a bit of thought. "But it's copyrighted."

"Don't worry, I'm not going to steal your intellectual property," I assured him.

"Though maybe you could, you know, sort the spelling and that," he said.

"Edit the text?" I asked. "Yeah, maybe."

He said he'd email me what he had so far. I am interested to see what he comes up with. Genuinely interested . . . and genuinely terrified too.

AUGUST 2ND

I'm not really sure I should do this. Not because of copyright issues, but because of taste issues. In the back of my mind I'm conscious that someone at West Meon Probation Services will read this journal at some point, which is a worry. And what of future generations of scholars tasked with poring over my writings? I must think of them, my devoted readers, before unleashing this. But of course I'm going to do it anyway. Here's an early version of chapter one of *Fifty Shades of Graham*:

There was this one time when I was walking past the public restrooms on my way home, minding my own business. I heard a voice coming from inside. I knew that no one had used these bathrooms since Lloyd Manning had his episode in there. So I was surprised. I stopped to listen. It sounded like a sob or crying.

I went in and called out, "Hello there, is there someone there?"

The noise stopped. I went in farther. It was dark, like a fridge with a broken light. But it was warm, like a microwave oven on low.

Then I heard a scuffling sound and I flung open the door to a cubicle.

The most beautiful girl I had ever seen was sitting there, tears on her face. She was wearing a very short skirt and had sexy legs and big b***s.

"What's wrong? Do you need the bathroom?" I asked.

She shook her head.

"I'm so sad," she said. "Because my dog died. And my kitten."

"You poor thing," I told her. "Come here."

I hugged her for ages until she stopped crying. Then she looked up at me.

"I'm totally grateful," she said.

"It's okay," I told her. "You're safe now."

"What's your name?" she said.

"Graham," I replied.

"Kiss me, Graham," she said.

That's enough of that for tonight. Sometimes reading is tiring, especially when the author can't even spell his own name. Still, I'm intrigued to find out what will happen between Graham and the toilet girl. Stay tuned.

AUGUST 3RD

Second knitting class last night.

On the way there Dad started talking about Frank Lampard again.

"I'm sure he's a fantastic player," I told him. "All I'm saying is that I, personally, have never seen him score a goal. It always goes over the top, or hits the bar."

"You aren't paying enough attention, then, because he scored sixteen goals for Chelsea last season," Dad said seriously.

"And how many did he miss?"

"Well, this is the thing," Dad explained patiently. "Frank's philosophy is that if you don't shoot, you don't score. He always takes a punt. He has a poor shot-to-goal ratio, but he still ends up scoring a lot of goals."

"I get that. I've just never seen it happen," I said.

"Right, you and I are going to a game this season," he said. "A league game, in London."

"No, Dad," I said, panicking. "We can't afford to go to Stamford Road."

"Stamford Bridge."

"Or Stamford Bridge," I said.

"Let me worry about the money," he said. "I've got some friends with season tickets. I'm going to make this happen."

"Great," I said weakly. "Amazing."

Before the class started, I went down the hall to class 3E, where Miss Swallow was teaching pottery. I popped my head round the door and smiled when I saw the coast was clear. I crept in and approached a giant lump of light brown clay sitting on a table. I was standing there, like Indiana Jones, just about to grab a handful when the door swung open behind me and I jumped my own height.

"Can I help you?"

I turned to see Miss Swallow, looking absolutely ravishing. Her top button was undone and her hair was tied back in a ponytail.

"I . . . um . . . I," I said suavely.

"Hello, Ben," she said, in a friendly way. "You're not in this class, are you?"

"No," I said.

"Aren't you doing knitting?"

How did she know? How?

I nodded.

"That's down the hall. 3G," she said cheerily, smiling her megasmile.

"Okay," I said, deciding I needed to seize the moment. "But before I go, do you think I could have some clay?"

"Oh . . . sure," she said, surprised by the request. She took hold of a thin wire with handles on either end and expertly cut a chunk of clay off the big block. Her elbow brushed against me as she did this and I caught a whiff of her perfume. It took everything I had to keep myself from closing my eyes and breathing in deeply.

"What's it for?" she asked.

"I need it for a school project." Having only had a few seconds to come up with a plausible reason why I wanted a lump of clay, I was pleased with my explanation.

"I see," she said, wrapping my clay in a thin plastic sheet. "What's the project?"

I cast my eyes around the room madly, trying to find inspiration in everyday objects. My gaze went full circle before coming back to the lump of clay, which was sitting on top of a box, which was itself on a table top.

"A ziggurat," I said blindly. "You know, like a pyramid?"

"Thanks, Ben. I know what a ziggurat is," she said.

"Well I have to build a Mayan ziggurat with people and priests and sacrificial victims and everything."

"Wow," Miss Swallow said. "That sounds amazing. I'd better cut you some more."

"No, no. This will do for now," I said. "I can always come back."

"That's right," she said, flashing me another heartbreaking smile. "You can always come back. I want to see that ziggurat when it's finished, okay?"

"Righto, Miss Swallow," I said.

"You can call me Jessica when we're not in school, Ben," she said.

"Okay, Jessica," I replied, grinning, then I ran for it.

Of course, it's a completely insane suggestion that Miss Swallow could have been flirting with me. Things like that don't happen in real life. Even Joz would have thought twice about using such a situation as a scene in *Fifty Shades of Graham*.

Mrs. Hooper was in 3G when I arrived at knitting. I stashed the clay in my bag and if she noticed she didn't say anything. I was the first one there again and Mrs. Hooper asked me to distribute everyone's work. I couldn't help but notice how much longer and neater my piece was than everyone else's.

"I'm glad to see you've come back," she said, smiling warmly at me.

"Why wouldn't I come back?" I asked. And then it struck

me that the idea of pulling out simply hadn't occurred to me. I could have switched to pottery. I could have phoned up Ms. Gunter in tears and demanded to know what classes were available on a Tuesday.

"Oh," she said, shrugging. "The men we've had on this course before have never lasted long."

"No stamina," I replied. I was pleased she'd bracketed me as a man, rather than a boy. That's what being an up-perclassman does for you.

People started arriving then, and I said hello to everyone as they came in, including Natasha and Amelia, the fuller-figured girls.

"Hey, Bob. Would you like to sit with us?" Natasha asked.

"It's Ben," I said, blushing. "But okay." I don't really fancy either of them, though they both have quite pretty faces, especially Natasha. But Natasha is a bit of a close talker and Amelia is a mouth-breather. I discovered that apart from knitting they both love cats and vampire novels.

Once the class got under way, Mrs. Hooper showed us how to knit in a complete circle, to do necks, and sleeves and things. Knitting in the round, it's called, where you join up the two sides to make a cylindrical object. I was starting to realize that knitting is basically just maths. Geometry. Once you'd worked out the mechanics of using the needles, then it was just about keeping the geometry of the piece in your head while you carried out the repetitions necessary.

The time flew and before I knew it we were packing up. Natasha told me about an illuminating knitting podcast, so I gave her my email address so she could send me some links.

As we headed down the hall I snuck away from the others so I could pull out my lump of clay and work it through my fingers. I even smeared a little on my cheek for extra authenticity before heading down to the workshop to find Dad.

I'm kind of getting the hang of the subterfuge now.

AUGUST 5TH

I once made the mistake of telling Joz how much I fancied Miss Swallow.

"We all fancy her," he'd said, hunched over his PS2 control.

"Yeah, but it's different with me," I said. I was feeling wistful, dangerous. "I think I might actually be in love with her."

"You should tell her," Joz said, blowing the head off a zombie.

"Yeah, good plan."

"No, seriously," he said, pausing the game to look at me. "Look, you know how old men fancy young girls, right?"

"Uh . . . yes."

"Well, it works the same with old women and young boys."

"Miss Swallow's not an old woman."

"She's got wrinkles," he pointed out. It was true; when she smiled she had little crow's feet that made my stomach flip. "Have you heard of cougars?"

"Yes, I've heard of cougars," I said, thinking of my dad's DVD collection.

"Joshua Wilkinson told me the Swallower was at Wicked nightclub a couple of weeks ago, sexy-dancing with Gareth Symons and Frankie Bell, and they only finished school last year."

"But she has a boyfriend," I said, shocked.

"And how old is this boyfriend?" Joz asked, raising an eyebrow.

"I don't know, thirty-four?"

"Well, maybe she's looking to trade him in for a younger model," he said, giving me a see-there-you-go look. Then he turned back to the game.

Could it be true? Could Miss Swallow be a cougar?

AUGUST 7TH

I've been looking up knitting online. It's actually quite interesting. There are tons of groups and all sorts of people involved. There's the Stitch and Bitch group, who have regular meet-ups in coffee shops and knit and bitch at the same time. There's the Purl and Hurl group, who have regular meetings in pubs to knit and drink, and there's one predominantly for male knitters too called Knit Club. Presumably they have regular meet-ups in a warehouse to knit and fight. There's this on their website:

The First Rule of Knit Club Is
Nobody Talks About Knit Club

The Second Rule of Knit Club Is
No Fair Isle Sweaters

There are some podcasts too, and I downloaded the one that Natasha recommended, called *Knitwits!*, which is recorded by two knitting obsessives from the U.S. I listened to a bit, and it did sound just like one of those spoof comedies on Channel 4, except these two are deadly serious. It's not a joke. Knitting is not a joke.

I'd become engrossed in a fascinating article on cast-ons, bind-offs and selvages (the sides of your knitted piece) when the door opened and someone came in. I slammed the laptop shut and looked up guiltily.

It was Mum, looking embarrassed.

"Okay. I know what that looked like . . ." I began. "But it's completely not what you think. . . ."

"It's okay," she said. "I read an article about this in *Modern Mother*."

"Since when do you read *Modern Mother*?" I asked, intrigued, despite the situation.

"They ran an interview piece with me and sent a free copy," she explained. "Anyway, it's perfectly natural to be curious about ladies, or boys . . . or, in fact, lady boys."

"Oh God, please stop," I groaned.

"Just don't let it get out of hand," she said, smiling.

"That had better not be a double entendre, Mum," I said, eyeing her suspiciously.

"I'm just saying that it's nothing to be ashamed of, exploring yourself and your . . . interests."

"It was a knitting website, Mum," I said. "I was looking at a knitting website, see?"

I opened the laptop and turned it around so she could see. She flinched briefly, but then looked.

"Oh," she said, sounding almost disappointed. "Right. Good. . . . So, you're serious about this knitting thing?"

"I wouldn't go that far." I laughed, with forced jollity. "But if you're going to do something . . . y'know. And it's actually quite interesting. Might as well do it to the best of your ability . . . right?"

She looked at me for a while thoughtfully, then nodded. "I understand, Ben. I used to knit, too."

"You did?"

"Yes. Wasn't much good at it, but I gave it a go when I was pregnant with you. Knitted a few booties, and a little hat, which was far too small. At the time I was blissfully unaware of just how massive that head of yours was going to be." A faint look of remembered pain floated across her face. She took off her glasses and began to clean them.

"I'll look in the loft, see if I can find my old needles," she said. "Still have some good yarn too, I think. Does yarn go bad?"

I smiled at her. She was daft sometimes.

"That'd be great," I said. "But Mum, would you mind . . ."

"What?"

"Would you mind if we kept this our little secret, for now?"

"Okay, sure," she said.

"It's just that if my friends found out, they wouldn't understand. . . ." We both knew it wasn't just my friends I was talking about.

She nodded; she understood.

She grinned at me, and I grinned back. A shared moment.

"Mum," I said eventually.

"Yes?"

"Why did you come in here?"

"Hmm?" she said. "Oh yes. It's to tell you my manager has managed to extend the tour, so I'll be off for another two weeks."

"From when?"

"Tomorrow," she said, grimacing sympathetically.

"Oh, okay," I said, trying not to let my disappointment show. I'm happy for Mum, that her career is finally getting somewhere, but I miss her when she's not around. I don't like it when we're not all together.

I'm losing it. Bellend Ben, missing his mummy, hiding knitting needles under his bed.

AUGUST 9TH

Dear Mr. Fletcher,

Another Waypoint on your Probation Journey is participation in the "Giving Something Back" victim support program. One hundred hours of your time over the next twelve months must be spent providing support or assistance to those affected by crime. We have contacted the victim of your crime, Mrs. Gloria Frensham, and she has confirmed she would like you to Give Something Back by performing basic maintenance and cleaning work at her residence, 47 Park View, Hampton.

You are required to attend Mrs. Frensham's residence weekly, for a two-hour period on Monday evenings from 4:30 p.m. to 6:30 p.m. You are not considered to be a danger to the public so these visits will be unsupervised. Please note though that we will contact Mrs. Frensham to assess your behavior, punctuality and attitude. Any failure to be punctual, polite and helpful will be a breach of the terms of your probation.

Yours,

Claudia Gunter

West Meon Probation Services

Sigh. I don't mind Giving Something Back, but do I have to Give It Back to Mrs. Frensham? She's mental, and hated me even before I smashed a bottle of Martini Rosso over her head. Something that everyone seems to have forgotten about in the fuss is that she nearly took my head off with a giant lollipop. Why can't I Give Something Back to another old lady—one who'll make me cakes and press some money into my hand and tell me I remind her of her youthful husband? Why can't someone else help Mrs. Frensham?

Someone like the waffle-cone killer.

AUGUST 9TH

Knitting was tricky tonight. We learned how to change to a different color wool halfway through. I got it, after a few false starts, and felt quite pleased with myself. Shame I can't tell anyone.

AUGUST 15TH

The upstairs toilet's blocked again. Dad blames me for using too much toilet paper, but the problem is clearly the noticeable kink in the soil pipe. The soil pipe that HE installed, I might add.

"Dad, you really need to get a real plumber in to sort out that bathroom," I said.

"I am a real plumber," he replied.

"No, you're a mechanic," I told him. "That's different."

"Ever heard of hydraulics?" he snapped. "It's plumbing for cars. It's just fluid going through pipes. Same for cars as it is for bathrooms."

"Well, then maybe I should take my dumps in the Citroën until the upstairs toilet's fixed," I said. "Let the hydraulics flush it away."

"Don't be a smart-arse," he said, and that was the end of that conversation.

God, I'm bored. I'm working on increasing and decreasing, which is gradually either adding or subtracting stitches from rows to make the piece thinner or thicker. You'd do that with a sleeve, for example, that you wanted to be thinner at the bottom than the top.

The funny thing is, when I start knitting I just get into it so quickly and next thing I know an hour's gone by. It's relaxing too. It helps me take my mind off my worries.

I think I might be starting to turn into a knitting bore.

AUGUST 27TH

So I went to see Mrs. Frensham today. That went well. Not. She lives in a terraced house on Park View, which isn't near the park and doesn't have a view. Unless the park is Sainsbury's car park and the view is Sainsbury's car park. I told Dad where I was going and he seemed really proud, like I was off to be knighted as opposed to what I was actually doing, which was fulfilling the terms of my probation by providing home assistance to an old lady I'd nearly killed. I suppose it's good to have his support, but if he's proud of me over this it does tend to suggest he has quite low expectations.

I clearly don't need to do much to earn his respect. If I'm ever in the dock at court facing a thirty-year stretch for a triple murder, I can be sure Dad will be there in the gallery wiping away a tear, beside himself with pride at the fact that I managed to tie my own tie.

Anyway, as I approached the house I was sweating bullets, frankly. Claudia Gunter had sent Mrs. Frensham a letter warning her I was coming, but that just gave her more time to plan her assault on me the minute I walked in the door. It wouldn't be just a lollipop this time. What other pieces of giant confectionery might she have in there? An eight-foot Twizzler? A mammoth tube of M&M's?

I walked up the path and rapped on the door, setting off a fusillade of yapping from inside. Oh Jesus, she's got a bloody dog, I thought.

She took ages to come to the door. I could see her approaching, a large dark shape visible through the pane of frosted glass in the door. She called out.

"Who is it?"

"It's Ben Fletch—" I began, in a strangled voice, made high-pitched by nerves. I stopped.

"What? Who? What?" she called back. "I'm an atheist!"

"Yap, yap, yap," went the dog.

I cleared my throat and tried again. "It's Ben Fletcher," I said in an exaggeratedly deep and gravelly voice, which in hindsight might have seemed a little threatening.

"Yap, yap, yap."

"Fletcher? Fletcher? Do I know you?"

"Yes, from the . . . accident, with the Martini Rosso?"

She went quiet, though I thought I may have heard a sharp intake of breath. Even the dog went quiet. Then I saw the dark shape retreat down the corridor.

"Hello?" I called. I stood there for a moment, rolling my eyes. "Mrs. Fletcher?"

Here I was, ready to start tying raspberry canes, or whitewashing the windows or whatever, and the old bat had disappeared.

A window opened on the second floor and I looked up just as a heavy object hit me on the forehead and I fell over in pain and surprise. It turned out to be an alarm clock. An old, heavy alarm clock. I looked up at her, gobsmacked, just as another object whizzed past my head and smashed on the crazy paving, something made of porcelain.

She had something else in her hand too, a hairbrush, I think, and as she curled her arm, ready to hurl it at me, I scrambled to my feet and backed down toward the gate, my heart thumping.

"You mental old witch," I yelled. A couple of people passing by had stopped to watch. "I'm not considered a danger to the public!"

"Come back to finish the job, have you?" she screeched and let fly with the hairbrush, which I was just about able to fend off. "Hoodlum!"

I wasn't even wearing my hoodie!

"I'm supposed to be here," I shouted. "Claudia Gunter sent you a letter."

"I didn't get any letter," Mrs. Frensham shouted, then she ducked back inside, presumably looking for more things to throw.

"Leave her alone," said a man carrying a Sainsbury's bag.

"I'm supposed to be here," I protested. "My probation officer sent me."

"You're frightening her," a woman said.

"I'm frightening her?" I spluttered. "I'm not the one throwing knickknacks."

"You should be ashamed," the woman said.

This was pointless. I dusted myself off and left as a bottle of hand cream bounced off my shoulder.

AUGUST 28TH

Dear Ms. Gunter,

It seems there may have been something of an administrative error. I attended the first Assistance Session at Mrs. Frensham's house yesterday, fully ready to Give Something Back, only to face an assault in the form of household objects being hurled at me from an upstairs window. I felt like King Harold besieging a Norman castle. Especially after a long, thin tube of Superdrug hemorrhoid cream hit me in the eye.

Under the circumstances I was reluctant to Give Something Back in case she Threw It Back at me.

While she was throwing things, though, Mrs. Frensham did mention that she had not received a letter from you about the visit and seemed surprised and upset by my presence. I am anxious to successfully complete all that is required of me during this probation period and would appreciate it if you could look into this matter forthwith.

Yours,
Ben

SEPTEMBER 4TH

Dear Ben,

I am sorry you had a difficult experience during your Assistance Session and I thank you for telling me about it in such descriptive language. I can assure you we did send a letter. Normally we would have followed up our letter with a phone call but I'm afraid on this occasion, due to short-staffing, I was unable to do this.

I appreciate your patience and your resolve to successfully complete your probationary requirements. I will contact Mrs. Frensham and rearrange your visit, ensuring she is fully aware of the process.

Once again, apologies for the mix-up and I look forward to hearing about the successful resolution to your frustrating siege!

Best wishes,

Claudia Gunter

West Meon Probation Services

SEPTEMBER 9TH

I'm dreading school tomorrow. I don't mind it normally, and as irritating as my friends are at least I've got some now. Before Gex showed up I was mostly on my own dealing with Lloyd "Psycho" Manning. I still can't believe I was the one who got in trouble for cracking that toilet when it was Lloyd and his friends who shoved my head into it. So I don't want to sound ungrateful or anything but recent events have caused me to worry that my friends are a liability, to say the least. See, Freya Porter is already advertising a massive party during break and everyone's invited. Even me. And I just know that if Gex and Joz and Freddie go, they will do something stupid and illegal and I'll somehow get caught up in it and it'll get back to West Meon Probation Services. And this could result in a recurring nightmare of probationary classes for the next ten years. Basically, all of my youth wiped away by hanging out with those three idiots.

On the other hand, Megan's going to be at Freya's party, and I've got a suspicion that Joz fancies Megan too, and I'm certainly not letting him try out any of his *Fifty Shades of Graham* techniques on her.

SEPTEMBER 10TH

First day of the new term today. I've decided to do both advanced math and English at AS level. On top of physics, chemistry, biology, geography and computer science.

Oh crap. Just read that back to myself.

I caught up with Freddie as we went into the main foyer and we stopped as we came face-to-face with a giant plasma screen giving us the hour in eight time zones and news tickers from around the world. We watched the scrolling text for a while and marveled at the fact that people in Mexico City were still in bed.

"What's all this about?" Freddie asked.

"I think we've been bought by someone new over the holidays," I replied.

I should explain that our school, including the upper-classmen, who are housed in a separate building, was turned into an academy three years ago. This basically meant installing a few Coke vending machines and a local office supply company donating four iPads. Then some outfit called Euripidia invested in us, became a "stakeholder" and built a new toilet block. Though why anyone would want a stake in any toilet used by Lloyd Manning is beyond me. Unfortunately Euripidia went out of business and sold their stake-holding to a U.S. bank, which also went under, and last year we were bought out, toilets and all, by a Brazilian hedge fund. Cue dozens of lame jokes from Joz about "Brazilian hedges."

Anyway, it looked like someone else had bought the school, and the toilets, which are no longer functional in any case, and had installed this spanking-new bit of technology.

I explained all this to Freddie, in simple language. He nodded and said, "But why are there all them clocks?"

I couldn't answer that, because I had no idea. There was a plaque above one of them, though. It said:

VIRILIA—INVESTING IN
TOMORROW'S ENTREPRENEURS

"I think they're looking for young entrepreneurs," I told Freddie as we headed up the stairs to our homeroom along with the throng. The sound of clattering shoes was deafening and we had to shout to be heard.

"What, like Marcus Grant selling dope to freshmen?" Freddie asked.

"Probably not," I replied.

"Or Holly Osman selling, you know . . ." he said, glancing around furtively.

"What does Holly Osman sell?" I asked.

"You know," he whispered. "In the broken bathroom stalls."

"I don't know," I said, stopping. Other students jostled me as the stream carried on up the stairs. Why didn't I know? "What does she sell?"

Freddie, for all his faults, is an excellent mime. He made it pretty clear what services Holly was offering, both of them. I was shocked, and a bit confused. I fancied Holly Osman. I had no idea she was getting mixed up in that sort of thing.

"How much does she charge for that?" I asked.

"What, this?" he said, miming again.

"No, the other one," I said.

"Ten pounds."

"That's actually quite reasonable," I said.

"It's fifteen pounds for this . . ." he said.

"Please stop doing that," I said, feeling sick.

"You have to wait to be asked," he said as we carried on.

"Are you sure about this?" I asked.

"Yes," he said, annoyed that I was doubting him. "Everyone knows."

SEPTEMBER 15TH

For once on a Saturday, the whole family was together and we celebrated by going to Tesco. After we'd done the food shop we packed the bags into the car before walking down the High Street. There are loads of empty shops these days. The butcher has closed now and Mum says the bookshop is on its last legs. Molly and I invented a game called

Death on the High Street. I got a point every time we passed a charity shop and she got a point for every mobile phone shop. I won 9–6.

There is one shop, though, that has always been on the High Street, and I've never really paid much attention to it before. It's a sort of hobby shop called Pullinger's. Not Warcraft or toy soldiers, but they do have model airplanes and ships, and they have billion-piece jigsaws in the window. It's the sort of place frequented by people who live alone, old ladies wearing raincoats and middle-aged to elderly men wearing anoraks. The thing I like about Pullinger's is the old-skool sign over the door. They've resisted the temptation to rebrand by losing the capital letter or the apostrophe.

I couldn't help noticing the display of knitting needles and brightly colored wool balls and I admit my attention was caught. I stopped to look.

I was so busy openly looking at a knitting display that I didn't notice Mum standing next to me until she nudged me with her elbow.

"Why don't you pop in?" she said. "You can catch up to us."

"What does he want in there?" Dad asked, clueless.

"He's looking for a present for Mrs. Frensham, aren't you?" said Mum. She clicked her fingers and a ten-pound note appeared, which she pushed into my hand.

I love my mum sometimes. I ducked into the shop before Dad could ask any more questions. The bell tinkled and I was in.

"Ben?" a voice said, from the depths of the shop.

I peered back there, my eyes still adjusting to the light. I relaxed when I realized who it was.

"Natasha?" I said.

She came down the aisle to greet me.

"Do you work here?" I asked.

"Yep. Three days midweek and Saturdays," she said. "Haven't seen you in here before."

"First time," I explained.

"Welcome," she said, bowing and extending an arm like a Moroccan rug-seller. "Have a look around and ask if you need any guidance."

I'd been passing this shop for sixteen years and never once entered before. It was amazing. Old-fashioned, with boxes and drawers on high shelves you could only reach with a ladder. The knitting stuff seemed mostly to be at the back, in an Aladdin's cave full of brightly colored yarns of a bewildering variety. I spent a long time inspecting a display of hundreds of knitting needles. They had U.S. sizes as well as UK and European.

In the center of the knitting room were racks of knitting patterns, new and secondhand. It was just like an old record store that sold LPs.

I was flicking through them when Natasha came wandering down to see how I was getting on.

"Retro," she said, peeking at the pattern for a vest I was holding. "Very in."

"Is it?" I asked, looking at it. I'd picked it up because it was cheap, it looked simple and I needed a vest.

"Yep," she said. She said yep quickly, like there was no point arguing with her. "You'll need washable wool for that. Thin strand."

"There are so many," I said, turning around to look up at the wall of wool.

"Lamb's wool there," she pointed out. "Here's merino, Shetland, Icelandic, fleece. The novelty wools are on the other wall; we just got some new chenille in. But novelty yarn's a bit tricky for beginners."

"Amazing," I said, doing a slow three-sixty. I loved the way they were shelved according to color, the way I'd wanted to do my books once, before I panicked and decided to abort. It really worked here. Pale blue graduated into darker blue, to indigo, through violet and beyond into the reds. Here green became yellow via a dozen stages. The blacks and browns ran vertically next to them. I found it deeply soothing, everything in its rightful place.

"Here's the washable section," she said, indicating a tall shelf in the corner. "It's treated chemically to destroy the outer layers of fiber. Otherwise it's too fuzzy and it collects dirt too easily."

She carried on showing me different varieties I can't remember now, but she was clearly very proud of her shop. It was like Q showing James Bond a selection of clever gadgets and weapon prototypes.

"This is sheep's wool, of course?" I asked, trying to sound as though I knew anything at all about wool.

"Yep. We do have goat, and even some angora."

"I thought angora was goat?" I said.

"There are angora goats," Natasha said. "Their wool is called cashmere. Angora wool comes from angora rabbits."

"I never knew," I said.

As we stood together staring at the many subtle variances of wool, something occurred to me.

"You know an awful lot about knitting for someone who's just started a beginner's knitting class," I said suspiciously.

Natasha shrugged. "I do a lot of cross-stitch and cro-chet, which isn't as tricky as knitting with needles, and I really want to learn to do it properly. The worst of it is it's my second time around in that class. I tried a couple of years ago, soon after I got this job, but I didn't have the time to practice. I didn't even finish the course. . . ."

She leaned even closer toward me and whispered, "Boy-friend trouble. Told him to take a hike eventually."

"Sorry to hear it," I said.

"It's fine, I prefer being single and available," she said, and I swear she winked at me. "Anyway, point is that I love the idea of knitting, and I read the magazines, and listen to the podcasts, but I'm not really that good at it. Not like you, you're a natural."

"Shut up," I said, blushing.

"You are," she said. "You've got skills."

There was an awkward silence for a few seconds until Natasha broke it.

"Shall we continue the tour?" she said brightly. She waved an arm casually at a selection of needles in various point sizes. "Impressive, huh?"

"Impressive," I agreed, nodding earnestly.

I hadn't really planned on buying anything when I went in, but Natasha's sales technique convinced me and I splurged on some merino in French navy, along with a couple of balls of chenille, which might come in handy for my grandma. I had just enough money.

As she handed me the bag with my goodies in it, she said, "So you're serious about this, then?"

"What?"

"Serious about knitting. You're not just doing it because you have to?"

I stiffened. "What do you mean?" I asked. "Why would I have to?"

She looked a little embarrassed.

"Sorry," she said. "I shouldn't have mentioned it. It's because of the probation thing. . . ."

"You know about that?"

Now she was bright red.

"Um . . . my friend Veronica does the admissions," she said.

"Great. So does everyone know?"

"No," she said quickly, but still the color of a ripe tomato. "Just me and Amelia."

"Great," I repeated.

Part of me was really cross about the lack of confidentiality, but another part of me was quite pleased that Natasha and her friend had been whispering about my shady past.

"Sorry," she said again. "If it's any consolation Amelia and I think it's quite cool."

"Don't worry about it," I said casually, forcing myself to avoid calling her dollface.

"See you on Thursday," she called as I left.

"See you Thursday," I replied as the bell tinkled.

SEPTEMBER 19TH

No news yet from Ms. Gunter about a new date to start Giving Something Back. I'm hoping the Mrs. Frensham gig falls through and they send me somewhere else, where

I'm less likely to be maimed. Until then, my Mondays are my own. I've started on the vest using the navy merino. I'm going quite slowly for now; I don't want to drop any stitches and there's no hurry. I've been doing just six or seven rows after I've finished my homework or just before bed. It's brilliant for helping me to de-stress.

Murder on my back, though. If I keep this up I'll be a hunchback by the time I'm twenty-one. Maybe I should take up yoga. I'm halfway to Loserville anyway, may as well take the train to the end of the line.

SEPTEMBER 20TH

There's definitely something wrong with the plumbing in the house. Taps cough and splutter, then spew out milky white stuff. The kettle doesn't work properly and last night Mum couldn't get the SodaStream to work. Of course, this has prompted my parents to ramp up the innuendos again.

"There's no fizz coming out of the nozzle," Mum shouted through to Dad.

"That's not what you said last night," Dad called back.

"No!" I screamed, putting my hands over my ears. "Just. No." Dad wiped away a tear and said he'd check the pipes.

"I'll check your pipes," Mum said and it all kicked off again.

I went up to my room at that point and unfortunately missed the rest of the double act.

SEPTEMBER 21ST

Natasha has this totally infectious laugh and had a fit of the giggles when I was telling her about the Siege of Frensham at knitting last night.

"You're funny, Ben," she said. "You do make me laugh."

I'll take it. Given that enrolling in Knitting 101 is a sure-fire repellent to most of the opposite sex I can't afford to be fussy when it comes to these random compliments.

"Thanks," I said, trying not to look too pleased.

I was still on a high as I was walking down the hall afterward and Miss Swallow popped out of her classroom and asked me how the ziggurat was coming along.

"Really well," I lied effortlessly. "I'm working on the sacrificial victims at the moment. It's a total bloodbath."

"Do you need more clay?"

"Er, yes?" As it happened, I had some in my pocket. I've been keeping a few lumps in wet newspaper under my bed, along with my needles and yarn in a cardboard box I'd begun thinking of as the Box of Shame. But I could hardly tell her that.

She popped back inside the class and came back a moment later with another lump, wrapped in plastic.

"Thanks," I said, shoving it into my other pocket.

"So. When can I see it?" she asked, leaning against the door frame in a provocative kind of way.

"See what?"

"The ziggurat!"

"Oh, it's a bit too big to bring in," I replied cleverly.

"So take a photo," she said.

"A photo?" I replied. "I could take a photo."

"Next week," she said, pointing a perfectly formed finger at me.

"Next week," I replied.

What an idiot. When am I going to have time to make a bloody ziggurat?

SEPTEMBER 22ND

Nearly got rumbled today. I wandered up the hill into town this morning. It was a beautiful, cold day, clear blue skies, with so many vapor trails criss-crossing the sky that it looked like a giant had been knitting. With jets. Badly.

Joz and Freddie had said they would be in town today too, possibly accompanied by the secretive Gex, who no one's seen for ages. I toured their usual hangouts; the low wall behind the hardware store, the rotten old park bench under the oak tree by the church, just outside Tesco Metro, where Freddie likes to stand and make the automatic doors open and close over and over, driving the checkout girls slowly insane. Apart from a thousand empty crisp packets and a million discarded Red Bull cans, I found nothing and no one, so I wandered up to Smith's shop to see if the October issue of *Knit!* was in yet.

It was! I grabbed a copy off the shelves and checked out the cover stories.

AUTUMN WEAVES: Eight New Yarns for the Fall Season

GOATS IN THE MACHINE: We Investigate
Animal Welfare in Industrial Yarn-Making

CABLE KNITS: The Industry Minister Vince Cable Puts Down His Red Box and Picks Up His Red Yarn to Show Us What He Can Do

JIMMY CARR: The Moon-Faced Comic Has Us in Stitches

GENERAL PATTERN: Our Regular Feature Returns, Bringing You This Year's Four Patterns You Simply Can't Do Without

Happy as a pig in shit, I started flicking through. It's not cheap, *Knit!*, but in my view it's the best knitting publication available, and the competition is stiff, let me tell you. The *Knit!* editorials are thought-provoking, rather than simply provocative. There are some highly investigative pieces too. The goat story was shocking, and last month they looked at child labor in the subcontinent and the economic woes of the knitting-machine industry.

I was deeply involved in an article about ecological damage caused by industrial wool dyes when I heard a cry from the front of the store.

"Bellend!" My heart rate accelerated as I looked up to see Joz, Freddie and Gex heading toward me at pace. How could I have been so reckless, so casual? I was going to get busted.

Thinking on my feet, I shot out a hand and snatched a copy of *Loaded* off the shelf and jammed it inside *Knit!*

"What's this?" Freddie asked, grabbing hold of the magazine. "*Knit!* You're reading *Knit!*"

I winked and opened the magazine and showed him the copy of *Loaded* inside. He looked at me as if I was a loony.

"Why're you hiding that?" he asked.

Gex and Joz peered over his shoulders to see what I was up to.

"In case Mum comes in," I said. "She thinks it exploits young women."

Joz looked puzzled. "In what way?"

Even Gex and Freddie looked a bit surprised by Joz's question at that moment, which was good for me. I silently thanked Joz for being such an idiot.

"Well, like that?" I said, showing him a picture of a girl who looked like she might be both cold and uncomfortable, bent over the wooden chair as she was, in that warehouse.

"Let's see," Freddie said, craning to look. He shook his head. "You think that's exploitation . . ."

He grabbed another magazine off the top shelf and tore open the plastic bag it came in. Opening it at a particularly intimate spread, he jammed a finger at it and said, "That's exploitation."

So then we all had to look through all the dirty magazines for half an hour until the manager came back from her break and told us to get out. It's not that I hate looking at that stuff but it gets a bit repetitive after a bit. And while they were there, examining each girl's boob or bum with such thoroughness that they seemed to be hoping to find the solution to the Da Vinci Code, I found my eyes wandering down, to the copy of *Knit!* I'd sheepishly replaced, or over to the left, where I'd just noticed this month's new knitting patterns had arrived.

I couldn't wait to get home and get to work with the vest.

SEPTEMBER 24TH

I had a dream last night that I was up at the top of the Shard, that new building in London that looks like it hasn't been finished off properly. I was in a dark office, after hours, just ambling around when something caught my eye. I looked at the window and saw there was a piece of paper on the outside, pressed against the glass by the wind. As I approached I realized it was a knitting pattern. But not just any knitting pattern. This was crazy, insanely complicated. I could make out enough of the detail to know that if I could just knit this pattern, all the way through, that something would happen. Something good. Things would be made complete. But it was just so complex. And how could I reach it, out there on the other side?

I heard something behind me and I turned to see Frank Lampard. He nodded and smiled.

"Go on, Ben," he said in his Birmingham lilt. "Go and get the pattern, mate."

Then it all got a bit confused and it wasn't Frank Lampard anymore and I was on a spaceship about to crash-land and Molly was there wearing my cycling helmet and I can't remember the rest.

But that must mean something, mustn't it? About the knitting pattern? And Frank Lampard?

SEPTEMBER 26TH

Finally gave Joz the edited text for *Fifty Shades of Graham*. We were in the common room, supposedly studying. The weather was crap. Icy rain outside.

Joz was really eager to see what I thought.

"Thanks," he said breathlessly as he read through it. "This is brilliant!"

"Let's not go overboard," I replied.

"I think we could really have something here," he went on, not to be discouraged.

"Are you sure about the title?" I asked.

"Oh yeah," he replied, nodding furiously. "I read a book about it. How to get your self-published ebook to the top of the Kindle charts."

"And it suggested you blatantly rip off the title of another book?"

"Yes. It's about what search terms people put in."

"What do they put in? 'Clumsy rip-off of badly written sex book'?"

"Something like that."

"Fair enough."

He looked at me and grinned. "Thanks for your help on this, Ben," he said. "I couldn't do it without you."

"Oh, shut up," I said suspiciously.

"No, really, I'm serious about this. I just want to be the best I can be."

I put my hand on his shoulder and nodded. "You already are, Joz," I said. "You already are."

"Thanks," he said uncertainly.

"It's just . . . well . . . ," I began, before trailing off.

"Well what?"

"It's just . . . one of the central characters is called Graham."

"Yeah? It's like Grey. Grey Am."

"I know why you chose it, I'm just not sure it's very . . . sexy."

"Hey, you just stick to the editing, Brainiac, I'll do the sexy."

Anyway, that made me feel a bit sick so I went outside after that.

SEPTEMBER 27TH

Tonight at knitting, Mrs. Hooper told us that there will be an assessment in the course. Apparently if we complete it successfully we get a Certificate in Knitting Proficiency—Level 1. I'm used to this kind of thing. Everything's tested these days. You can't go thirty seconds at school without someone quizzing you on what you learned twenty-five seconds before.

So the assessment is in two parts. There's a brief written examination, which she says will be pretty simple, mostly multiple choice. The other thing is that we have to Complete a Garment of at Least Moderate Complexity. Extra credit is given if you design your own pattern.

I'm definitely going to create my own pattern. I now know what the Shard dream was about! I have some brilliant design in my head which is locked away just now but if I learn the right codes I can unlock it and access the pattern. I'm going to sit down tomorrow with some blank sheets and see what I can come up with. There's no hurry, the garment doesn't need to be finished until Christmas.

SEPTEMBER 28TH

Dear Ben,
I'm pleased to let you know I have successfully rearranged your Giving Something Back session with Mrs. Frensham. Your first appointment is at 4:30 p.m. on Monday, October 8th. I have spoken to Mrs. Frensham in person. She is expecting you and has promised she will not hurl hemorrhoid cream at you.
Best wishes,
Claudia Gunter
West Meon Probation Services

SEPTEMBER 29TH

Dad's embarked on another mission to get me interested in soccer. He dragged me down to Hampton FC again today. The field is located about a mile out of town. They used to play on a field in the town center but the council sold it to Tesco and the club moved out. There isn't a tree for miles, it's right on the edge of the South Downs and the wind comes howling up from the sea from October to April. The few supporters who can be bothered to come all the way out here sit together in a clump in the uncovered stand, like male emperor penguins protecting their eggs, waiting for the females to come. Freddie wasn't there, unfortunately, so I ended up having to make conversation with Dad while we watched Joe Boyle running rings around everyone else on the field.

"He'd still be playing for Portsmouth if he hadn't done his knee in," Dad said.

"His knee looks all right to me," I said as Joe nutmegged a defender and scored Hampton's third goal. He turned and held out his arms like an airplane, a huge grin on his face. He looked like he was the happiest man in the world just then.

"Go on, my son!" Dad yelled, standing up and clapping.

"All right, calm down, Dad," I said quietly.

"He's not so quick on the turn as he used to be," Dad mused. "It was a bad job; he was out for two whole seasons. No coming back from that, not at thirty-five."

"Shame," I murmured.

"He's doing all right," Dad said. "Doesn't earn much now, but I heard he invested wisely while he was getting the big wages."

"His girlfriend's nice," I said, a bit out of my depth and looking down at the front row, where Miss Swallow sat.

"Not half bad," Dad agreed, dragging his eyes away from Joe Boyle for a moment.

Miss Swallow was wearing an attractive cowl-neck top, quite loose. From where we sat, we could see just a hint of her modest cleavage. We sighed as one, then turned our attention back to the game.

"Chelsea had a good win yesterday," Dad said.

"How'd Lampard do?" I asked politely, but not caring.

"Couple of near misses," he said, sounding slightly

embarrassed. "But that's the thing about Chelsea, someone'll step up when they need to."

"Better a champion team than a team of champions," I said, feeling quite pleased with myself.

He nodded. "Fancy coming to watch them sometime? Up to London?"

"Yeah, maybe," I said, my heart sinking. Last time he'd taken me to a game in London it hadn't ended well. He'd forgotten I was with him in the pub afterward. A fight had kicked off and he'd bolted. I managed to get out eventually but was accidentally kicked in the face by a Man City fan.

But Dad is persistent, I'll give him that. He promised he would ask his friend about some tickets for Chelsea.

"That would be amazing," I lied. Soccer's so dull. If only you could do something else while you were there. Like watch something more interesting, for example. Hmm, I wonder what would happen if I pulled out my knitting during the first half. I couldn't do that to Dad.

Speaking of knitting, the vest is coming along nicely. I was right to think it was a simple pattern. It's taking a long time though, because the yarn is thin and I have to use tiny needles to get the tight weave. Vests aren't supposed to be fluffy, they should be sheer and smooth to the touch. I think I was wise to go with a dark color.

If only I could talk to Dad about knitting. Then I wouldn't have to rely on clichés to make conversation with him.

Hampton 6, Haslemere 1.

OCTOBER 1ST

My bike is in the shop for repairs, by which I mean it's at Dad's garage waiting for him to get around to fixing it. I may have seen the last of the bike this term, to judge by previous experiences having Dad fix it. He's so cheap, why won't he pay for me to get it repaired down at Evans's?

"Why don't you pay?" he said, when I suggested this.

"I don't have any money," I pointed out.

"What about your allowance?" he said.

"Dad, the last time you gave me allowance Britney Spears was happily married."

"So your mum doesn't give you allowance, then?"

"She sometimes lets me keep what she finds behind my ear," I told him.

"And what's that, usually?"

"Fifty pence, maybe. Occasionally a pound. Sometimes not even money, just stuff she's carrying around. Last week she gave me a dishwasher tablet."

"Well, then you should get a job," he said, exasperated.

"When would I find time to work?" I asked. "On Mondays I'm at Mrs. Frensham's, Thursday night I'm at kn— pottery. You have me helping at the garage on Saturdays. I'm supposed to be studying for AS levels this year."

"What about a paper route?" he suggested. "Try getting out of bed a bit earlier."

"How am I supposed to deliver the papers without a damn bike!" I shouted.

He stopped and turned to me, pointed a buttery knife.

"You get yourself a paper route, and I'll fix your bike for you, how's that for a deal?"

"Aaaargh!" I yelled, before storming off to my room.

Mum's away AGAIN. I feel uneasy when it's just me and Molly and Dad around the house. I'm not convinced about Dad's parenting skills. Bedtime causes him particular difficulties. Last week we paused *Band of Brothers* while he went up to read Molly a story. He was gone ages so I went up to check and found him asleep in her bed. She was sitting up next to his snoring frame watching *Harry Potter V* on my Kindle Fire. *HPV*! I find *HPV* too scary. And he never remembers to turn her lava lamp off.

"Switch off after eight hours use!" I tell him, pointing to the instruction manual, which I kept for future reference.

"Stop fussing," he says.

I wish Mum would come back. We're okay for a few days, the three of us. And I don't mind Dad trying to do guy things with me, not at first. But after a few days we start to really irritate each other and bicker. Mum smooths all that stuff over, neatens everything up.

OCTOBER 3RD

I finished the vest tonight. I've got to say, it looks amazing, and it fits me perfectly.

OCTOBER 4TH

Popped into Miss Swallow's pottery class before knitting tonight as I needed some fresh clay for the ziggurat I'm pretending to make.

"You promised me a photo of it ages ago," she remarked. "I'm intrigued, I must say."

"I've decided you have to wait until I've finished," I said. "I want it to be just right."

"Fine," she said. "But it had better be good."

For half a second I wondered about suggesting she came to my house to inspect it. Imagine that, having Miss Swallow in my bedroom, checking out my ziggurat. But of course I didn't have the nerve.

"Have you knitted anything so far?" she asked, handing me a lump of clay in a plastic wrapper.

"I knitted this," I said, indicating my vest.

"You knitted that?" she asked, feeling the vest, her fingers brushing lightly against my chest.

"It's brilliant! You're amazing." She looked up at me and gave me one of her megasmiles, and a close-up of her slightly imperfect teeth.

"No, you're amazing," I wanted to say.

Then a thoughtful look came over her face.

"Look, I don't suppose you'd knit one for me, would you? I'll pay. How much, twenty-five pounds?"

"You want a vest?" I asked.

"Not for me, for my boyfriend."

"Oh," I said unenthusiastically.

"It would need to be a bit bigger than that one," she said.

I nodded. So he's huge and I'm tiny. Rub it in, why don't you?

"A lot bigger, in fact, around the chest."

"Okay. Got it," I said a bit snappily. "Can you find out his chest measurement?"

"Sure." She megasmiled at me again, turning back to her pots. I was just shuffling out of the door when she called my name.

"Ben?" she said. "I've just thought. You know I sell my pots on Etsy, don't you?"

"Um. Etsy?"

"It's a website. Like eBay, but specifically for people who make their own products," she said. "You should start up a page there. Sell your vests, and . . . anything else you make. People will pay for handmade things, you know?"

"I'll check it out," I said, feeling a bit better.

After the encouragement Miss Swallow had given me, I showed Mrs. Hooper the vest. She was astonished.

"Ben, you have a gift. Look at these tight purls, these could have been made by a knitting machine."

"Nah . . ." I began modestly.

"Really, Ben. You have natural talent. You should be proud."

She was still going on about my natural talent when I tried to leave after the class. I was starting to feel slightly uncomfortable. I haven't had so much praise since I stopped wetting the bed.

"Ben, I meant what I said before, about you having a natural talent," she said.

"Now, this might not be of interest to you. And you might feel you don't have the time, but the All-UK Knitting

Championship is getting under way soon. They're having regional heats, and there's a junior category."

"Championship? Are you serious?" I asked. "I've only just started."

"Ben, those patterns you designed, they are seriously impressive. Your technique is brilliant. You won't have to take on anything complex, they'll just be looking for basic weaves at the junior level. It's about technique, pattern design and speed."

"So what, I just submit some pieces of work and they judge them?"

"Yes, but there's also a showcase event. You have to knit in a room with other contestants. You won't know what the pattern is until the event itself, then you're given two hours total to complete two tasks."

"Like *MasterChef*?" I thought about it.

"Yes," she said. "Except without the TV cameras."

"But will anyone be watching?"

"Yes, of course." She nodded. Like that was a good thing. "There'll be a live audience."

She gave me a brochure about the event that featured a rather uninspiring photograph of a group of round-shouldered knitters sitting in rows in a convention center. They all looked like they could do with a few yoga classes.

I'd have to think about this. On the one hand, the idea really excited me. Proving myself against others my age. Challenging myself. And if I'm serious about maybe selling things on this website Miss Swallow told me about, then winner of the UK Junior Knitting Championship, or even finalist, would look good on the CV.

On the other hand, was I ready to go public? It would be

hard to keep my knitting habit under my beanie should I achieve any kind of success.

Also, I was enjoying the quiet escape offered by the class. Did I really want to try to take that further? Surely this was about simple pleasures? Sitting with nice people, in a room, knitting garments that no one was likely to wear. Success might change all that, turn me driven and goal-focused. Did I really want to be the Frank Lampard of the knitting world?

"Anyway, think about it," Mrs. Hooper said, with eyebrows slightly raised at the intense expression of concentration which I guess had come over my face.

"I will," I said, a hand in my pocket squeezing clay between my fingers. "I will."

OCTOBER 5TH

School was good and bad today. Good because I had double maths in the morning and I can't get enough of quadratic equations. They're very like knitting in a way. It's about using a simple tool, a pencil in this case, to turn basic values into complete patterns. When I'm deep inside a calculation, my mind just shuts everything else out and all I can see is the equation itself. Nothing else can bother me. I'm totally engaged in a single-minded pursuit of just one thing.

The bad bit happened when I went out for lunch. I was looking for Joz and as I walked down past the science block, I ran slap-bang into Lloyd Manning. He gave me a shove.

"Watch where you're going, Bellend," he snarled.

"Sorry," I said, backing away. But of course one of his huge friends, Jermaine, had walked up behind me and I bumped into him instead. He shoved me from behind.

"What's wrong with you?" Jermaine said. "You a retard?"

"Look, guys," I said, "I don't want any trouble."

My heart was beating fast. Last term George Foxwell had made the mistake of mentioning Lloyd's episode in the sponsored bathrooms and ended up with a broken nose and gravel rash from being dragged across the netball court.

"Then stay out of my way, retard," Manning growled.

He shoved me against a wall. Though Lloyd and his friends are only underclassmen, they are all much bigger and fatter than me. I felt my cheeks redden with the humiliation.

They didn't take it any further though, and walked off after that, Jermaine pretending to slap me as he passed, causing me to flinch. They sniggered and disappeared round the corner. I brushed myself off and carried on, only to spot Megan across the court. She was looking my way, presumably having watched the whole thing. Great.

I've been waiting for an opportunity to go and talk to Megan. I've sent her a friend request on Facebook but she hasn't accepted yet. If she does, maybe we could DM and that might help get things moving. Today, after the incident with Manning and his gang, was not the time to make my move.

OCTOBER 7TH

Dad has finally admitted he doesn't know anything about pipes and has contacted a proper plumber about the water problem. It's getting ridiculous. There's no pressure, and the little water that does come out is all filthy.

Started designing my pattern today. I've come up with something I'm just calling Pattern Mk 1 at the moment. It's a loose-fitting top with a tight, complex weave. It has a wide neck but I'm not sure about that. It's supposed to be unisex but I think it looks distinctly feminine. It would help if I could draw better, but the pictures in my head never look the same once I've drawn them. I wish I could ask Joz to help, he's so good at drawing. Still, a work in progress, and I'm feeling positive about it.

OCTOBER 8TH

Despite lacking a bike, I took my helmet with me over to Mrs. Frensham's today and put it on as I approached, not wanting to take any chances. I'd been psyching myself up on the ride over and I knocked on the door a bit nervously, triggering the yapping dog again. I was worried about that dog. I heard Mrs. Frensham come shuffling down the hall and then the door opened.

"Hello, Mrs. Fren—" I managed before having to reel away from her walking stick, which she was waving at me aggressively. Simultaneously, the little dog shot out and sank its teeth into my ankle, making me scream with pain. Understandably, I kicked.

"Leave him alone, you bully," Mrs. Frensham shouted at me, unfairly. She came at me with the stick again.

"Mrs. Frensham, it's me, Ben Fletcher," I called, hands held up in surrender. "I'm here to Give Something Back."

"I'll give you something back," she cried, lifting up the cane to finish me off. *What would Katniss do?* I thought as I closed my eyes and waited for the blow.

But the blow never came.

"Fletcher, you say?" Mrs. Frensham stood over me, the warrior queen, weapon held high.

"The one they called about?"

"Yes," I replied, nodding furiously. "The probation service." The dog was emitting little growls, still chewing agonizingly on my ankle.

"Get off him, Jasper," she said, aiming her own kick at the dog. Jasper leaped back, looking disappointed.

Mrs. Frensham finally lowered her club and nodded at me. "Better come in, then."

I kept my helmet on and followed her into the house. It smelled like lavender and potpourri and some kind of boiled meat. Human flesh, possibly.

We walked right through to the back and Mrs. Frensham took me outside into the garden. She walked toward the shed. I limped after her, my ankle aching and a little damp, though whether that was with Jasper's saliva or my blood I wasn't sure I had the courage to check. Why were we going to the shed? I suddenly thought. What was in there? Body parts?

Mrs. Frensham opened the door and we peered inside. It wasn't body parts, it was junk. Old junk, mostly piles of paper. It all looked like it had been there a long time.

"My late husband was a bit of a hoarder," Mrs. Frensham explained. "This was his shed. Been like this since he died."

"You want me to clear it out?" I asked.

She nodded. "Never been able to bring myself to do it," she said. "But it's silly, keeping it all there."

"And what should I do with it all?" I asked. "Do you want it all thrown away?"

"If you find any photos or letters," she said, "keep those. Everything else can go, unless it looks important."

"Important?" I asked.

"Use your common sense," she snapped. "Or maybe you don't have any common sense."

"I have plenty of common sense," I replied, stung.

"We'll see," she said, and handed me a roll of trash bags before stalking off back into the house. Jasper gave me a look of contempt and waddled off after her.

I looked back at the shed, groaning with dusty piles of old newspapers, pieces of broken furniture, old bike parts, moldy cardboard boxes and thousands and thousands of mouse droppings.

And then it started to rain.

I sighed and began work, first trying to clear enough space in the shed to stand out of the rain. Once I'd started though I went solidly at it for two hours, until Mrs. Frensham came out to check on me. It all took a long time as the piles of papers that were nearest the door weren't just newspapers, but had other documents in there too. Old accounts, files of business correspondence, magazine clippings. I had to go through everything to make sure it wasn't important. The stuff I wasn't sure about I put into a separate box, out of the rain.

I'd filled maybe a dozen bags with trash when Mrs. Frensham darkened the doorway behind me like the reaper come to take my soul. She nodded briskly at the work I'd done, even though I felt I'd hardly made a dent in the junk pile. She had a quick look at the documents I'd thought might be worth keeping and then added the box to the throw-away pile.

"All right," she said. "You can go."

And that was that. When I got home my back killed from all the leaning over. My fingers were covered in paper cuts, my face was covered in filth from the dust and I didn't smell nice. But it didn't matter, because I was Giving Something Back.

OCTOBER 9TH

On the way home from school today I ran into Megan. That's one advantage of not having my bike. I saw she was a hundred yards behind me so I stopped to tie my laces for about an hour before she caught up, then I stood and looked all surprised to see her.

"Oh, hiya, Megan," I said.

"Were you waiting for me?" she asked.

"Er, yes. I suppose I was."

"Pretending to tie your shoelace?"

"Kind of."

"For ages."

"Yes. Well, you walk very slowly."

"I slowed down when I saw you because I was a bit freaked out about what you were doing."

"Oh. Well, I was pretending to tie my shoelace so that you'd catch up."

"Yeah."

There was a pause.

"Shall we walk together?" I suggested.

"Okay," she said, smiling.

"Haven't seen you for ages," I said.

"I saw you this morning in history," she pointed out.

"Yes, but not to talk to."

"No," she agreed. "Not to talk to."

"Not since the Great Trolley Robbery at Waitrose."

"Ha!" she said. Then clapped her hand over her mouth.

"It's okay," I said, grinning. "You can laugh at me."

"I missed you at Seneira's party," she said.

"Yeah, it would have been good."

"It was wild," she said, in a tone that made me wonder who she'd been wild with. But I didn't ask.

"You know Freya Porter is having a party soon?" she went on.

"Yeah, I heard that. Are you going?" I asked as casually as I could manage.

"Yeah, I think so, are you?" she asked, looking straight ahead.

"I will if . . . yeah, I'll go."

Ask her if we can go together, ask her if we can go together.

"So this is me," she said.

We'd arrived at her house. A neat, tidy semidetached place with a perfect garden and a classy absence of cars on bricks at the front.

"Okay," I said. "See you tomorrow, I guess."

"Yep," she said. "See you tomorrow."

Apart from asking her if we could go to the party together, which I think might have sounded a bit needy anyway, I can't think what I could have done better during that exchange. And yet I don't really think I made any progress at all. I know, I should have asked for her number, that's it.

Still, things are okay. We're going to be at the same party at the same time. And she did say she'd missed me at Seneira's party.

She missed me.

OCTOBER 10TH

Just eaten a bad clementine. The one just before it was amazing and sweet and juicy. How does that work? Seems these days that it's fifty-fifty with clementines, just like people I suppose. Not much else happened today. Mum's back tomorrow. Thank the Lord. Dad and I are seriously running out of conversation, as well as celementines. Also Molly is becoming increasingly feral.

Last night I came upstairs just before nine, well after her bedtime, to find Molly come sprinting past, completely naked and singing a Katy Perry song with explicit lyrics.

"Molly?" I said. "Did you know you have toothpaste on your bottom?"

She stopped and twisted around to look.

"Not *again*," she said, and ran off again.

Doing Miss Swallow's vest, making it really tight, trying to see if I can get it smooth, like it's been done by a machine. If I can get these right I can sell them on the Etsy site.

OCTOBER 11TH

Incredible. Mum's been back less than twenty-four hours and she and Dad have started with the bloody double entendres again. If they keep this up I'm calling Child Services.

> *Mum:* I don't think you boys have been eating properly while I've been away. I'm going to make you a hearty meal tonight. What would you like?
>
> *Me:* What about chicken pot pie? That's hearty.
>
> *Dad:* Yes, please. I do like a bit of your mum's pie.
>
> *Me:* *Suspicious pause*
>
> *Mum:* What would you like in it?
>
> *Dad:* I know what I'd like to put in your pie, Susan.
>
> *Me:* Gross. Stop it.
>
> *Dad/Mum:* Stop what?
>
> *Molly:* Yes, stop what?
>
> *Me:* The pie talk. Stop the pie talk.
>
> *Mum:* You don't want my pie?
>
> *Dad:* I want your pie.
>
> *Me:* I'm going to my room.

I did actually want Mum's pie, having said all that. Her pies are pretty good, though I found it hard to look Dad in the eye while we were eating.

"How about dessert?" Mum offered when I'd finished.

"Yeah. Your mum's getting her muffins out tonight," said Dad, with his mouth still full.

I rose from the table in protest, a look of disgust on my face.

"Shut up, Dave. Ben, sit down," Mum ordered. "Can't we just sit together for two minutes at a meal for once?"

Giving Dad a warning glare, I sat back down stiffly.

"How's the pottery going, Ben?" Dad asked, on his best behavior now. Mum glanced up at me quickly.

"Fine," I said. "I'm not sure I'm going to be the next . . ." I stopped.

"I can't think of any famous potters," I said.

"Harry?" Molly suggested.

"Beatrix?" Mum said.

"I mean, potmaker, or . . . um, ceramicist? Or whatever they're called. I don't think I'm going to be the world's first famous potwrangler, is what I'm trying to say," I carried on. "But I'm not doing too badly."

"So when are we going to see some of the fruits of your labor?" Dad asked before cramming a huge forkful of mashed potato into his mouth.

Mum raised an eyebrow at me.

"Next week," I said firmly.

"Not tonight?" he asked.

"No, nothing ready yet," I said. "I'll bring something back next week."

"Great!" he said. "What is it?"

"It's a surprise," I answered confidently.

Surprise is an understatement. What the hell am I going to show him?

And I've got to make the ziggurat, too. Why am I doing this to myself?

OCTOBER 12TH

We tried something a little more complicated in knitting last night, and I'm afraid to say I struggled with it. Mrs. Hooper gave us patterns for a tea cozy, which seemed simple enough. The way I like to work though is to get the whole pattern in my head, rather than just work on it stitch by stitch. And I just couldn't get my head around the tea cozy, for some reason. A hole for the spout, then a hole for the base, and a hole for the lid, and a hole for the handle, all different sizes. Add in some stranded colorwork, which I find difficult and . . . well, I just didn't like it.

"Just follow the pattern," Mrs. Hooper said to me. "Don't worry about the holes till you come to them."

Easy for her to say. As far as I'm concerned the best time to worry about something is well before you come to it. That way you're prepared.

OCTOBER 15TH

I've spent two useless hours trolling the charity shops around Hampton, looking for pottery pieces I can show my dad and pass off as my own work. It's all a bunch of crap. Everything's either chipped, old-fashioned or stamped with MADE IN STOKE.

I need something amateurish and recent. Mum suggested I go to the craft fair, but that's not on until Sunday and I promised Dad I'd have something for him on Thursday after class.

What a bloody stupid tangled web I've weaved.
. . . or knitted.

OCTOBER 16TH

On the *Knitwits!* podcast I was listening to today, they were talking about the Ocean Spray sweater that seems to be all the rage at the moment in U.S. knitting circles. I checked it out online and it is really nice.

I've downloaded the pattern from an illegal pattern-sharing site, which I feel pretty bad about, but to do it legally would have cost $19.99, which is about £12.50.

How mad is that? You could buy a sweater for that at Mackays. Admittedly Mackays isn't the most upmarket clothing store, and their sweaters aren't as nice as the Ocean Spray, but still.

Anyway, it looks pretty complicated, but I think I'll give it a go.

OCTOBER 18TH

I'm a genius, and sometimes it takes a genius to see the simple answer to a complex set of problems. Take these four statements:

Dad thinks I'm taking pottery.

I need some convincing evidence of my pottering, or pottaging activities.

Miss Swallow is teaching the pottery class.

Miss Swallow wants a vest for her boyfriend.

Now pop these statements into the mind of a genius. Stir vigorously, simmer for an hour. Season to taste and serve with crusty bread.

"I'll do a deal with you," I said to Miss Swallow. I'd got there early again and had popped into the pottery class before anyone else arrived. She had her hair tied back and had a smudge of clay on her left temple. I had to keep my hands clenched to stop myself trying to wipe the smudge away.

"Go on," she said as she carried on cutting lumps of the slick, brown clay and slapping them down onto individual desks.

"I need a present for my mum's birthday," I said. "I'd like to get her a nice set of coffee mugs. Handmade."

"Ah, I see where this is going," Miss Swallow said, stopping to grin at me. "You want to swap the vest for some mugs?"

I nodded.

"But your vests are lovely," she said. "They're worth far more than a few misshapen mugs."

"I think your pott . . . ing is amazing," I said. "I saw your products on Etsy. They're fantastic."

"Thanks, Ben, that's sweet," she said. "Still, four coffee mugs don't seem like much. Can I throw in a plant pot?"

"Go for it," I said. Deal done. I grabbed a little more clay "for the ziggurat" and left, rubbing my hands evilly.

And in knitting tonight, I finally finished that stupid tea cozy. I didn't enjoy it but I finished it. I'll never do another one again. Say No to Cozies!

OCTOBER 19TH

Result! Miss Swallow gave me the mugs and flowerpot today at school. I've hidden the flowerpot under some old tarp behind the shed. I can use that later. The mugs I'll present to Dad after next week's class.

I'm a genius, I'm a genius.

In other news, the plumber came today, finally, and apparently told Dad the pipes were all clogged up. Brilliant. I could have told him that. Turns out there's something in the water! The city council have been contacted. I knew it. This is why I'm so weedy and have no facial hair. I'm being slowly poisoned. Am going to start taking water bottles to school to fill up there. I'll be burly and hirsute within a month.

I've not got a thing to wear to the party tonight. I'm feeling nervous now it's here. If it wasn't for Megan, there's no way I'd be going. I hope my friends don't embarrass me.

I hope I don't embarrass myself.

OCTOBER 20TH

So. The party.

Could have gone better, could have gone worse. . . .

Gex and I met up with Joz, who was on his bike, and we walked to Freya's house, which is a big classy place in a new housing development. On the way Gex opened his bag and gave us all a bottle. Mine was Martini Rosso.

"Is this supposed to be a joke?" I asked, staring at it.

He looked surprised.

"I thought that was your drink, isn't it."

"Really? You thought my drink was Martini Rosso?"

"Well, what is it, then?" Freddie asked.

"Yeah, what is it, then?" Gex repeated.

"I—I don't know," I said. "But it certainly isn't this."

"Look, it's just to get you into the party," Gex said. "You're not going to drink anything anyway cuz you is a pansy."

"I is not a pansy," I retorted. "I mean I am not a pansy. I just don't see why it's necessary to get drunk and vomit on the carpet in order to have a good night."

"Whatever, Bellend," Gex sighed.

So the first sign of foreboding was when Brianna Moore answered the door and claimed she didn't recognize us.

"ID, please," she said suspiciously.

"Brianna . . . it's us," I said. "You know . . . from school?"

She peered at the three of us, frowning.

"Oh, right. Maybe."

"So, gonna let us in, then?" asked Joz.

"How did you even find out about this party anyway?" she said, ignoring the question. "It's not on Facebook."

"Freya invited us," Gex piped up. "She invited every-one, totes."

"Only sixth form," Brianna said.

"We are upperclassmen," I said. "You and I were in the same geography class last term, remember?"

"You and me?" she said, peering at me.

"You and I," I corrected. "You sat right behind me." I was astonished at her poor memory.

"No way, there was some little dark-haired loser in front of me," she said.

"That was me!" I said. I turned around to show her the back of my head.

Thankfully, at this point Freya and her friend Jasmine came to the door and let us in. Freya warned us that her father was upstairs with a headache and a five iron and that no one was to go up there on pain of death.

Once we got inside, the party was the usual sort of thing. Everyone just talking to their friends, getting drunk on mixed drinks and fighting over the music. This must have been going on for some time as Freddie had nearly slipped in a pool of vomit as we'd walked up the drive earlier.

"We should of brought mixers," Freddie said.

We poured ourselves glasses of our various drinks (no one wanted my Martini Rosso, including me) and stood awkwardly in the kitchen. I kept looking out for Megan, who was the only reason I'd agreed to come, but she didn't seem to be there.

"Imagine if you were always drunk," Freddie said.

"Like Mr. Carter?" Joz said.

"No, I mean, what if everyone was always drunk. Like it was your normal way to be. And when you drank alcohol it made everything seem normal, not like really fuzzy."

There was a pause while we all thought this over.

"Yeah," Gex said. "People would, like, get up in the morning and go, 'I simply can't start the day without a double vodka and oatmeal.' You know, instead of a cup of tea or whatever?"

"Soccer players would have to start drinking forty-eight hours before an important game," said Freddie. "Just to, like, function properly during the match."

"School would be a bit more fun," Freddie pointed out.

"Makes you think," Joz said.

"Def," Gex said, sipping his whiskey and ginger ale.

"I think there's already a term for what you're describing," I said.

"Really?" Joz asked.

"Yes, it's called alcoholism."

Thankfully Freya and Jasmine came over to talk after a while. They're actually quite nice as it happens. Freya's kind of plain and ordinary looking, but Jasmine is, well, pretty, with big dark eyes, and she's always smiling and even Joz stopped being vile about the female species for a bit. Gex didn't say a word to Freya, which I know is his way of showing a girl he likes her. Freddie tried his own pickup technique on Jasmine—he offered her drugs that he doesn't have and has no way of getting. After a while the girls went off but Jasmine came back later and handed Gex a note.

Gex looked at it and then gave it to Freddie to read. Gex struggles a bit with handwriting.

"Freya wants to meet you in her room at eleven," he said. "Top of the stairs, second door on the left. But be careful of her dad. Try to distract him so he goes downstairs, then you can sneak up."

"Right, we need a distraction," Gex said, and started telling us his plan. Now, before I go any further, I'd just like to say that I, for one, voted against the plan. I thought it was dangerous and wouldn't work. But I was outvoted, as usual. So, just before 11 p.m. Joz and Freddie went outside and after a couple of minutes Joz rang the doorbell, I opened it and Freddie shot in on his BMX, sweeping through the house and out through the sunroom doors at the back, leaving chaos in his wake.

Girls were screaming, boys were shouting and throwing stuff at him, lawyers were called, someone set up a helpline for anyone affected by the issues raised and I think the government briefly called a state of emergency. Of course, Freya's father heard the racket and came charging downstairs, waving a golf club. He ran into the garden, after Freddie. This left the coast clear for Gex to nip up the stairs. Joz had disappeared, as usual. I went back into the kitchen, which was now empty as everyone had run out the back to watch Freya's dad beat the intruder around the head with his club. I later found out he'd chased poor old Freddie all the way to the canal, which Freddie tried to jump on his BMX, like at the end of *The Great Escape*. He had to go back this morning and fish his bike out.

In the kitchen I found my still-untouched bottle of Martini Rosso.

"You going to open that?" said a soft voice behind me. It was Megan. She looked quite nice, though she had so much makeup on it made her look like a cartoon version of herself, as though she'd been replaced by her own avatar.

"Sure," I said, suddenly feeling nervous. I opened the bottle and grabbed a couple of plastic cups.

"You know what goes well with that?" she asked. I shook my head.

"Apple juice," she said, and raised an eyebrow as she went to the fridge to get some.

She was right; Martini Rosso and apple juice does work, and doesn't taste alcoholic at all. Megan drained her cup quickly and held it out for another one.

"What's this drink called?" I asked. "Applosso?"

"Rossopple?" she suggested.

What do you talk to girls about? They don't watch *The Shield* or *Dave*. I wondered if I should talk to her about knitting? No, don't be a fool, Ben, I told myself. You've come so far. You might as well just go ahead and tell her you fancy her mum.

But I was saved from not knowing what to say by a scream from upstairs. We rushed back into the hall to see Gex leaping down the stairs three at a time, a look of blind panic on his face. He was followed by a disheveled woman in a nightie who I was guessing was Freya's mother.

"Wrong room," he shouted as he passed me in the hall. "Wrong freakin' room!" Then he was out the front door and away into the suburban night.

People had started to come back in to watch the latest entertainment. To get away from the crowd Megan suggested we go to the sitting room.

"I don't think we're allowed in there," I said. "I think the door's locked. Freya said they've got a new white carpet."

"I know another way," she said. "I've been here loads of times."

So she led me through the laundry room and into the empty, dark sitting room.

"Are you sure about this?" I asked, meaning was she sure we should be in this room, but she said, "Yes, I'm sure," and she kissed me.

I was a bit gobsmacked, to be honest. I've never really had a proper kiss before. I'm not sure how to describe it really. It was sort of . . . meaty. She was almost chewing my lips. Without breaking off, I put the bottle down on the table behind me and started chewing right back.

Then light entered the room as the door opened and Freya's mother was there. "What the hell . . . ?" she said, and turned on the light. Megan turned to face her, leaving me standing facing the door.

"What's that?" Freya's mum screamed, pointing in the general direction of my crotch.

Megan turned to look. "Oh my God!" she said.

What? I thought, suddenly panicking. What's going on down there? But it wasn't my crotch they were looking at. I whipped around to see that damned bottle of Martini Rosso had fallen off the table and was on its side busily glugging bright red liquid all over the Porters' new white carpet. I was relieved to discover they weren't horrified by a problem in my trouser department, but this was nearly as bad.

I'm ashamed to say we ran for it. I lost Megan in the crowd in the hallway and that was the end of the fun for the night. I thought it better to quit while I was, if not ahead, then at least even on points. Bad times regarding Martini Rosso on the carpet, and I'm worried there's going to be a call from Freya's mum on that one. But this all pales in significance on account of the fact that Megan snogged me.

Surely now she'll accept my friend request? I don't think Megan's big on FB but she must check it sometime, surely? And she wouldn't reject my request now, would she? I'm a bit worried though that the experience might have put her off.

Anyway, when the lads and I compared notes this morning, sitting in the sunshine on the wall outside Freddie's house, Gex had to be coaxed into telling his story. It turned out he'd crept into the darkened bedroom as instructed, saw someone lying in the bed and, deciding Freya must be "up for it," threw all caution to the wind and leaped onto the bed with a cry of "Yahoo!" Only then did he discover the bed was occupied by Freya's mum.

"What were you thinking, you muppet?" Freddie gasped through his laughter.

"You said third door on the left, right?" a furious Gex told him.

"No, I said SECOND door on the left," Freddie replied. "Why would I say third?"

"You said third, you moron. Didn't he say third?" Gex asked me.

"Can't honestly remember," I said, and shrugged, my mind already on other things. I still couldn't stop thinking about the kiss. And whether my parents were going to get a call from Freya's mum. I hadn't told my friends about my kiss with Megan. They would only have said something revolting.

"It was a disaster," Freddie said. "The whole night was a friggin' disaster."

"Not disastrous for all of us," Joz said, showing us a fresh hickey on his neck.

We stared at him in amazement.

"Jasmine," he said. "Under the stairs."

Well, this was an unexpected curveball.

Maybe it's time to take *Fifty Shades of Graham* more seriously. . . .

OCTOBER 22ND

I think I might be making some progress with Mrs. Frensham. We actually had a conversation today. She brought me out my tea and stood around for a while, watching me sip it intently, as though she'd put cyanide in it and wanted to make sure I drank it all down like a good boy. She didn't say anything, just stood there, holding her own cup but not drinking from it.

"Were you born in Hampton?" I asked, feeling I needed to break the ice.

"Portsmouth," she said.

"Do you have family here?" I asked after a pause while I sipped from the chipped Eeyore mug she'd brought me.

"Family," she spat, in a tone that suggested her family had already been given their mugs of cyanide tea.

"Do you not get along?" I asked, trying to look sympathetic.

"Who wants to know?" she said.

I shrugged. "Sometimes it helps to talk."

"People do too much talking," she said. "Why do people always dig up things best left buried?"

"Dunno," I said.

She didn't make any move to go back inside though, and after a while, she said, "I don't like them. My family."

"Fair enough," I said, wishing she'd put my mind at rest by drinking her own tea.

"My niece is okay," she went on. "She keeps me up to date with what's going on."

"But you don't talk to anyone else?"

"No," she said, then finally she sipped her tea. I breathed a sigh of relief. "There was a fuss over my mum's wedding ring when she died."

"When was that?"

"Nineteen sixty-nine."

I spat tea.

"Nineteen sixty-nine? How old were you?"

"Old enough to know my sister was trying to steal from me," she said. "It all went downhill from there."

"Good that you have your niece, though," I said.

"She's an odd one," Mrs. Frensham said after a pause. "She's called her baby Spector."

"For real?"

"For real. Stupid name."

"I suppose we'll all have stupid names in the future," I said.

That was about it. A bizarre sort of conversation. I think she'd be more suited to Freddie's brand of chat really. Maybe I should introduce them.

I'll phone Ms. Gunter about it tomorrow and let her know how I'm doing. Speaking of phones, I looked for Megan at school today but she's out sick. She still hasn't accepted my friend request. I did see Jasmine though, and I know she's friends with Megan. Jasmine was wearing a scarf, which suggested to me Joz wasn't the only one with a hickey.

"Hi, Jasmine," I said casually.

"Hi, Ben," she replied warily.

"Do you have Megan's number?"

"Yes."

"Could I have it?"

"Why do you want Megan's number?"

"I was going to send her a text, to say thanks for Saturday night. . . ."

"Why, what happened on Saturday night?"

I paused, surprised. "She didn't . . . say anything?"

"About what?"

Why are girls so protective of each other in these situations? It's like they think us men are sharks, circling a huddled group of shipwrecked sailors. Jasmine should be facilitating. She should be bringing me and Megan together. She shouldn't be putting up barriers or firing spearguns into my eyes.

"About me," I said.

"No," Jasmine said. "She definitely didn't say anything about you. She was totally drunk and doesn't remember anything about that party."

Jasmine stood up and walked off, giving me a contemptuous look, as though I'd just made her an indecent proposal.

"Nice hickey," I said as she strode away.

Could Jasmine be believed? Megan had already looked a bit bleary when she'd found me, and then she had had another couple of drinks. A drunk Megan would certainly explain why she'd been so willing to make out with me. But what did that mean? That she didn't actually like me? Was it just the alcohol speaking? Or had the Rossopple merely stripped away the inhibitions, revealing her true, yearning desires?

Cripes, I think I've been reading too much *Fifty Shades of Graham*. Speaking of which, Joz gave me six or seven more pages to edit. It's getting marginally better. Things have moved on and Graham and Daisy have plunged into the world of big business, with all its attending temptations and moral dilemmas. The pages are in the Box of Shame under my bed, along with the clay, three back copies of *Knit!*, my actual knitting and some racy mags down the bottom that quite frankly don't get much of a look these days.

OCTOBER 23RD

Finally caught up with Megan at school today; she was walking around with Freya Porter. I stalked her for a bit, waiting for my opportunity, keeping well out of sight. I thought it had come when Freya went into the bathroom and it looked like Megan was going to wait outside. But then Freya said something to Megan, apparently convincing her she needed to go as well, and they popped in together. Girls do like company when they're in the bathroom. What do they do in there together? Is it like midwives? Do they offer each other encouragement, hold hands? Coax it out?

I had to wait until the bell was about to ring before the girls could finally bear to be parted from each other and I sprinted around the science block to get ahead of Megan.

"Oh, hi," I said, affecting surprise and puffing slightly.

"Were you just following us?" she asked.

"What? Following you?"

Megan carried on walking; we had to be in class in a couple of minutes.

"Me and Freya," she said. "Wherever we looked, you were there. Like Kim Kardashian."

"Just coincidence, I suppose," I said breezily. "It was a good party last Saturday."

She rolled her eyes. "I don't remember. I think I had too much to drink. Are you going this way?"

"Yes," I lied. We were, in fact, heading in the opposite direction from where I needed to be. "You don't remember anything?"

"Not really," she said. "I heard about Freddie steaming through the house on his BMX."

"Yeah." I laughed a little too hard, accidentally snorting like a pig. "Do you remember anything else?"

"Freya's dad chasing after Gex with a golf club?"

"That was hilarious, yes," I said, impatient now. We were nearly at her classroom. "But anything else? Something that happened a bit later?"

She turned to look at me, smiling. Aha, I thought, she's been playing with me. She remembers.

"No," she said. "Not really."

She walked off toward her classroom and I watched her go with a heavy heart. How could she not remember?

But then she turned around as if to see whether I was still watching her. She smiled and said, "Oh, apart from our kiss, of course."

Then she was gone, swallowed up by a river of students pouring into the classroom.

I grinned, spun on my heels and raced off to geography and Mr. Grover.

OCTOBER 24TH

The lift doors closed and we started to go up.

Suddenly, before I knew it, Daisy was clinging on to me and kissing my lips with hers. She was wearing glasses and had her dark hair tied up. She had on a tight, short skirt and a blouse that clung to her heaving bosom beneath. She looked dynamite.

"What are you doing, Miss Field?" I said. "We're on our way to an important meeting that could make us a million pounds!"

"I don't care about the money," she said, hitting the red button with a sharp stiletto. The elevator quivered to a stop. "I just need you desperately." She began taking off her blouse, revealing the black bra that I had given her for her twenty-first birthday.

I grinned a wry smile at her.

"I can see you're not going to take no for an answer. I'm

going to have to quench your passion before you'll be able to con-
centrate on this important business meeting."

The bra dropped to the lift floor and she came close, breathing
softly in my ear.

"I always think you need to be properly prepped before any
meeting," she said.

"Take a note, Miss Field," I said, and began unbuckling my
belt.

Twenty minutes later, I was pulling my trousers back on and
helping Daisy zip up her skirt when I noticed that we had an
audience.

"Hmm," I said wryly. "Maybe we shouldn't have taken the
panoramic elevator."

Daisy turned around to look at the dozens of clapping and
cheering office workers in the building opposite, who'd just had
the show of their lives.

"I've got nothing to be ashamed of," she said, waving. Then
she turned and grabbed my trouser department.

"And neither have you. . . ."

Will Daisy and Graham's passion derail their fledgling
business venture? Or will their hunger for business success
match their hunger for one another? I really can't see where
this is heading and I don't much care either.

OCTOBER 25TH

I presented Dad with the mugs after class tonight. He looked
really impressed. I felt quite proud for a while. Before I remembered I hadn't made them and my life is a tissue of lies.

He drank his tea out of one when we got home and kept grinning at me, giving me the thumbs-up.

"What are you going to make next?" he asked.

"A flowerpot," I said, once again rejecting the opportunity to come clean.

I'm going to hell.

OCTOBER 26TH

In knitting last night Mrs. Hooper showed us how to design a pattern and how to write it in such a way that it can be followed by others. It's a little like machine code, a programming language. Mrs. Hooper asked us to just write out the pattern for a simple scarf to begin with, but then she showed us how to introduce more complex weaves and wefts. The symbology of casting off and so on. I found it quite fascinating but some of the girls looked a little blank. It's probably not because they're girls, in hindsight, or that they didn't find it all quite as engrossing as I did, but more because they're not all a bunch of total nerds like I am.

She reminded us that part of our coursework for submission is to come up with an original pattern.

"It doesn't have to be anything complex," Mrs. Hooper explained. "Just a normal sweater will do, but maybe you could add some darts on the cuffs, or flares. Or perhaps you could make it unusually long. Just something that shows you've thought about it and that you understand how to adapt a standard pattern to incorporate a variation."

She gave us ten minutes to work on it and I lost myself in the code for a while. I started thinking of different patterns, mad stuff, like sweaters with three arms and onesies with wings. The original pattern, or Pattern Mk 1, was quickly superseded. I decided to move on to Pattern Mk 2. Or 2Patz for short.

"Ben?" someone was saying. "Ben?"

It was Natasha.

"Sorry," I said.

"You were miles away," she said, grinning. "Thinking about your girlfriend?"

"I don't have a girlfriend," I said.

"You must have loads of girls hanging around," she said.

I laughed. "Thanks for the ego boost, but no."

Not officially anyway, I thought to myself, remembering what Megan had said to me at school on Monday. I smiled shyly at Natasha and got back to my pattern.

They're like that at knitting. So supportive.

I've now got quite a large pile of clay that I've been taking from Miss Swallow bit by bit and hiding in the Box of Shame under my bed, keeping it wet with damp newspaper. I should really start building the ziggurat before Dad finds it and asks awkward questions.

Anyway, I've done no homework tonight. I've been doodling most of the day, coming up with ideas for my grand pattern. I don't just want to do something boring. I want to come up with something new, something brilliant. Something that I could sell on the internet, maybe.

2Patz promises to be just that.

OCTOBER 28TH

Dad's bereft about Lance Armstrong turning out to be a drugs cheat.

"Not him too," he said. "Are there no heroes left?"

"Frank Lampard?" I said.

"Boris Johnson?" Mum suggested.

"Harry Potter?" Molly added.

Dad shrugged. "Yes, I suppose so," he said. "But sometimes I think it's just a matter of time before even they let us down. Get caught stealing, or cheating or lying." Just as he said that last bit he happened to look up at me and my stomach flipped.

Does he know? I hate this. I'll have to tell him.

NOVEMBER 1ST

I made a decision yesterday.

"Okay," I said. "I'll do it."

"Do what?" Mrs. Hooper replied absently. She was busy sorting out knitting needles into thicknesses. I admired the way her slim, nimble fingers sorted and shifted the thin rods, making everything neat. Turning chaos into order.

"Enter the competition," I said. "The Knit-Off."

"You mean the All-UK Knitting Championship? Oh, that's brilliant news," she said, beaming. For one exciting moment I thought she might be about to hug me. She didn't.

"But I have one condition," I said. She blinked.

"You can't tell anyone about this. Well, no one outside of the class. I'm not ready to come out just yet."

She tried not to smile. "Okay, Ben. I promise."

"The brochure said I'd need to submit a garment and an original pattern."

"The sweater you did will be perfect as a piece to submit," she said. "You've already done your clever pattern design, so it's just the event itself."

I wasn't sure I wanted to submit Pattern Mk 1. I'd started to become a little uneasy about it, and was thinking of showing 2Patz instead, but 2Patz wasn't ready yet. It wasn't the time to say, though. No point broadcasting my psychological issues.

"When is it?" I asked. "The brochure doesn't give the dates for the regional heats."

"December fifteenth," she said.

"But that's only six weeks away!" I cried.

"Don't worry," she said, "you'll be fine. That gives you plenty of time to practice."

"What should I be practicing?" I asked.

"Simple patterns," she said. "Small things. It'll be a scarf, or a beanie or something. It's about getting your knits nice and tight."

"So you don't know what the pattern will be?" I asked. "What exactly I'll be knitting at the event?"

She shook her head. "Oh, no, that's a very closely guarded secret. You won't know until half an hour before the event itself, but it's unlikely to be anything unusual."

"Hope it doesn't involve stranded colorwork," I said nervously. "I have a mental block about stranded colorwork."

"Don't worry about it," she said, laughing. "You'll be fine."

Don't worry about it? She's told me not to worry about it? She clearly doesn't know me at all.

I mentioned it to Natasha when she arrived.

"That's fantastic news, Ben," she said, giving me a massive hug. Natasha is quite a touchy-feely sort of person. She often touches me on the shoulder or puts an arm around me. I think she sees me like a little brother. "I'll definitely come along to watch, if that's okay?"

"Yeah, I'd love that," I said. After all, no one else would be there. Maybe Mum, if she was around. God knows what I'm going to tell Dad. December 15 is a Saturday; maybe I'll tell him I'm going to church.

He'll take that better than the knitting.

NOVEMBER 2ND

What a weird conversation I had with Ms. Gunter today. I decided to call, rather than email, because I was confused about something I'd read in my probationary terms, which I just happened to be rereading.

"Hello, Ms. Gunter," I said. "It's Ben Fletcher."

"Oh, hello, Ben," she said. She sounded exhausted. "I'm glad it's you."

"Really?"

"Really. You don't know the day I've had. So many phone calls, so many breaches. You're not calling with a problem, are you?" she added guardedly.

"No, not really," I replied, looking at the document in my other hand. "It's just that it says here we're supposed to have arranged face-to-face interviews during the probation.

At least one here at my home. I was just wondering if you were going to be in contact about that."

She was silent for a while.

"Yes, Ben, don't worry, I'll get around to that very soon. Do you feel . . . do you think you need to see me urgently? Has something happened?"

"No, not at all," I replied.

"No more sieges outside old ladies' houses?"

"Not for ages," I said.

"Good, I'm really pleased to hear it," she said. "Because you know what, Ben? You're just about the only success story I've got at the moment."

"Oh," I said, not sure what to say. What bizarre universe is this in which I am a success story? "Sorry."

"They've cut the staffing again," she said. "There are just three caseworkers here now, handling over two hundred files each."

"How's the waffle killer doing?" I asked.

"Who? Oh, yes, him. He's back in jail, I'm afraid. Breached the terms of his probation."

"He didn't eat someone else's kidneys?"

"No." She laughed.

"Liver? Spleen?"

"No, no. If you must know, there was a restraining order stopping him from being within a hundred meters of an ice-cream van."

"Let me guess," I said. "He was apprehended whilst in possession of a Nutty Buddy."

"Worse than that," she said. "He walked into my office with the damn thing." We laughed then, but I was shocked to hear her laughter suddenly turn to sobs.

"I'm sorry, Ben," she said. "This is totally unprofessional."

"It's okay," I said, not sure what else to say.

"It's just so shortsighted," she went on. "They're trying to save money, but cutting the probation service will just mean more crime, more people going back to jail; the costs of that dwarf the salaries of a few caseworkers."

"You should tell them that," I suggested.

"I've tried," she said, sniffing. "We all have. I wrote to the Home Office about it just this week, telling them about the good work we've been doing."

"Well, that's great," I said. "I'm sure they'll notice."

"Problem is, though," she said, "I'm not really having much luck with anything at the moment."

"That's because you're overworked," I said.

"Yes," she said. "That and the fact that my clients are all criminals and nutters."

"Except me," I pointed out.

"Yes, Ben," she said. "Except you."

NOVEMBER 5TH

Stopped off at Pullinger's after school to collect some wool and had a chat with Natasha while I was there. It's good to have someone to talk to about knitting. I told her I was going to try the Ocean Spray sweater.

"Good for you," she said, impressed. "I've been hearing about that. You like a challenge, I'll say that for you."

"Always up for a challenge," I replied, with feeling.

"Are we talking about knitting here?" she asked. "Or have we moved on to your love life?"

"I've given up on love," I said. "I'm never going to get

the girl. Every time I get close some cruel twist of fate denies me. I'm like that squirrel thing in *Ice Age*, forever chasing that damn acorn, never quite managing to catch it."

"I think you'll get the girl, Ben," Natasha said. "I don't think you realize just how special you are."

"Not sure everyone agrees," I said.

"Fancy someone out of your league, do you?"

"Possibly." I laughed, blushing.

"Megan?"

"Well, her too, but there is someone else I like. An older woman."

"Really?" Natasha said, playing with her hair. "Anyone I know?"

"That's classified," I said, turning a bright red. What was with all the questions?

"Well, I apologize," she said, winking. "Let's go and look at some yarn."

I got some lovely goat's wool, dark gray, treated to smooth the fibers. I loved the feel of it and kept slipping my hand inside the paper bag I carried it in to stroke it on my way to Mrs. Frensham's.

There's definitely something wrong with me.

NOVEMBER 6TH

I'm in a quandary. A moral dilemma. I was listening to *Knitwits!* this morning on my way to school and they started talking about illegal pattern downloading. Apparently it's a huge issue in the States. There are pirate knitting sites where you can go and download pretty much anything you want, either the original pattern itself or a knockoff. There's a collective called OpenSource Patterns who think everything should be free and they mess about with other people's designs and add things or adjust them. It's a real gray area, morally. The worst thing was, the *Knitwits!* girls mentioned the Ocean Spray pattern and also the site where I'd downloaded it!

"I'm telling you, this sort of thing is destroying the knitting industry in this country," Marie said, going a bit over the top, I thought.

"It's theft," Alana said. "Pure and simple. Would you steal a car? No. Would you steal a sandwich? No."

"Would you steal a hot dog?" Marie asked.

"No . . ." Alana said. "I—"

"Would you steal a bag of potato chips?" Marie asked.

"No, I thin—"

"Would you steal bacon?"

"That's enough examples," Alana said. "The point is, people spend time and effort creating these things and they deserve to be rewarded."

Well, of course, how could I disagree with that? When I got home after school I deleted the pattern from my hard drive. But now what? I don't have enough money to download it legally. I've bought all this wool.

I am a certifiable muppet.

NOVEMBER 7TH

"... but how can you fancy Craig Revel Horwood?" Dad was saying to Mum in disgust as I sneaked past the sitting room and went up the stairs. "He's not even a dancer. He just judges dancers."

"He can judge my Bossanova anytime he likes," Mum said.

Usually I'd join them for *Strictly Come Dancing*, but I've lost interest in TV lately. All I want to do is knit.

I'd been over at Joz's place all day playing Xbox until the quitting knitting cold turkey drove me back home again. I had crept in this time and tiptoed down the hall, hoping for an hour or two to work on the sweater before anyone realized I was home.

Here's my plan to deal with the lack of a pattern for the Ocean Spray. I've decided to knit it anyway, without a pattern. Just from memory. I think it's a good mental exercise; it'll help me learn how to hold the idea of a garment in my head and just knit it, without constantly checking the next line. It's sort of ripping off the design, but they don't have a copyright on gray sweaters with cabling, do they?

I'll make sure I don't get too close to the Ocean Spray design; I'll make it my own, that way I won't be breaching copyright.

NOVEMBER 8TH

Have I mentioned before how disgusting my dad is? He's gruesome all the time, but especially bad when Mum's not around. Even if I have mentioned it I'm sure I can't have got across the totality of it all. Especially as he seems to have a new revolting habit each week. Last time it was constant burping. Not loud, openmouthed belches like a normal disgusting person. He makes a pretense of being polite by doing them with his mouth closed so that his cheeks blow out like a frog's dewlap. Then he slowly lets the burpy air out of the side of his mouth in a slow hiss before saying "Excuse me."

This week though is even worse. He's been obsessively cleaning his ears with a metal skewer. He says he likes the sensation of the metal scratching against his inner ear.

"I have an itch," he said one day at breakfast. "A terrible, maddening itch. This is the only thing that works."

"You're like a Roald Dahl character," I said. "Seeing your doctor is out of the question, I suppose?" Molly was staring at him as if he were a creature from outer space. When even Molly notices something is out of the ordinary there's a serious problem, Houston.

"Dr. Gilhooly?" he spat. "She'll just tell me to use Q-tips."

"Or maybe she might prescribe some appropriate medicine? You probably have an infection."

He ignored me, sighing with pleasure as he worked the skewer around.

I went off to be sick.

I love my dad, but he is getting more repulsive every day.

NOVEMBER 9TH

I've now cleared an area in Mrs. F's shed a couple of meters squared, or cubed, I suppose. I've uncovered an old wooden chair so I can sit in there, out of the rain, listening to Spotify on my phone, or maybe a knitting podcast on my iPod while I sort through the papers and assorted junk.

I'd just finished a big pile of papers, which were mostly old tax returns. But then I found a manila folder full of letters which looked like they might be personal, so I put them aside. The pile of papers had been squashing an old cardboard box, which I opened. You know what I found?

Knitting things. Balls of yarn, a stack of old yellowing knitting patterns, slightly nibbled by mice, and about sixty knitting needles. Not cheap knitting needles either. I picked the box up and sat with it on the chair, rummaging through in peaceful silence.

So Mrs. Frensham was a knitter too. Or had been. No active knitter would have abandoned needles of this quality.

After a while Mrs. Frensham came out with a cup of tea. I showed her the letters, which she nodded at and snatched out of my hand. Then I showed her the contents of the knitting box. When she saw it her shoulders sagged a little and she looked deflated.

"Everything okay?" I asked, wondering if the sight of the knitting things had brought back some unwelcome memories.

"I'm fine," she said, a little snappish. "Why wouldn't I be?"

I decided not to push it. But, "What should I do with these?" I asked, indicating the box.

"Chuck them," she said. "They're worthless."

"They're not, though," I said. "I mean, the yarn is too old, of course, and the patterns are out of date, but these are KnitPro acrylic needles. And these ones are Pony brand; they're quality."

She eyed me curiously. "What's wrong with you, boy? Had a knock on the head, have you? How is it you know so much about knitting?"

I thought it over quickly; what harm could it do to tell her? She didn't know any of my friends and if she was ever in a room with any of them she'd clobber them with a giant lollipop before they had a chance to raise the subject of my hobbies.

"I like to knit," I said firmly. "I'm taking a class, every Thursday, down at the college."

"A knitting hoodie?" she said. "Now I've heard everything."

"I hardly ever wear a hoodie," I said, exasperated.

"You take the needles then, if you want them," she said, turning to go.

"You don't want them for yourself?" I called after her.

She spun around looking cross.

"What would I want with some silly old needles?" she growled. "Knitting's for girls." And with that parting dig, Mrs. F stomped off back up to the house.

Bristling a little bit, I carefully replaced the knitting gear in the box. I wasn't that bothered by her insult, but I felt bad taking something that seemed to have a history, nor could I bear to throw away those needles.

NOVEMBER 10TH

"Graham," Daisy sighed breathlessly. "I've not seen one that big before."

I smiled ruthlessly and put the egg whisk down.

"I'm saving that for later," I said to Daisy, where she lay on the snooker table. She groaned in frustrated impatience. Her large chest heaved angrily at me. She needed something, and fast.

I quickly walked toward her and checked the silk scarves were still holding her tight.

"Kiss me," she moaned. I kept her waiting a bit longer as I chalked my cue. Then I decided it was time to score.

I'm not really sure what "the author" is trying to say here. He might be trying to approach this from a feminist perspective but I'm not too clear about the snooker table metaphor. Does Daisy's position atop the table represent her elevated place in society? Is Graham chalking a real cue? Is this a postmodern reference to the works of Camus? I guess I'll have to read on to find out.

NOVEMBER 11TH

At some point, I suppose I'll have to tell Dad my secret. He's not going to like it, especially the fact that I've been lying to him for so long, but this can't go on. Tonight was the closest I've come to being caught red-handed. I was sitting on my bed, needles in hand, yarn everywhere and deeply engrossed in the sweater. The cabling is quite complex and really, I wish I'd picked something simpler, or put my hand in my pocket and paid for the pattern. Anyway, the bit I was doing involved using needles of three different sizes. I was getting more and more frustrated, especially as I knew I should be studying for maths.

Then I lost a needle. A U.S. size 3.5. It's one of my favorites and I just couldn't find it anywhere.

"I just had you a minute ago!" I said, looking under my bed and lifting the duvet.

"Who did you have a minute ago?" Dad asked, walking into the room behind me, and nearly giving me a heart attack. I quickly dropped the duvet over the cardigan on the bed.

"You got a girl in here?" he asked, laughing.

"Lost my . . . protractor," I gibbered, but he wasn't listening. He was looking past my left ear. I turned to see what he was looking at, but it was just a poster of the periodic table. I turned back.

"Huh?"

"What's that behind your ear?" he asked.

He reached out a hand and grabbed hold of the U.S. size 3.5 knitting needle I'd tucked behind my ear earlier. That's where it went.

"What's this, Ben?" he asked.

"No idea," I said weakly.

"It's a knitting needle," he said, stating the bleeding obvious as usual. He looked nonplussed.

"I think it might be one of Mrs. Frensham's old needles," I said. "She was throwing it out."

"So you took it off her hands?" he said. "What for?"

"I thought it might be useful as a . . ."

Dad's eyes were boring into me. I had never seen him look quite so concerned about anything.

"... as a flagpole for my ziggurat," I finished.

"A flagpole?"

"Yes."

"Do ziggurats have flagpoles?"

"Well, I had to Google that."

"And?"

"Turns out they didn't."

"Oh."

"No flags."

"I see." He inspected the needle carefully, then looked up at me. "So you don't need it?" he asked.

"No!" I snorted. "Why would I want a knitting needle?"

He nodded. "Mind if I take it?"

"Um . . . suuure," I said, quite pleasantly, considering.

It's only my favorite needle. U.S. sizes in nickel are hard enough to get at the best of times, but that's a quality product. An Addi brand. Practically irreplaceable. But right there in my bedroom, in front of me, Dad jammed the pointed end of my Addi Turbo nickel size 3.5 into his manky old ear and began grinding it about.

"Ohhhh yes," he groaned. "This is perfect."

"Great," I said, trying not to gag. "Glad to help."

Dad finished grinding and inspected the end of the needle with a satisfied smile.

Gross. It will need sterilization now. If I ever manage to get it back.

NOVEMBER 12TH

Aman came round from the council to test our water. He said there was too much zinc. Is this why the Soda-Stream's stopped working? There's nothing about it on my *Guardian* periodic table wall poster. I should Google this later.

NOVEMBER 13TH

I've finished the Not-the-Ocean-Spray sweater. I calculated that it took twenty-two and a half hours of actual knitting time. I think that's pretty quick. I'm looking at it now, laid out on my bed. One of the arms is slightly longer than the other, which puzzles me as I'm sure I used the same number of rows in each. Also, there are a couple of dropped stitches from the other night when Mum and Dad were out and I was watching *Dallas* and my attention was caught by a particularly dramatic confrontation between Christopher and John Ross.

I'm not one hundred percent happy with the sweater. But the cabling on the front is quite neat, I suppose, and I added a couple of impressive flourishes that just came to me. I'll take it in to class tomorrow night and get some constructive criticism from Mrs. Hooper.

NOVEMBER 14TH

Googled zinc. Apparently, excess zinc causes lethargy and ataxia. So this is why I'm horrible at soccer. The good news is that I can now blame my dad, who probably bought cheap zinc pipes when he installed the bathroom and kitchen suites. He can't really argue with Google.

And if I fail my tests that'll be down to him, too.

NOVEMBER 15TH

Mrs. Hooper LOVED the sweater.

"This is astonishing," she said as she examined it.

"Dropped a couple of stitches watching *Dallas*," I mumbled apologetically.

It was before class and a few of the others had wandered in and joined Mrs. Hooper to exclaim over my work. I did feel a bit proud.

"This cabling, was this from a pattern?" Natasha asked.

I shook my head, slightly embarrassed. "I just thought of it as I was doing it. The sweater itself is inspired by the Ocean Spray design."

"I see that. It's brilliant," she said, her eyes shining.

"One of the arms is longer than the other," I pointed out. "I think I must have miscounted."

"Or it could be that you've made the knits slightly larger on one side. That's natural for a beginner, until you've settled into your natural action."

I was pleased to hear that. I hate getting calculations wrong and it had been bothering me.

"What are you going to do next?" Mrs. Hooper asked excitedly.

I shrugged. I hadn't really thought about it.

"Why don't you go down to the bookshop? They have quite a wide selection of new patterns down there. I think you're probably ready to tackle something quite complex now."

"You do?" I asked.

"Definitely," Mrs. Hooper said.

Everyone smiled at me and it felt pretty amazing, just for a moment.

NOVEMBER 19TH

I'm nearly done clearing out the shed. It's really quite spacious now. Dry and warm. I can see why Mr. Frensham spent so much time in there. It would make a nice, relaxing place to sit and reflect and maybe get away from Mrs. Frensham from time to time. It would also make a nice place to sit and knit, in peace.

Mrs. Frensham brought me a radio today, along with my tea. I paused the *Knitwits!* podcast I was listening to on my iPod and smiled at her.

"Found this in a box," she said gruffly. "You might as well have it, instead of listening to that thing all the time." She pointed to my iPod, clearly thinking it was a portable radio.

"Actually, I'm listening to a podcast," I told her. "About knitting."

"Whatcast?"

"A podcast. It's like a radio program, but you download it off the internet and put it on your iPod."

"What's wrong with the radio?" she asked.

"Well, they don't always have the program on that you want to listen to."

"So change it to Radio Two," she suggested. "What program did you say you were listening to?"

"*Knitwits!* It's two girls who talk about knitting a lot."

She stared at me for a while, an odd look in her rheumy eye.

"You're a bit odd, aren't you?" she said.

NOVEMBER 20TH

You know in *The Apprentice* where one of the contestants flaps about, talking to potential customers without actually selling anything and they later get accused in the Boardroom of being unable to "Close the Deal"? Well, that's like me with Megan Hooper. There's lots of talking going on. Lots of face-to-face interaction, but no contract. Not yet.

Take today, for example. I saw her at lunch; she was on her way to the library. I was heading off to the staffroom to talk to Mr. Grover. We smiled at each other. I said hello. She said hello. Then I couldn't think of what to say next, so I said, "See you later." She said, "See you later," and we smiled at each other again and that was that.

As it is pretty obvious that I really don't know what I'm doing here, why can't Megan take charge? Maybe she's really not interested, and that kiss we had was like an experiment that has somehow failed? Maybe she instructed Jasmine not to give me her number? Why does it sometimes seem as though she's avoiding me at school?

The reason I'm not giving up hope entirely is because it's so bloody awkward with her and everyone knows that's a good sign. If we were just friends, then we'd chat, or just make stupid faces at each other in the corridor as we passed and not think anything of it. If looking at me made her want to stick forks in her eyes, then she'd just ignore me, or run away, like the other girls do.

But there's something there. I know it. Something there that makes it impossible to have a normal conversation with her, something that makes me trip over my shoelaces, and makes her drop her books. Something that makes both of us act a bit mental around each other.

Or am I just kidding myself?

NOVEMBER 22ND

Apparently I'm just kidding myself.

Hated today. I had another run-in with Lloyd Manning. Plus Megan seems to be not just avoiding me now, but deliberately ignoring me. So much for the mutual-awkwardness theory. I couldn't get close to her because she was always with a group of friends, helping one another with their quadratic equations, or pretending to. I hung about for a bit, feeling like an idiot, and when it was clear she wasn't going to even look up, let alone come over and talk to me, I gave up and went off to the library, which is where Psycho Manning caught up with me. I was sitting, staring at a page of logarithms and he just walked past and slid all my books off the desk onto the floor.

"Shh," Carter the librarian hissed at me.

"Sorry," I mouthed. Then I turned to glare at Manning, who was metaphorically ROFLHAO. What was he even doing in here anyway? Manning can't read. I'd always imagined he couldn't cross the threshold of a library, like a vampire unable to enter a church.

I'd just got engrossed in the book again when he walked past and this time he snatched my notebook and walked off with it.

"Hey!" I yelled, scrambling after him.

"Shh!" hissed Carter again.

But I ignored him and kept after Manning, who walked quickly out of the library and ran off across the quad. I ran after him. It was windy today and leaves were being whipped around as I sprinted after him, furious. I wasn't sure what I was going to do but I wasn't going to back down, that was for sure.

Then I saw his two bodyguards walking along toward us. He slowed as he approached them and turned to watch me.

"Problem, Bellend?" he asked.

"Give me that back," I said, less sure of myself now there were three of them, but blood still boiling.

"What? This?" he asked, looking at the book. He flicked through a few pages. It was then that I remembered the Pattern. Or the revised pattern. 2Patz.

"Oh, how pretty," he said. "Bellend's been drawing. Lovely cardigan here. And here it is again, with a hood, and now there's arms. Very nice, Gok!"

Jermaine and the other one were peering over Manning's shoulder, laughing and whispering. I felt my face grow hot.

"It's a project for art," I lied. I didn't actually do art, but they wouldn't know that.

"Need some assistance, Ben?" a familiar voice asked behind me. I turned to see Gex, with Joz behind him looking nervous.

"Thought you were suspended," Manning grunted at Gex.

"Nope, it's finished," Gex said. ". . . I think."

Manning's gang fell about laughing at this.

"Give him his drawings back," Gex said, impressively focused given the situation.

"Or what?" Manning said, not laughing now. The three of them walked over to us and Manning stood nose-to-nose with Gex, who didn't flinch.

"Forget it, Gex," I said. "It's just a dumb notebook." The last thing I wanted was a fight. Not just because I'm a coward, but also because I'd be breaching the terms of my probation. And Gex would certainly be suspended again if he was caught fighting. That's assuming he wasn't already suspended but had forgotten about it, which has happened before.

"Yeah," Manning said, still eyeballing Gex. "It's just a dumb notebook."

"But it doesn't belong to you," Gex said. "It belongs to my friend."

The end-of-lunch bell rang. I was supposed to be on my way to geography. I felt agitated.

"Your boyfriend, you mean?" Manning said. "Is that why he's drawing a pansy cardigan? Is it a present for you?"

"Come on, Gex, let's g—" I started to say, but before I could finish Gex and Manning were on the ground in a tangle of limbs. Manning's gang piled on top of the two of them, rolling around, fists flailing. Joz and I looked at each other with a WTF look, then rushed forward to try to pull the fighters apart.

"Hey, you boys!" Carter had emerged from the library for once. He came rushing up and yanked Jermaine off Gex. Then Mrs. Fowler came huffing up. "I saw the whole thing," she said. "He started it," she said, pointing at Gex.

"No, he didn't," I cried. "It was Manning, Miss."

At this Manning shot me a filthy look, presumably adding "snitch" to his list of reasons he wanted to pummel me.

"You and you," she said, pointing to me and Joz. "Get to class."

"But . . ." I started.

"Now!" she snapped. I gave Gex a sorry look and walked off. He didn't seem bothered, to be honest. Gex hadn't wanted to finish school anyway. He wanted to go off and be a deejay, but his parents told him they'd kick him out if he didn't keep going to school, and he's not really got anywhere else to go.

I called Gex straight after school. He'd been suspended again.

"Sorry, mate," I said. "I feel responsible."

"I had to do it," he said.

"No, you didn't," I said. "It was just a notebook."

"He was bullying you," Gex said.

"Yeah, but who got suspended?" I said. "Not Manning. And I nearly got caught up in it. I'm on probation, remember?"

"You gotta fight for your turf, you feel me?"

"Oh, don't give me that *Wire* crap," I said. "I appreciate what you did, but it was still a dumb thing to do."

"You are such a pussy," he said. "I was standing up for you, okay?"

"I didn't ask you to," I snapped.

"Next time I won't bother, then," he sniffed.

"Please don't," I told him. "I don't want to go to jail, okay?"

He laughed. "You won't go to jail. . . ."

"I might, if I breach the terms of my probation," I said, angry now. "Thank you for standing up for me, I mean it. But next time, please let me deal with it, okay?"

"Whatever," he said.

Why can't he see it from my point of view? I need to keep out of trouble. So does he, for heaven's sake.

The only thing that kept me going today was the thought of knitting class tonight. How sad is that?

Nobody judges me in that class. Or at least no one is critical of me. We all help one another with our problems. It's got to the point where we talk about other stuff now, not just knitting-related stuff. I know that Mrs. Simpson is having trouble with her cat bringing in birds and ripping them limb from limb on the kitchen floor. And that Amelia is having trouble finding a suitable guy on her dating website, and that Mrs. Grissome has had mysterious problems with her waterworks, which she refers to in a code that all the women seem to understand but which leaves me mystified. At first I thought she meant her actual waterworks, as in the plumbing in her house. When I told her I had the same problem and was suffering from a buildup of zinc she and the rest of them gave me a very funny look.

Myself, I steer clear of talking about Lloyd Manning, or

my dubious friends. But I have told them about my efforts to ensnare the beautiful Megan. Of course, I never refer to her by her real name. I call her "the girl" or "Miss X." I am kind of attached to Miss X.

They calm me, these Stitch and Bitch sessions. It's like the girls on *Knitwits!* keep saying. Knitting is more fun with company. Company is more fun with knitting.

NOVEMBER 24TH

Dad and I were watching a recorded *Great British Bake Off* tonight and one of the contestants was carrying a man-bag in one of the background sequences they do.

"What a pansy," Dad said.

"Why?" I asked. "Just because he has a man-bag?"

"Not just that; look at his pointy shoes. You wouldn't catch Jeremy Clarkson wearing pointy shoes. Or James May."

Dad thinks Jeremy Clarkson and James May are ideal role models. Fortunately for me, there's a third presenter on *Top Gear*.

"Richard Hammond might," I said.

"Exactly," he scoffed. "He's a metrosexual."

"What's wrong with metrosexuals?" I asked. "They're just men who look after themselves. You know, they're comfortable with their feminine sides?"

"Being comfortable with your feminine side is one thing, cuddling with another man's feminine side is something else."

"Are you saying Richard Hammond is gay?"

"What? No, well, I don't know, he might be."

"Frank Lampard probably wears pointy shoes," I said.

"He bloody does not!" Dad yelled.

"You're such a homophobe," I said.

"I am sodding not," he replied, annoyed. "I don't care what blokes get up to in the bedroom. The thing I don't like is when they pretend to be girls."

"What are you talking about?"

"You know, shoes with heels, handbags, ballet . . . bloody needlework! These are not things for men."

I nodded wisely, inwardly thinking, HE MUST NEVER EVER KNOW ABOUT ME.

NOVEMBER 30TH

Mum's away again, and Dad's struggling a bit without her. We'd run out of dishwasher tablets this morning so he put a mixture of salt, rinse aid and Palmolive in the dishwasher and when I got back from school the kitchen was full of soap bubbles. It's like living with Paddington Bear, sometimes.

DECEMBER 2ND

Mum's back! She got home tonight, looking exhausted, and collapsed into an armchair. Molly came and sat on top of her to watch *Strictly Come Dancing*. Dad offered to cook a celebratory meal for us all; we could hear him clattering away in the kitchen. He popped his head round the door after a bit.

"Drink?" he asked Mum.

"Whiskey and soda, please," she replied, sighing contentedly.

"Stiff one?"

"Just the drink, thanks."

After we'd sewn all our sides back up again, I asked how her tour had been.

"Good, mostly," she said. "A bit of an awkward moment in Crewe, when the member of the audience I invited up on stage to help me with a trick turned out to be shit-faced."

"What's shit-faced?" Molly asked.

"Oops," Mum said. "Forgot you were there. It means had a bit too much to drink, petal. Anyway, she's stumbling about all over the place, and everyone's laughing. I managed to get her into the wardrobe, and then when I opened the doors, she'd completely disappeared."

"So?" I asked. "Isn't that the point?"

"No, she wasn't supposed to disappear at all. She was supposed to still be in the wardrobe but wearing a different color dress," Mum said. "It's a very sophisticated trick. It subverts the audience's expectations."

"But it was your expectations that were subverted," I said.

"Welcome to my world," she said.

"So where had she gone?"

"Not sure. Her husband came and accosted me after the show. She turned up eventually, in the upstairs bar."

"Wow, good trick."

"If only I knew how I'd done it," Mum said, face screwed up in concern.

I laughed. It was good to have her back.

"Have you told him?" she asked me quietly.

"Eh?"

"Have you told him about the you-know-what?"

I shook my head and she gave me a look.

"I will," I said. "I will tell him."

"Good."

After a bit Dad came in, looking worried.

"Susan," he said, "I've dropped a Toblerone in the stew."

"Honestly, it's like living with experimental chef Heston Blumenthal," Mum said, pushing Molly off and climbing to her feet. "Step away from the stove. I'll fish it out; you go and open some wine."

What with the zinc in the water, and Dad's cooking, I'm amazed I've made it to seventeen.

DECEMBER 3RD

Just got back from Mrs. Frensham's. Mum's making tea so it's taking forever, of course. Not that I mind, she cooks proper food. Spaghetti Bolognese tonight, with nice Sainsbury's garlic bread. When Mum's away it's usually just eggs and bacon on toast or sausages and baked beans from a can. British Cassoulet, Dad calls it.

Mrs. Frensham was in a funny mood today. She smiled as she let me in, almost as if she was pleased to see me. And when I got out to the shed, I noticed straightaway that the knitting box had gone. Had she thrown it away? I wondered. But when she brought the tea out, she didn't go straight back in. She stood for a bit and seemed like she wanted to talk. She was asking me what I'd found today, but didn't really seem to be interested in the answers. I offered her the chair but she shook her head.

"I'll stand while I'm still able," she said.

"Okay," I said, nibbling a cookie and watching her suspiciously. I tried to think of suitable topics of conversation. Should I ask after her hemorrhoids?

"So how long you been knitting, then?" she asked eventually.

"Um . . . a few months," I told her.

"You like it, do you?"

I nodded. "I actually do, I find it calming."

"Yes, it is," she said. I watched as her heavy features scrunched themselves up into a smile before flopping back.

"So you used to knit, but not anymore?" I asked.

"I was crazy about knitting as a girl," she said, her face taking on a reflective look. "We'd use anything we could get our hands on. We'd knit with string, when we couldn't get wool."

"Was it rationed?" I asked.

"What do you mean rationed?" she shot, snapping out of her reverie. "How old do you think I am?"

I shrugged. "I dunno. Eighty?"

She stared at me, her jaw sagging a little. "I'm sixty-one," she said. "Rationing ended when I was three."

"Sorry," I said, blushing. "My eyesight's gone a bit funny since I started knitting. . . ."

"I used to knit a lot when my husband was alive," she went on. "First when we were just married, I knitted baby clothes, you know, booties, bonnets, that sort of thing."

I nodded encouragingly.

"But the baby never came," she said.

"Sorry," I said awkwardly. Her eyes were beginning to look a little moist.

"So I knitted for him," she went on. "Scarves, socks, a beanie for winter. He gave me a kiss every time I finished something and told me I was a marvel."

"He sounds nice," I said.

"He was," she said. A tear ran down her cheek. Was I expected to hug her? Put a reassuring hand on one of those great shoulders? And it struck me then that this Mrs. F, so strong and warriorlike (and a tad violent) on the outside, was scared and lonely and sad on the inside. Maybe all adults are unraveling a bit inside? Like they've dropped a couple of stitches somewhere. And not just adults. I felt a bit unraveled myself sometimes.

"Wasn't until years later I found out from his sister that he'd always hated woolen clothes," she said. "Couldn't stand the feeling of it against his skin. He liked rayon."

"Rayon," I said, shaking my head sympathetically. *"Rayon."*

"Yeah," she replied.

"But he never told you," I said. "He didn't want to hurt your feelings."

"That's right," she said, nodding. "He'd never have hurt a fly."

"No," I said gently.

"Though he did once shoot a burglar up the arse with an air rifle."

"Well, fair enough," I said.

She stood for a while longer, lost in her memories. I stood awkwardly, waiting, not sure what I was expected to do.

We settled on an exchange of smiles in the end. Then Mrs. F picked up the tea mugs and the cookies and went back into the house. I can't say it was the most comfortable ten minutes of my life, but I'm glad I was there today when she needed someone to talk to. I'm glad I found the knitting things. I think maybe I didn't completely mess things up today.

DECEMBER 7TH

Dear Ms. Gunter,

I thought I should email you to let you know how I'm getting on and to thank you for your efforts. Mrs. Frensham's shed is nearly cleared now, and we're moving on to stage two of the shed renovation project, namely painting the door. I'm looking forward to that. Mrs. Frensham and I are getting on quite well now, you might be surprised to hear, considering our relationship got off to such an abusive start. She now comes and drinks her tea with me. My tea breaks are getting longer and longer. We chat about all sorts of things: radio, TV, the Youth of Today, and knitting. Apparently Mrs. Frensham used to be a keen knitter; she gave it up years ago but it seems having me around is starting to rekindle her interest. I found an old box of knitting things early on, and although she told me to put them with the pile to throw away, I saw on Monday she'd actually moved it into her sitting room and taken some things out. Maybe she'll start knitting again. I hope so. Also, I've been bringing her knitting magazines, once I've finished with them.

I've been telling her about the people at my knitting group, and also about my friends. I think she's starting to recognize that Gex, Freddie and Joz are actual, real people, not just Symbols of Broken Britain.

She's been telling me about the perils of being a lollipop lady. Mad drivers, crazy (ahem) cyclists, rude children. I'm starting to understand now why she comes across as a swivel-eyed warrior queen. You have to be tough to do that job. Tough and possibly insane too.

Anyway, I hope things are okay for you. How's it going with the Home Office?

Best wishes,

Ben

DECEMBER 8TH

Went out to get more wool today for the prototype of 2Patz. Natasha wasn't working in the shop. Another girl was there, which was okay with me. Natasha's great, but she can talk for England and I was in a bit of a hurry to get back and crack on with my practice.

When I got home I made the mistake of coming in through the front door. Dad heard me.

"Want to come and watch the second half, Ben?" he called as I passed the sitting room. I stopped, groaning inwardly.

"I'd love to, Dad," I said, popping my head round the door. "It's just I've got loads of homework." This was true, though I had no intention of doing it.

"Oh," he said, sounding disappointed.

"How are they, er, how are Chelsea getting on?"

"Two–one down," he said, "but we're getting most of the ball."

"Lampard scored our goal, did he?" I asked hopefully.

"No. Hit the crossbar a couple of times," Dad said.

"Oh, never mind. Game of two halves, I'm told."

"You're not wrong," he said, pointing his beer bottle at me.

I ducked out then and raced up to my room, anxious to get my hands on those needles.

It's like a drug.

Hang on. Needles? Drugs? How have I not made that connection before?

DECEMBER 11TH

Embarrassment newsflash! Just had a man-to-man chat with Dad. Mum's been away this weekend and for some reason he's gone all role-reversal. Cleaning everywhere, washing sheets, stacking the dishwasher properly. Not sure what that's all about, but the upshot was when I got home from school today, Dad called me into the sitting room. He had a very stern look on his face. He doesn't do stern very well, actually. He's about as forbidding as Louis Walsh, the wet one from the *X Factor* judging panel. Nonetheless, I was suddenly nervous. There was stuff I didn't want him to know about.

"Please sit down, Ben," he said. "We need to talk."

What is it about that phrase that can reduce even the bravest person to jelly? If Darth Vader's dad came into his bedroom and said, "We need to talk," poor Darth's twisted heart would skip a beat and his breath would grow even more ragged. What have I done? he'd think. Was it the planet I blew up? Cutting my son's hand off? Did I leave a skid mark in the Death Star toilet?

"I was tidying your room this morning, Ben," Dad said.

Uh-oh, please don't tell me he's looked under the wardrobe.

"I found a magazine."

Just one? Probably not the wardrobe then.

"This magazine," he said, holding up the November issue of *Knit!*

"Right," I said. This was even worse. How was I going to explain *Knit!*?

"Is there something you're not telling me, Ben?" he asked.

"What do you mean?" I asked, playing for time.

"Well, this is clearly not yours," he said, "and your mother doesn't knit. Not anymore."

"No," I said. Then suddenly I noticed he had a sly grin on his face.

"You've had a girl in your room, haven't you?"

"Um . . ."

"I don't mind, Ben," he said. "Good for you, is what I think. If you only knew the things I used to get up to at your age. But you don't have to go skulking around, you know?"

"Oh, okay."

"Introduce her to me, will you?" he said, nodding encouragingly. "To me and your mum. She's not a loony, is she?"

"I'm not going out with a loony, no," I replied carefully.

"Well," he said, standing up and handing me back the magazine. "I look forward to meeting her. Oh, and Ben?"

"Yes?"

"Don't screw it up, will you?" He laughed and left the room.

Next week I'll give the magazine to Mrs. Frensham. In

fact I think I'll keep all my magazines in her shed. The knitting ones, I mean. The others can stay under my wardrobe.

DECEMBER 12TH

How can it be Wednesday again already? It's always Wednesday. I hate Wednesdays, that's the day Mum and Dad go out. Date Night, they call it. Apparently, it's traditional. I pointed out once that Dad still goes out on Wednesdays even when Mum's not here so how could it be Date Night then, but I was ignored as usual. The main reason I hate it is because I have to make Molly's tea. She's incredibly fussy and if it's not Mum doing the cooking she only eats three things. Life cereal with semi-skimmed milk, tinned sausage and baked beans on toast or chicken fingers with pasta—no sauce.

Problem is, she doesn't like it when I cook these things, even if I make them in exactly the same way Dad does. But on Wednesdays she doesn't have a choice and after a bit of shouting and slamming doors, and duels with pistols and armed sieges she generally ends up eating something. She does this whilst pulling the most revolted faces and gagging every few seconds. It's not very complimentary. Tonight she actually threw up some half-masticated beans onto the table.

How rude. Not even the angry one on *MasterChef* has ever done that.

After I'd cleaned up the vomit, I asked her, as I am required to do by the Ancient Law of the House, if she wanted any yogurt.

"No," she said.

"No what?" I asked.

"No way," she said.

"No way what?"

"No way, Jose."

"Bath time," I said, giving up.

Anyway, the kid's in bed now and after half an hour's studying, I'm going to work on 2Patz some more.

It's really, really quiet now. Kind of peaceful. Maybe Wednesdays aren't all bad.

DECEMBER 13TH

"I have a secret," Daisy said. She was looking upset. Like she did whenever I went away from her.

"I know all your secrets," I said, downing the glass of expensive vodka I'd just poured and reaching for the bottle again. "You can't hide anything from me."

I walked to the window and stared out at the Beijing skyline. In the reflection of the glass I noticed she wore nothing but the silk negligee I'd given her for her twenty-second birthday. I couldn't bear to look at her. I couldn't allow her to win me over with her soft, porcelain skin.

"You're angry," she said.

"Yes," I agreed.

"Is this because you found me in bed with your lawyer?"

"No."

"Your accountant?"

"No."

"The estate agent?"

"I was angry about him, yes. He is my brother, after all," I said. "But, Daisy, don't you understand? Really?"

"No, Graham," she said. "I really don't."

"Then it's over, Daisy," I said. "I'm flying to New York tonight. And I'm not coming back."

What a cliffhanger! Joz says he's not giving me any more until after Christmas. I'm on tenterhooks. I'm not sure I entirely understand what Graham's problem is, as it happens, and am very much in Camp Daisy at present. He's usually remarkably understanding about her affairs, so what could she have done this time to make him decide to leave?

DECEMBER 14TH

Tomorrow night's the regional heats of the All-UK Knitting Championship (AUKKC). Dad's going to watch Hampton play in Basingstoke and won't be back till late. I can make my own way there and back. Dad got sick of me moaning about not having a bike and brought it back from the shop yesterday with a new chain and the gears reset. I'm delighted about that, but when he does nice things like that it all just adds to the sense of guilt I feel about lying to him. I'm going to have to tell him sooner or later. Aren't I? But part of me thinks that if I get knocked out in the first round, then maybe I won't have to? I don't know. I've got too much to worry about at the moment. Lloyd Manning tripped me on the stairs today and I fell against Yasmin Tench and accidentally touched her boob and she screamed and it all turned out to be my fault, of course, and tickets were issued and official statements had to be made and witnesses were taken into police protection. I hate Lloyd Manning. I won't say that all my problems would be solved if he had the top of his head taken off and the insides scooped out and eaten by badgers, but one of my problems would be solved and I'm sure the badgers would appreciate the protein, however scant.

Bit worried about what the pattern's going to be tomorrow. What if it is stranded color? I know there's no reason I shouldn't be able to do it. I just have this irrational fear of stranded color. I tried to talk to Natasha about it, but she doesn't understand. Knitting's like that. Sometimes you just get a bad feeling about something. Or maybe it's just me.

DECEMBER 16TH

Didn't have time to write last night. I got back very late. Dad was still out, which we were pleased about. Mum is still going along with our subterfuge, but she's giving stronger hints that it might be time to tell Dad about the knitting.

Anyway, the regionals. I'd expected a few losers standing around yawning at the Arts Center venue, which is huge. But it was packed. I suddenly realized I was in at the deep end when I arrived. And I immediately wanted to go home. But I'd come too far to back out now, so I stayed. There were two categories: junior knitting and senior knitting, and man those SKs are scary—a couple of them were actually knitting and making small talk with the public at the same time. Now, I like a good conversation when I'm working on something simple and repetitive, but these ladies were doing complex weaves, cabling, experimental selvages, all the while carrying on proper conversations. When I'm doing anything remotely complicated I have to stop talking immediately. I go into a trance and my tongue pokes out.

There was a small knitting fair going on at the same time and there were stands staffed by fabric companies, yarn makers, machine designers and so on. There was even a pen with four very attractive goats. Not to mention the angora rabbits, in runs. There were workshops, lectures and seminars.

This is so cool, I thought, wandering about, before realizing that perhaps "cool" wasn't the most appropriate term.

In fact, "not cool in any way" might have been more accurate but I didn't care. I was in my element and amongst like-minded people.

I was standing, gazing in awe around me, when my eyes fell on a sight that struck terror into my heart.

Megan Hooper.

Maybe it was inevitable that she'd find out eventually. She was standing with her mum as I approached the room where the competition was to take place. She looked up and saw me and I realized there was no escape. Oh well, I thought. It's not as if it was ever going to happen between us, anyway. At least now I could tell myself that it was her prejudice against knitting that put the kibosh on it, and not the fact that I was so hopeless with girls.

"Ben? Hi," Megan said, blinking in surprise.

"Oh, hi, Megan," I replied.

"What are you doing here?" she asked. Over her shoulder Mrs. Hooper was making "I'm sorry" faces at me. I shrugged.

"I'm here to knit," I said.

Megan laughed. "Funny," she said. "But really, why are you here?"

I looked her in the eye. Time to be a man. "I'm really here to knit, Megan. I've been taking your mum's class for the last few months. I'm in the junior category."

There was a long pause during which my life flashed before me. Then I watched her face closely. She has lovely eyes, does Megan. Green with hints of hazel. What could I see in those eyes? Shock? Maybe a touch of betrayal?

"That's b-brilliant!" she said eventually. "Erm, it's not . . . I mean, you don't normally see . . . many boys knitting."

"Some of the world's most successful knitters are men," Mrs. Hooper pointed out.

"Well, good luck, Ben," Megan said, straight-faced. "I'll be cheering for you."

Was she mocking me? I couldn't tell.

"There's no cheering allowed," Mrs. Hooper said. "They need to concentrate."

"I'll be cheering on the inside," Megan said.

"Megan, I need to borrow Ben for a moment," Mrs. Hooper told her daughter, leading me away a bit more forcefully than necessary.

As I was dragged off I felt regretful. I'd missed my chance with Megan for good. If only I'd been a bit more impulsive. I should have just grabbed her arm and said in a gravelly voice, "Look, Megan Hooper. You're a woman, I'm a man. Let's stop playing games and make this happen."

But the moment had passed. I'd blown it now. Put the final nail in my own coffin.

"Sorry about that," Mrs. Hooper whispered. "I hadn't expected to be bringing her but she asked if she could come along. She said she needed a break from studying."

"Don't worry about it, Mrs. Hooper," I sighed.

"Naomi, please."

"Okay, Naomi. See, I've been thinking it's about time I man up and start telling people. It's nothing to be ashamed of, after all."

She shook her head. "It really isn't. You have a wonderful talent."

"Thanks."

"Now, go in there and win this thing," she said.

"What's the pattern?" I asked.

"Ah, yes. About that . . ."

"It's stranded colorwork, isn't it?"

"Yes, it is."

Honestly, what's the point of trying to be positive when everything conspires against you?

My competitors in the junior category of the All-UK Knitting Championship (Hampshire Regional Heat) were an odd-looking bunch. All girls, as you'd expect. They all looked a lot older than me, which I was suspicious about until Mrs. Hooper showed me the eligibility criteria and I realized the junior category went up to age twenty-three.

They were quite sullen too. I'm used to chatting while I knit, and knitting while I chat. I tried to kick off a conversation as we all took our seats.

"First time?" I asked the girl sitting behind me. She was thin and angular, with sharp glasses and dry skin.

"No," she said.

"This is my first time," I said, to the room at large. One girl gave me a brief smile but most just ignored me. I got the impression that chatting to the other contestants was bad form. I suppose it's like the Wimbledon final, you don't get

Roger Federer asking Rafael Nadal where he has his hair cut moments before the start.

I turned back to my desk and inspected the kit. There was a selection of high-quality needles and hooks. There were six green balls of yarn and six red, all different weights.

A dumpy lady wearing a name badge I couldn't read stood up in front and held up a sheaf of papers.

"These are the patterns," she called out, causing a frisson of murmured excitement from the other contestants.

"Ooh," I said, joining in.

She walked down the aisles between the desks, slapping a sheet on each, facedown.

"Please turn over your patterns . . . now!" the dumpy lady sang out.

I flipped mine over and saw, with an inward groan, that it was for a neck warmer. Simple enough but with a rose design in it. Stranded colorwork in the round. My worst fears had been realized. Correction: it could have been worse. It could have been a tea cozy.

I looked up to see the angular girl eyeing me carefully; she'd seen the look of disappointment on my face.

"I can handle stranded colorwork," I told her. "I can handle knitting in the round. Just not together, you know? I find it hard to keep everything in my head at once; it bothers me."

She nodded briefly and turned back to inspecting her yarns.

"There is only one place in the national finals available," Dumpy went on. "So there can only be one winner."

"Like *The Hunger Games*," I whispered to Miss Angular. This time she ignored me completely. Okay, I thought to myself. If that's the way you want to play it.

"Okay, contestants," the Official Lady said once she'd finished. "You have ninety minutes to complete as much of the pattern as you can. You don't need to finish it. Some extra marks will be given for completed patterns, but more important are neatness, precision and technique. Officials will be walking around inspecting your technique as you work."

She checked her watch, counting down the seconds until 7:30 p.m. I looked up at the viewing gallery and saw Mrs. Hooper and Megan. Mrs. Hooper gave me the thumbs-up; Megan was looking off into the distance, apparently bored already. Then I saw Natasha and Amelia threading their way along the aisle to sit next to the Hoopers. Natasha sat, saw me looking and waved. I smiled weakly back, utterly nauseated.

"Contestants, your time starts now," the Official Lady said. There was a mass clicking as the other contestants picked up their needles of choice and began work immediately. I took a deep breath, tried to clear my head and picked up two needles of my own.

The reason I don't like stranded color when knitting in the round is that I like to picture the whole garment in my head, the whole time. I like to know where everything is, where it was and where it will be. I have to think in 3D, otherwise I get confused and my stitches start to slip. Other people I know can concentrate on one thing at a time. Complete that stitch, that purl, that row, then think about what to do next. I don't think like that. It's all got to be there before I start. Then the process itself becomes almost automatic.

So for me leaping right into the pattern, like the others had, wasn't the plan. I had to focus, get the job completed in my head first, then keep it there while my fingers did the rest. I must have sat there, eyes closed, visualizing for four or five minutes. I could hear people whispering in the gallery, the outside hubbub of noise from the show, the soft bleating of goats. I blocked all this from my mind and thought about nothing but the pattern.

There were 60 rows, 50 columns, 3,000 stitches, 798 red, the rest green. Knitting in the round, locked into place, stranded colors, locked into place. Overall garment shape, size, locked into place. Estimated time of completion—77 minutes.

I opened my eyes and started to knit.

I cut out all the noise, all the distractions. I didn't care about school, or Lloyd Manning, or my friends, or Megan, or Mrs. Frensham or anything; the only thing I was thinking about was that pattern.

I knitted, and I purled and I knitted some more. The needles were perfect, the yarn was silky smooth and unraveled easily. I completed the first ring without a dropped stitch, then the second and the third. I didn't look at the clock, I just kept going. My fingers flicked and twisted, the needles flew, the neck warmer started to take shape. The loops were the perfect size, not too loose so as to let warm air escape, not so tight that the fabric would be too thin.

It was going well. Very well.

So well, in fact, that something just had to go wrong. I'd completed thirty-five rows and was ready to bring in the different color when suddenly there was a huge crash to my left. I nearly jumped out of my skin.

Miss Angular had knocked a stack of knitting needles off her desk onto the floor.

"Sorry," she mouthed.

"Is everything okay?" the Official Lady asked, walking

over to help collect the needles. I nodded and gave her the thumbs-up.

"It's okay," I mouthed back to Miss Angular. But as I did, I noticed something. Suddenly she was smiling. Just a hint of a smile. A sly smile. The sort of smile people give when they've just done something mischievous.

She'd dropped the needles on purpose! To break my concentration. The minx! I stole a quick glance at her neck warmer. It was good, nice loops, strong weft. But she'd only completed twenty or so rows. A survey of the other contestants told me that she was, in fact, ahead of most of them, except me. I was well ahead. Or had been until the crash of needles dropping broke my concentration. Now everyone else was furiously knitting, catching up to me.

I was stung by this treachery. I couldn't bring myself to look up at Megan. I had to get back into the Knitzone. Concentrate, Ben. Concentrate.

It took me longer this time. The mental image I had in my head had been deleted. I had to reconstruct it. But as I was a third of the way through, it was more difficult. I was also worried that Miss Angular might try the trick again. I couldn't let her beat me, not now. I hadn't cared so much about winning beforehand, I just didn't want to embarrass myself. Now though, things were different. She'd laid down the challenge and I wasn't going to back down.

I closed my eyes, took another deep breath and then suddenly, with a little ping, the image was back. The area I'd done was filled in bold, the bits still to do grayed out. I just had to complete this row, then I'd bring the next color in.

I resumed knitting. Not so fast this time, not so smooth. I dropped a stitch here and there. But I was determined. The image remained in my head, spinning slowly, the colors filling in as I carried on. The first flash of red appeared, then started to grow. Another row completed, then another, then three more.

Then Miss Angular started coughing. Loudly. Clearly faked.

"Could I have some water, please?" she croaked loudly. I stared straight ahead, trying to shut her out, but my hands slowed and I lost the thread again. I stopped and waited for her fit to pass.

As the Official Lady walked off, after delivering the water, my nemesis turned to look at me. She had a fierce glint in her eye. Though, in fairness, that could have been the overhead lights reflecting off her glasses.

"You're right, this is like *The Hunger Games*. And you can call me Katniss," she said sarcastically. The she returned to her knitting. She'd sped up, I saw, or maybe I'd slowed down. And she was now just a few rows behind me. I swallowed, my mouth dry, wishing I had some of her water.

Once more, I closed my eyes and tried to bring back the image. I got it back, but again, the distraction had knocked my confidence. Damaged my focus. I dropped more stitches. One row was so bad I had to frog the lot. Damn her. Damn her!

When time was up, I hadn't finished. I was sure I could have completed the garment in the time had I not been interrupted twice. An official took my work, saying nothing. She attached a tag to it with my name on it, then did the same for Evil Miss Angular. I refused to look at her, I was so angry.

"The judging process will take half an hour," the Official Lady called out. "Please do take a look around the fair while you wait. There are refreshments available at the bar or café. We'll see you back here at nine thirty p.m."

I waited for my nemesis to leave before standing and shuffling out into the main hall, where the Hoopers and my knit class pals were waiting.

"You were brilliant," Natasha said, giving me a hug.

"That girl next to you was a bitch," Amelia said. "We could see her keep looking at how fast you were going, and she was sweating bullets."

"We think she might have dropped those needles on purpose," Megan added, apparently having found watching a knitting competition more engaging than she'd expected.

"She definitely did," I said. "Put me off." I could see Miss Angular across the hall, eyeing up the goats, perhaps planning to sacrifice one of them to thank the gods for her win.

"Your knitting was better than hers, though," Mrs. Hooper said. "And so fast. I'm astonished to watch your hands, Ben. You're a blur with those needles."

"Thanks," I said, feeling a bit better.

"Let's go and have a cup of tea," she said. "Are you hungry?"

I was ravenous, as it happened, and ate a tuna sandwich and a packet of chips that Mrs. Hooper bought for me. She went off to see how the judging was coming along. Amelia had disappeared to gaze longingly at a wefting machine. I was left alone with Natasha and Megan. There was a bit of an awkward pause, which I filled by jamming half a sandwich in my mouth.

"So you're the famous Megan?" Natasha asked as I munched away.

Megan looked at her in surprise, and nodded.

"Ben's told me all about you," Natasha said.

"Have I?" I asked, finishing my mouthful.

"Has he?" Megan said.

Natasha nodded. "You talk about her all the time in knitting class."

As if I wasn't embarrassed enough already. That was exactly the wrong thing to say. Hi, Megan, this is Bellend Ben, he's a weedy knitting loser and is totally obsessed with you. Unfortunately I couldn't say anything to defend myself because I'd shoved the other half of the sandwich in by then.

"So you two are in knitting class together?" Megan asked Natasha with a thin smile.

Natasha nodded. "Yes, it's very sociable."

"Chat, chat, chat?" Megan said. There was a bit of a tone to her voice.

"Yes. We have lovely chats, don't we, Ben?"

I nodded, chewing and forcing a smile, wishing I was watching *Top Gear* with Dad.

Thankfully Mrs. Hooper came back then and told us the judges were ready to announce the winner. As I stood, brushing crumbs from my tank top, Megan grabbed my hand and squeezed it. It felt like a good-bye.

"Good luck, Ben," she said.

"Thanks," I said, taken aback.

The desks had been cleared from the Knitzone and we all gathered around to hear the winner. I wasn't holding out any hope that they might call my name.

Please let it be someone else, I thought to myself. Not Miss Angular. She's not Katniss.

"Ladies and gentle*man*," the Official Lady began, having apparently developed a sense of humor. "The officials have given us their reports on technique, and the judges have examined every stitch of each contestant's piece."

She paused for effect. "This was the closest heat we've had in years," she went on. "We hadn't really expected anyone to complete the garment in the time allowed, but one contestant came very close."

Mrs. Hooper stood right next to me on one side and turned to smile at me supportively. I saw Megan standing off to the side, just watching.

"This has been a very difficult decision," Official Lady went on.

I noticed Natasha had crept up on my other side. I turned to grin at her.

"There can only be one winner. But we have smaller prizes for three runners-up."

I noticed Miss Angular standing at the front. She held her hands in front of her, slightly apart as if she were about to begin praying. Was it possible I might be one of the runners-up?

"The third runner-up is Ella Gower!"

There was a loud shriek from Ella, followed by a warm round of applause. Ella was a reedy girl in a red cardigan who I hadn't noticed up to now. An Assistant Official Lady ducked through the crowd to deliver a paper bag full of knitting goodies to her. I craned my neck to get a better look at the contents. Did I see some organic angora?

"The second runner-up is Denise Hancock," Official Lady called out. A second shriek, even louder, and another round of applause. This was a blow. Denise had produced a piece that I had thought might just win the whole thing. Miss Angular seemed to agree; she turned and smirked at Denise, clapping slowly. Ooh, I hated her so much. The Official Lady's assistant delivered a second goody bag to Denise and made her way back to the front.

"The first runner-up is . . ."

We held our breath. I felt Natasha grab hold of my hand. She was nervous too.

"Jeanette Fairbanks!" My heart sank.

There was no shriek this time. Heads turned as people looked for Jeanette.

"Is Jeanette still here?" the Official Lady asked.

"She must have gone," someone called.

But then I saw something that lifted my spirits. The crowd had shifted slightly and I had a clear view of Miss Angular, who looked utterly furious. So not Katniss after all, but Jeanette. I grinned with satisfaction.

"Jeanette Fairb—"

"I'm Jeanette Fairbanks," she shouted. She virtually snatched the goody bag and walked off into the crowds. It seemed to me she was very careful to avoid catching my eye.

Mrs. Hooper gave me a wink and I grinned back. So I hadn't won any prizes, but at least the cheating Jeanette had got her comeuppance.

"And so the winner of the junior category of the Hampshire heat of the All-UK Knitting Championship is . . ."

Silence fell as we all waited. The Official Lady gave it the full *X Factor* sixteen-second delay before shouting out the name.

"Ben Fletcher!"

You know that whooshing sound you get when you come up for air after being underwater for a while? I had that.

Was this for real?

I realized the place was in uproar. Mrs. Hooper slapped me on the back.

"Well done, Ben," Amelia cried, grabbing my upper arm. "Woohoo!" she shrieked as I blinked in surprise.

Then Natasha grabbed hold of me and gave me a great bear hug, spinning me around. I could see Megan over her shoulder. She'd come forward, presumably to offer congratulations, but Natasha accidentally stepped backward, standing on her foot. Megan stumbled away, looking cross and was swallowed up by the crowd.

Then Natasha kissed me.

DECEMBER 17TH

Like I said, it was a strange night. Emotions were running high. I had a brilliant time and was thrilled to have won but, as ever, my obsessive mind wouldn't stop poring over the details, trying to figure things out. Trying to solve mysteries that might not have even existed in the first place.

So that was that with Megan. After the result was announced she disappeared. Part of me was annoyed at her. Even if she found the knitting a turnoff, she could have hung around to congratulate me. Couldn't we be friends at least?

The rest of us went back to the café for a celebratory cupcake. After congratulating me, Mrs. Hooper went to find Megan and came back a while later to tell us Megan wasn't feeling well and that she was going to take her home. I'll have to find her at school tomorrow and explain about being too embarrassed to come out of the knitting closet. She'll understand. I hope. But I'm also terrified that she might tell other people about my little secret.

Secondly, Natasha. Her kiss had been a bit . . . wet. It didn't seem like a congratulatory peck on the cheek. But then again, she is quite a touchy-feely person. Did Natasha fancy me? Was she my cougar? Surely not.

The third thing bothering me was the fact that I'd just

won the regional heat of the AUKKC (Junior Category) which means that I now have to go to London for the final. My first thought was to reject the idea. I couldn't possibly keep that a secret. But how could I turn it down? What a disappointment it would be for Mrs. Hooper and the others who came to cheer me on. And worse yet, it would mean Jeanette bloody Fairbanks would go instead.

I can't let that happen, can I?

DECEMBER 18TH

Dark days for the *Knitwits!* podcasters. Alana desperately wants to knit the Rocky Coast cardigan, which I checked out online, and it is pretty impressive. She has the right needles, size 10.5. Problem is, she's having a tough time deciding what yarn to use. The pattern calls for a worsted-weight yarn. She has an impressive stash at home, including a single-ply organic alpaca at the right weight, but only in a navy blue. Oh no. Alana doesn't wear navy! Why spend all that time knitting a beautiful cardigan that you're never going to wear, right? Also, a darker color won't show the attractive cabling. On the other hand, she has a pretty pale blue Malabrigo worsted that is the perfect color. It would make a nice cardigan, but it would pill like crazy.

Well, Alana, I'm no expert, but that's the problem with single-ply!

Marie, as usual, is totally useless at coming up with a solution. She doesn't say much anyway, Marie. And she's a total yarn snob. It's got to be organic, it's got to be unusual. Normal, boring old merino isn't good enough for Marie, oh no. I sometimes think I should be Alana's partner on *Knit-wits!* I wonder if I win the final I could get a guest spot, and start elbowing Marie out. Alana sounds quite cute, too. I wonder how old she is.

DECEMBER 19TH

I looked for Megan at school today but couldn't find her anywhere. I did run into Jasmine though and asked her if she'd seen Megan. She put that look on again.

"No," she snapped.

"Is she avoiding me?"

"Why would she avoid you?"

"Because . . . I dunno."

"Well then."

"Look, if you see her, just tell her . . . sorry."

"Sorry for what?" Jasmine said, smirking at me. A cold hand clutched at my heart. She had clearly been talking to Megan about something. Did she know about . . . ?

"Did Megan say something to you?" I asked tentatively.

"About what?"

"Nothing," I said, backing away from her.

DECEMBER 20TH

I mentioned to Mrs. Hooper tonight at knitting class that Miss Swallow had asked me to knit a vest for her boyfriend and wanted to pay me for it.

"Great," she said. "Actually, I've been meaning to talk to you about this. Now that you're a regional heat winner, you should use it in your favor."

"How do you mean?" I asked.

"Have you heard of Etsy.com?"

"Yes, Miss Swallow told me about it."

"Well, if you want to, you could set yourself up as a supplier. With the endorsement you get for being a junior finalist, you'll likely get plenty of orders."

Well, that got me thinking. Could I actually make some money out of this? I had another look at the site when I got home. It was pretty simple to set up my own page. Reading through the comments section it seems that a few people actually make a living out of it. I checked out the competition and there was a lot of quite shoddy work on there. I was sure I could do better.

The only slightly sticky bit was that the website asked me to upload some photos of my garments being modeled. Who am I going to get to model for me?

DECEMBER 21ST

Last day at school before the Christmas break. I left a Christmas card and a small box of chocolates on top of Megan's locker. But I didn't have the chance to talk to her.

I gave the vest to Miss Swallow today, along with her card. She was thrilled. She even kind of hugged me. At school. Just outside the staffroom. Where people could see us. She smelled faintly of lemons. I'd never thought of the lemon as being one of nature's sexier fruits before now.

Natasha? Miss Swallow? I'm like a babe magnet now. Well, not all babes. Not the babe I like. Maybe I'm only attractive to older women?

"This is brilliant, Ben, thanks so much," she said.

"Miss Swallow," I said as she turned to go.

"Yes?"

"Do you think. I mean, would you mind taking a picture of your boyfriend, wearing the vest?"

She looked puzzled. "Er, okay. Why?"

"I need a male model. I mean, I need a man to wear it so I can use it on my website, for advertising. I'd cut his head off if he wants to be anonymous."

She looked thoughtful.

"I'll ask him, but why don't you just use yourself as a model?"

I laughed. "I'm a little . . . small for that. It needs someone with a proper chest to show it off properly."

She gave me a curious little smile.

"Okay, Ben," she said.

As I walked off she called after me:

"But just remember, Ben. A big chest isn't everything."

I think it is, Miss Swallow. I think it kind of is.

CHRISTMAS DAY

3:34 p.m.

A very merry Christmas dinner's over. Molly was very funny and Mum got a miniature magic set in her cracker and actually managed to make the tricks work. Then she did some other brilliant tricks of her own. It's amazing the number of places she can pull a Brussels sprout from. I even laughed when Dad suggested he liked filling a big bird with his special sausage stuffing. They got me a new phone, which is totally amazing.

"What are you doing for New Year's Eve?" Mum asked me over pudding.

"Nothing," I said.

"Really? Not going out with your friends?"

"No. Look, it's always a disaster. I'd rather just not bother and stay in, get an early night and catch up on my studies."

"Maybe we could watch *The Big Fat Quiz of the Year* together?"

"Sounds good, Mum, yeah," I said. What I really wanted to do was crack on with my knitting, of course. But I couldn't say so with Dad in the room.

"You could invite your friends over, if you like?"

No way, I thought. They're nothing but trouble. I think it best for all of us if I have a bit of a break from my friends, especially Gex.

11:38 p.m.

Just finished half a Terry's Chocolate Orange. Feel sick.

We all stayed up late to watch *Murder on the Orient Express*, which is one of Mum's favorites. Dad claimed not to remember who'd done it. We all stared at him in disbelief, but he's like that, he never remembers films or books once he's finished them. Unless they're about the Second World War, of course, in which case he'll bore you to death with the details.

As it turned out, he went to sleep twenty minutes before the end of the film and has only just now gone to bed, still with no clue whodunnit.

Might have the rest of this Terry's Chocolate Orange, then head up myself. Ooh, just heard comedy ringtone on new phone.

It was a text from Megan.

Merry Xmas, Ben, thanks for the card and chocs. Sorry haven't had chance to congratulate you on your win last week. You around tomorrow? Will pop by and drop off present.

So she isn't avoiding me after all? I texted back to let her know I would indeed be around. I wonder if she now thinks Natasha is my girlfriend, or more likely doesn't care one way or the other. Her text contained distinct tones of friendliness, which suggests to me she's well over whatever feelings she might have had for me. No kiss, though. What does no kiss mean? Friends get one kiss, don't they?

Either way, I'm stoked that she's coming over, and that she's bringing a present. Crap! Just thought, what am I going to wear? I currently have on a festive wooly sweater (shop-bought) with a snowman motif. That's got to go, as do the comedy monster slippers Molly gave me for Christmas.

DECEMBER 26TH

So Megan came this morning to give me my present. I wore skinny jeans and a Gap hoodie and think I looked pretty good. Shame I forgot to take off the illuminated reindeer antlers but I suppose it shows I don't take myself too seriously. She wore a Santa hat that was a little too big for her. It was a good look. She has lovely big eyes with long lashes, Megan Hooper. I sighed inwardly.

"It's knitting-related," she said. "Hope that's okay."

"That's perfect," I said. I was glad she'd told me before I went ahead and opened it in front of Dad. I opened it later to find some lovely two-ply merino wool in a dark blue. She has good taste.

"Do you want to come in?"

"I can't," she said. "Going to Gran's for lunch."

"Okay. Look, Megan?" I began.

She stood for a moment, looking at me expectantly.

"Sorry about . . . you know, the other night."

"What about it?" she asked.

"Oh, don't you start," I said. "You sound like Jasmine. I just meant that it must have been a shock for you."

"Yeah, a little," she said after a slight pause. "I'm surprised you didn't tell me."

"You haven't told anyone else?"

She shrugged. "I told Jasmine."

I knew it.

"Why, is it a secret?" she asked sniffily.

"Yes, it is."

"But—"

"Strictly confidential," I said firmly.

"Okay, Ben. I'll tell her to keep it zipped," she said a bit frostily. "Merry Christmas." Then she was gone. Why is she annoyed at me? What did she expect me to say?

DECEMBER 27TH

Be still my heart. I've just received an email from Miss Swallow. She wrote:

Hi Ben,

Here's a couple of pictures of Joe flexing his pecs, though you can't really see that under the vest. Hope they're okay (pics not pecs). Joe is delighted in his new role as knitwear model and is happy for you to show his face.

Good luck with the website!

Jx

P.S. How's the ziggurat coming along?

I now have Jessica Swallow's email address. Or should I say J's email address? She's just Jx to me now. And I'm B to her. Or Bx. She signed her email with a kiss! Should I respond? If so, should I kiss her back? Up the ante with another kiss? A smiley face. No. It's only girls who put kisses and emoticons on emails and texts. As Dad would say, it's "not a thing for men."

I waited an hour, so it didn't seem desperate. Then I waited another seven minutes so it didn't seem like I'd waited exactly one hour.

Hi there,

Thanks! These are perfect.

B

Pretty smooth. Pretty, pretty smooth.

DECEMBER 28TH

I put the pictures of Joe up on my Etsy page today. It all looks brilliant. Joe looks great, which must be because of the vest. I added captions to the photos saying things like "Hampton FC striker Joe Boyle wears a classic vest in four-ply navy merino." Maybe I'll get some hits from Hampton FC fans!

DECEMBER 29TH

So my divorce from Gex lasted all of three days. I'm like Michael in *The Godfather*. I can't escape the Family, no matter how hard I try; they just pull me back in. Joz and I were cycling through the park today and we saw Gex and Freddie hanging out by the broken swings. They called us over. I could tell Gex had a plan as soon as I saw his face. He was looking all shifty and scanning the area constantly. He couldn't have looked more suspicious if he'd had a twirly moustache, a cackling laugh and was standing over a screaming blonde he'd just tied to a railway track.

"What?" I asked guardedly.

"What you doing for New Year's?" he asked us.

"Nothing," Joz said immediately.

I hesitated. I had intended to spend New Year's Eve with Mum before sneaking upstairs to get on with the knitting. I'm working on a particularly complex neckline pattern Mrs. Hooper had told us about and that I was thinking of introducing into 2Patz, but I could hardly tell him that. In fact, I had recently made wholesale adjustments to the pattern and was no longer calling it 2Patz. It was now Patt3rn.

"Good," Gex said. "You two is coming wiv us to Wicked."

"The musical?" I asked. "I've seen it."

They looked at me in contempt. "Oh," I said, suddenly getting it. "You mean the nightclub in Haslemere retail park, don't you? Classy."

"Yep," Freddie said. "We're going clubbing."

"I'm not," I said. "I hate clubs, and we're underage. I'd be breaching the terms of my prob—"

"Stop crapping on about your probation," Gex said. "This place is wall-to-wall girls, isn't it?"

"I'm supposed to be Giving Something Back," I pointed out.

"Well, think of it as Giving Something Back to the ladies of Hampton," Joz said.

"What am I giving back to them?" I asked.

"How about the knickers you stole off their washing lines?" Gex suggested.

When everyone had stopped rolling around laughing, Freddie explained that his friend Baz works at Wicked and can help us get in.

"New Year's is free for girls, only guys have to pay, so he says they always end up with loads more girls than guys. The girls go a bit mad without so many blokes around. You know. Sexy dancing with each other, bit of girl-on-girl snogging and toward the end of the evening they're ready to grab hold of anything in a pair of trousers. Even you won't have any trouble, Bellend."

"Thanks for the ego boost," I said.

"Baz tells me he gets fistfuls of phone numbers shoved

in his pockets," Gex went on, eyes wide at the thought. "He gets felt up the whole time. He loves it."

"Gex," I said. "Baz is in that position because he works there and is over eighteen. How are you going to benefit from this, considering you won't be allowed in? Are you going to wait outside with a sign?"

"We're going to dress up as bar staff," Gex said, his eye glinting at the sheer genius of his own plan. "No one's going to be asking you for ID when you have a staff T-shirt."

"Where are you going to get the T-shirts from?" I asked.

"Baz grabbed me some old uniforms, said as long as we wash them and return them next week no one will miss them."

"Why would Baz do this?" I asked, suspicious.

"Because he got fired, right?" Gex said. "He doesn't care anymore."

"And why did he get fired?"

"Got caught snogging a girl in the ladies' bathroom."

"He's a legend," Freddie said.

"So, you in?" Gex asked.

"No," I replied.

"Why not?" he asked, genuinely astonished.

"Look, for a start, the plan is not going to work," I told him. "Even if we manage to sneak in without being caught and arrested, we'll hardly be able to wander about the place chatting up girls. We'll either be spotted and thrown out right away, or else we'll end up having to pour drinks all night."

"That place is dark," he said witheringly. "It's noisy. On New Year's Eve it'll be heaving like a dieting ballerina. No one's going to notice us, and even if they do, we'll just say we didn't know we weren't supposed to be there."

"And how will we explain the uniforms?"

"All you do is ask questions, Bellend," Gex said,

exasperated. "Try not to see the problems, try to see the opportunities."

"You know who's going to be there, Ben?" Freddie asked, a sly look on his face.

"Who?" I asked.

"A teacher."

"Mr. Grover?" I asked. I knew perfectly well who he was thinking of.

"A teacher who likes to shove big things into her hot oven."

"All right, all right," I said. "Drop the double entendres, I get enough of those at home. So Miss Swallow's going to be there. So what?"

And then Freddie dropped his bombshell. "So she's single now. She's split up with Joe, that's what."

Shut the front door.

DECEMBER 30TH

Apparently it happened on Friday. Freddie says Joe came around to their house for some family thing. He was all morose and told everyone about it then.

"So why did they split up?" I asked him.

"I dunno," he said, shrugging.

"You didn't ask?"

"He did tell Mum," he said, bored with the conversation now. "But I was playing Xbox. I wasn't really listening."

"Freddie, this is important information," I said, annoyed. "Did he cheat on her? Or did they just drift apart? Is she upset? Vulnerable? Does she hate all men? Is she looking for revenge or a rebound relationship?"

"Come clubbing wiv us," Gex said, "and you might just find out. . . ."

"I'll think about it," I told him coolly.

Damn him. Damn him!

JANUARY 1ST

I don't even know where to start about last night. First of all I had trouble getting out of the house. I was nervous about possibly seeing Miss Swallow in an erotically charged situation and I spent ages getting ready. I put some aftershave on. Possibly too much, actually; I had a choking fit and can still feel it in the back of my throat nearly twenty-four hours later.

I'd dressed in a simple white T-shirt, skinny jeans and proper shoes, like Gex had instructed. Only problem was that the only proper shoes I have are the ones Mum got me for Gran's funeral, which are a bit dressy for Wicked, I think. But Gex had said "no Converse," and the only other shoes I have are my school shoes. So I borrowed a pair of my dad's two-tone shoes, the ones he wears when he and Mum go to Back to School '80s Night in Guildford. I don't know much about fashion but those are clearly dancing shoes. You do not want to hear what else they wear on these date nights, but it includes leg warmers and marble-wash jeans.

"Where are you going with those shoes on?" Mum asked as I clattered down the stairs.

"Out, just over to Gex's house." This was true, but only because we were meeting there before heading off to the club.

"I thought we were having an evening in?" she said. "I'm off on tour again tomorrow."

"Sorry, Mum," I said. "I arranged this ages ago."

"You said you were staying in."

"Did I?"

"Yes. What are you doing at Gex's?"

I thought furiously. Why hadn't I prepared an answer?

"Watching telly?" she suggested. "Playing computer games? Studying? Shooting up?"

"Yes," I said. "All of those. Except for the shooting up."

"And the studying," Mum said.

"Yes, that's right, except for the shooting up and studying."

"You're supposed to be doing advanced classes this year," Mum reminded me.

"I know, Mum, but it's New Year's Eve. . . ."

She frowned at me. "Okay, off you go, then; we'll just sit here and watch *The Big Fat Quiz of the Year* without you."

"Can you record it?" I asked.

"Already am."

"Thanks, Mum."

She stood up and walked over to me. "I know you very well, Ben," she said, looking down at my shoes, then at my hair. I could see her nostrils flare as she sniffed my aftershave.

"I know you do," I said, shifting uncomfortably.

She held out an empty hand, palm up.

"Put your hand over mine," she said. I did so.

Mum pressed her palm against mine, and flipped our hands over so mine was underneath, then she took her hand away to reveal a twenty-pound note.

"What's that for?"

"In case you want to buy your young lady friend a drink. Or a McFlurry. Or an iTunes card, or whatever it is you teenagers buy each other to express affection."

I grinned. "Thanks, Mum."

I hightailed then, running down the hill and along Foster Street to Gex's house. Gex lives in a manky old terrace. His dad hasn't worked for a while. There's always a mattress out in the front garden at Gex's house. Oddly enough, it's not always the same mattress. I'm curious what the situation is with the mattresses. Who puts them there? Who takes the old ones away? Who decides when all of this should happen? I'm always too scared to ask.

They were all waiting out front when I arrived. Gex and Freddie were sitting on the hood of Gex's Ford Fiesta while Joz sat on the low garden wall. Freddie was smoking.

"Where you been?" Gex asked.

"And why are you wearing bowling shoes?" Joz added.

"They're dancing shoes," I replied.

"Where do you usually go dancing?" Freddie asked. "Bowl-a-Rama?"

"It don't matter," Gex said. "No one's going to look at his shoes. Come on, let's go."

He handed us all our golf shirts, emblazoned with the Wicked logo. We put them on and got in his car. I was sweating a bit, to be honest. I didn't think it likely we were going to be arrested or anything, but we were certain to get caught and chucked out. What if someone saw us and word got around? What if Mum found out? She'd be disappointed in me. What if Mrs. Hooper found out? That would almost be worse. What if Claudia Gunter found out? I'm supposed to be her model client? It was all right for the others. No one has any expectations of them. They've been written off by the world already. Or at least Gex has. Why can't I be written off?

JANUARY 2ND

Couldn't finish the Club Night story yesterday. Found I was writing in more detail than I'd meant to. Mum interrupted me and reminded me I've got maths mock exam in three weeks. Did a bit of studying last night and will do some more tonight. But I wanted to get this down while it's still fresh in my memory.

Freddie was doing his Deep Thought thing in the car. He goes quiet for ages, obviously concentrating on some big concept, then he suddenly comes out with it, slowly and portentously, and it's always completely pointless. We were speeding, literally, along a country road, Gex having decided to avoid the highways as he happened to know there weren't any cameras along this particular route.

"Is it okay? That you're speeding?" I asked, trying not to seem anxious even while clutching the door handle. "You've already lost your license once." Gex is eighteen. He lost his license three weeks after he got it, for six months. "Remember you had to do that safe driving course?"

"Advanced Driving course, okay?" he said. "Not Safe Driving. I got seventy-three percent on Advanced Driving."

"What happens if you're faced with a situation from the twenty-seven percent you failed on?" I asked, wincing at how close Gex had come to swiping a cyclist. I craned to watch the poor guy shaking his fist at us in the rearview mirror.

"Look," he said. "Because of you, we're late. Our shift started ten minutes ago."

"We don't have a shift," I pointed out. "We're not actually employed by anyone. We can turn up whenever we like."

"Do you think mice who live in Legoland think they're giants?" Freddie said, apropos of nothing.

There was a silence in the car as we all thought this over.

"They might," Joz said eventually. It's best just to go along with Freddie when he's in this mood.

"I think there are probably a lot of animals confused by Legoland," I added.

"Yes, you're right," Freddie said. "Like birds flying overhead. They probably think, 'Whoa, I'm really high!'"

Gex shot through a red light, nearly knocking another man off his bike.

"Another flipping cyclist," he spat. "They're everywhere. It's like Beijing round here."

"At least you saw him this time," I said.

Gex grunted.

"So what's your plan of attack with the Swallower?" Joz asked.

"I don't have a plan," I said. "I'll ask her if she wants to dance, and she'll shoot me down. Nothing is going to happen between us. Obviously."

"Obviously," Freddie said.

We arrived twenty minutes late for our "shift" but at least we were in one piece. Gex led us up to the door, where two bouncers were checking IDs. Gex unhooked the red rope, cool as you like, and walked in. The bouncers looked up.

"Who are you?" one of them asked. He was huge, both tall and broad. Imagine if Dennis Rodman and Shrek had got into a teleport machine together and ended up fused into one person. You might have got something that looked a bit like this bouncer.

"Mike called us over from the other club," Gex said coolly. "Said you were short-staffed."

"News to me," said Dennis Shrek.

The people in the crowd, mostly girls, true, were staring at us suspiciously. Did they sniff a fast one being pulled?

Gex shrugged and just stood there, looking at the man. I kind of admired his nerve. All I wanted to do was run.

Eventually the monster twitched his massive head toward the doorway. "Go on, then," he said. "Good luck with this lot."

We were in. We headed straight for the bathrooms and took off our shirts, then it was back out onto the dance floor. Now that we were inside, some of my fear fell away and I started to quite enjoy myself. The music was rubbish, of course, but it was so loud, and the dance floor was so crowded that it didn't really matter. We surged into the gyrating mob, shouting at each other, jumping up and down, not caring how we looked. No one was looking at my shoes. No one was looking at me.

I was actually having fun.

Then a gap opened up in the crowd and, for a moment, I saw her. Miss Swallow, dancing, apparently alone, her eyes closed. Looking like class on a dance floor. Time slowed, I was deaf to the music, blind to everything but Miss Swallow. She wore a loose gray top, short, which showed off her midriff and, if I wasn't mistaken, was made from angora wool. The stitches were loose, open, which made the top slightly see-through; she wore a black bra underneath and very, very tight white jeans.

Then she opened her eyes and saw me. She stopped dancing and came over. I stood, trying to keep my tongue in my mouth, trying to stop my eyes from popping out of my head.

"What are you doing here?" Miss Swallow shouted over the music. "You're underage."

"Not much," I protested. I was trying to avoid staring at her top. I was fascinated to know what yarn it was, but I was worried if I had a good old stare she might think I was looking at her boobs.

She looked doubtful. She also looked drunk. She shrugged and said, "Oh, what the hell, come and dance with me."

I wanted to move, but I was in a state of shock. And panic.

"Come on," she persisted, grabbing hold of my arm and pulling me with impressive force. "Time to see what you're made of, Fletcher."

She did sound a bit "buzzed," as my grandma terms it, but this was a call to arms. It was now or never.

"If you insist." I grinned.

Only problem was, I have absolutely no idea how to dance. Not only that, but all that freedom I had felt, that confidence, the devil-may-care feeling when we'd first walked onto the dance floor? All gone. I was going to look like a total muppet in front of Miss Swallow.

I tried to dance, to follow what she was doing, but my legs felt like planks. My arms wouldn't bend properly, one of my hands felt incredibly heavy and the other one like it was full of helium. I must have looked like a malfunctioning Cyberman.

To her credit, Miss Swallow carried on dancing with me till the end of the song. I only caught her smirking at my shoes twice. After the dance, she leaned close to me and for a mad moment I thought she was going to kiss me, but of course she wasn't.

"Thanks for the dance," she shouted, her breath hot in my ear. "I have to go and find my friends."

"Okay," I bellowed into her ear, causing her to wince.

She was so close, I wanted to place my hand on her back, just to touch her. Just to have the pretense of intimacy, just to have a feel of that gorgeous yarn.

"Be good," she mouthed as she disappeared off into the crowd.

"Wait!" I called. I couldn't leave it there. I had to try, at least.

She turned and gave me that curious smile again.

"I heard that you'd broken up with Joe, is that true?" I asked.

She nodded. She didn't look angry that I'd brought it up. Or even that upset.

"Was it the vest?" I asked.

She looked at me for a long time as the new song thumped and blared and shining dancers swept around us.

Then Miss Swallow laughed and shook her head.

"No, Ben, it had nothing to do with the vest."

I grinned. "Phew."

She leaned in again and kissed me on the cheek. "You're very sweet, Ben Fletcher," she said. But before I could respond, she was gone, off into the crowd, lost from sight.

And that was that. My opportunity gone. Let down by my malcoordination and weak, knitting-based humor. Oh well. At least I tried, I thought. I drifted to the side and stood, lost in thought, until the song was finished.

After that I went off to find the others, which wasn't difficult. The next song was some hard, thumping dance track and Gex, Freddie and Joz were doing their Gangnam routine in a circle of onlookers. I shrugged and joined in. I'm good at Gangnam Style. Who isn't?

The time flew by after that. Gex got us some beers. I'm not usually that keen on alcohol, but it was cold and refreshing and I drank it down with the others. I remember laughing a lot and dancing till sweat streamed down my face. It was great, like knitting in a way, at least in the sense that I could forget about my worries for a while and just jump up and down with my idiot friends.

When midnight came, we all linked arms and put our heads together, counting down the seconds. Then we all grabbed as many girls as we could for a kiss and a cuddle and it was all brilliant and friendly. I was so happy, even when they put Katy Perry on.

And then disaster struck. As it always does when things are going well for me.

I was jumping up and down to Katy Perry, beer sloshing onto my jeans, when Joz tapped me on the shoulder.

"Isn't that Megan Hooters?" he yelled into my ear.

I looked over to where he was pointing. Megan was here?

Megan was indeed there, by the cigarette machine. She wore a very short skirt and a spangly top and I think she had acquired a fringe since the last time I'd seen her. It was hard to tell, though, as her face was obscured by the head of some guy she was snogging.

I stopped jumping. I dropped my cup.

"Is he eating her?" Joz asked.

It certainly looked that way.

"Who is he?" I asked, as someone crashed into me from behind. Suddenly I wasn't enjoying myself so much. We made our way over to the edge of the dance floor, to get a better look at the snogging couple.

"I know him," Freddie said. "Played soccer with him. He's at Petersfield Comp and his name's Sean, I think."

"Sean? Who's named Sean?" I spat, disgusted.

"Sean Bean?" Joz suggested.

"Sean the Sheep?" Freddie said.

"Shaun of the Dead?" Gex added, after a moment's thought.

"Loads of people—" Joz started.

"You're not helping, guys," I said.

"Never mind, Bellend," Gex said, slapping me on the shoulder. "I'll get you another drink."

But we didn't get that drink. Suddenly the bouncer was there and grabbed Gex without warning. The crowd scattered, forming a circle immediately. I spotted the floor manager standing nearby, looking furious.

Joz reacted quickly. He sprang over and kicked the hulking bouncer sharply in the shin. Shrek howled and let go of Gex.

"Time to go, lads," Joz hissed.

At this point, the manager strode past me and made a lunge for Freddie. Almost without thinking, I stuck a foot out and he went down in a heap and we scarpered, ducking through the crowds and busting out the front doors into the cool of the New Year.

When we realized no one was coming after us, we sat on the hood of Gex's car, in the far corner of the parking lot. He had a few Cokes in the trunk and we drank those.

I sat and tried to be philosophical about Megan. It's not as if we were actually going out. That boat had sunk the minute she'd found out about the knitting. Still hurt, though.

Movement caught my eye and I looked up to see Miss Swallow walking unsteadily to her car. Without thinking, I sprinted over to catch up with her. Surely she wouldn't drink and drive?

"Miss Swallow, are you okay?" I called as I approached.

She turned in surprise and I stopped suddenly, shocked.

Mascara had run down her face, over those delicate cheek-bones. Her hair was disheveled. She looked tiny and fragile.

"I'm fine, Ben," she said. "I'm fine."

"Are you okay to drive?"

She peered at me quizzically, then she laughed briefly.

"I'm not drunk," she said. "If that's what you're thinking."

"Okay," I said. I shivered as a cool gust of wind swept across the car park, carrying chip bags and plastic cups. An unextinguished cigarette skittered along the asphalt behind her, casting sparks.

"I've been drinking Diet Coke all night," she added. "Which was bloody noble of me, considering. Anyway. Do you want a lift back into town?"

"Yes, okay," I said, a bit thrilled that she had said a swear word in front of me. I was honored.

So I got into Miss Swallow's car and we drove off together, passing Gex, Freddie and Joz, who turned to watch us go, openmouthed.

I couldn't resist winking at them.

JANUARY 4TH

Nothing happened between me and Miss Swallow. Of course. She was very upset. Turns out I'd been wrong to think she wasn't that cut up about her split with Joe. She'd been putting on a brave face.

"I really loved him," she said as we drove slowly back into town. The streets were dead; everyone still at their parties, or tucked up in bed.

"What happened?" I asked.

She shrugged. "He's a soccer player. They're not known for being faithful."

He only plays for Hampton in the UHU Glue Conference League (South), I thought. He's not David Beckham.

"He made a mistake," I said. "If you're this upset maybe you should give him a second chance?"

"I don't really think he's that bothered, to be honest," she said. "He didn't pay much attention to me when we were together."

I directed Miss Swallow to my house and she pulled up outside.

"Wanna come in and see my ziggurat?" I asked jokingly. Though then got slightly worried she might say yes. I don't have much of a ziggurat to show her.

She laughed. "Tempting, but no."

"Sorry to unload on you," she said as I got out. "Totally unprofessional."

"That's okay," I replied. "I won't tell the principal if you don't tell my probation officer about me being in a nightclub."

"Deal," she said, then winked at me and drove off.

JANUARY 7TH

First day back at Mrs. Frensham's after the Christmas break. It was too wet to paint or sand. So she came out with a big pot of tea, some cookies and her box of knitting.

"Look what I got," she said, her wrinkled old face shining. She opened the box to show me some fat balls of merino wool in pastels.

"Amazing," I murmured, dropping to my knees like a pirate inspecting a treasure chest. It was good-quality wool.

"Four-ply?" I asked. She nodded.

"Scarf? Sweater?"

"Ski mask, I think," she said. "I remember how to do them."

"When are you going to start?" I asked.

"No time like the present."

The shed renovation abandoned, Mrs. F and I sat around and knitted and drank tea and ate cookies and listened to the rain drumming on the roof. At first I wished I'd brought Patt3rn so I could work on that, but then I realized that it wasn't the right time. Mrs. Frensham liked to chat while she knitted and Patt3rn required concentration.

I decided to start on a new vest, borrowing both needles and wool from Mrs. Frensham. She talked about her job, her niece and her other, estranged family. She asked me about school, and girls and my parents. She seemed fascinated by the fact that Mum is a magician.

There's an old cupboard in the shed, uncovered now I've cleared it all. When it was time for me to go, she suggested we store the knitting there and have another session the next time it was raining. I remembered the magazines and we put those in there too, except for one that she wanted to take into the house with her.

We parted very amicably. I'm starting to think that maybe knitting has healing powers greater than I ever imagined.

JANUARY 12TH

Went to see Hampton play today with Dad, Freddie and Freddie's dad. It was freezing, but I didn't mind for once. Not because I have suddenly developed a liking for the sport, but because I was curious to see how Joe was and whether there would be a new blonde cheering him on from the sidelines.

There wasn't, as it happens, though a few of the locals in the crowd were concerned about Miss Swallow's absence, if you count "Where's the posh bird, then?" as concern. But Joe looked tired to me. He played back, not coming up the field as he usually does. Even a soccer idiot like me could see Joe wasn't at his best.

"What's wrong with him?" Dad said.

"Broke up with Jessica, right?" Freddie's dad replied.

"That was weeks ago," Dad said.

"Move on, Joe!" Freddie's dad yelled as Joe jogged past, head down.

Joe clearly heard this and I watched him as he ran back to his spot. He stopped and put his face into his hands, almost as if he were crying.

After the game (Hampton 1, Godalming 4) I asked Dad to wait while I ran down to the sidelines where I could see Joe signing autographs. The line of small boys clutching bits of paper was noticeably shorter than it usually was, and I joined the end. I wasn't really sure why I was doing this. I just felt I needed to see him. To see how he'd been affected by the breakup.

When it was my turn, Joe looked at me and held out his hand. He looked terrible. Gray-faced, red-eyed, gaunt. I looked at his hand for a moment, wondering if he wanted me to shake it, before I guessed just in time. I jammed a hand into my coat pocket and found a pen. I was relieved to find a notebook in the other pocket. I pulled it out and presented it to him for his signature.

He grabbed the pen and notebook, then stopped, staring at it in surprise. It was then that I realized it wasn't a notebook at all, but a pattern for a winter skirt I was planning on knitting for Mum's birthday.

Joe Boyle looked up at me, as if registering me for the first time.

"You're that kid," he said. "The knitting kid."

My heart sank. Joe Boyle, local hero, first among alpha males, had recognized me as "the knitting kid."

"Er, yeah," I said, looking around to check no one else had heard.

"You're mates with Jess, yeah?"

"Well," I mumbled, "I wouldn't say mates. She's my teacher."

"She talks about you all the time, though," he said, a bit miserably.

Uh-oh, I thought. Was he actually jealous of me? Did he somehow blame me for the breakup? Maybe he thought that vest was a curse?

"Come on, Ben," Dad yelled. I looked over to see them headed off toward the parking lot.

Joe leaned in to me.

"Do you have time to chat?" he asked.

I looked back at Dad and the others, shrugged and nodded.

"I'll just let my dad know," I told him.

"Let me grab a shower, okay?" he said. "Meet me back here in fifteen minutes and I'll drive you home."

When I told Dad Joe was driving me back he looked surprised, but then nodded at me. I hung around outside the small clubhouse in the cold, wondering what this was all about.

"Cheers for waiting," Joe said as he appeared twenty minutes later. The other players drifted past, ignoring us as we got into Joe's flash Beemer. It was only when I got inside that I realized the car had seen better days. The gear stick was slightly worn and some of the trim looked a little shabby.

"The thing is—" Joe said as we drove off. "What's your name?"

"Ben."

"The thing is, Ben," he went on, "I've made a terrible mistake."

"Okay," I said.

"I suppose you heard that Jess and I broke up?"

"Yes, I heard," I said.

"Did you hear why?"

"Um . . ."

"Yeah, you did. And it's true. I played away. I cheated on her. I'm scum. I know it."

"You made a mistake . . ." I said limply, echoing my words in Miss Swallow's car, on a similar journey I'd made with her two weeks before.

It seems like he doesn't care, she'd said.

"I love Jess," he said. "I love her so much. My life feels empty without her." We'd stopped at a red light and he turned to me, a desperate look in his eye.

"When I got injured, and Pompey didn't renew my contract, I thought my life was over," he said. "Two years of rehab, and I end up here. After the Premier League, this shit hole . . . no offense," he said.

"None taken," I replied as we pulled off again and headed onto Jermaine Street.

"But then I met her, and she turned it all around," he went on. "I realized that I didn't need all the fame and the money and the new cars. I've got enough to live on, I have a nice house and can play soccer again. I have Jess. I only figured it out recently." He paused for a moment, then said, "But I'm happy. I was happy."

"You need to tell her this," I said.

"No, it's over," he said. "She won't take me back. My mate Johnny says he saw her down at Wicked straight after we split up, dancing with some kid. I can't blame her. What would she want with an old wreck like me after what I've done?"

I directed Joe to my house.

"So why are you telling me?" I asked as he stopped and turned off the engine.

He shrugged but said nothing.

"Do you want me to talk to her?"

He said nothing, his head low over the steering wheel.

"Joe?" I said, peering to see his face. It was then I realized he was crying.

"Sorry," he said after a while.

I sat for a moment, shocked and uncertain what to do. A part of me thought he deserved to suffer for a while. Throwing away a goddess like Miss Swallow. But here he was, reaching out to me, man to man. It was hard not to feel sorry for him.

I sighed, and thought for a minute.

"Okay, Joe," I said after a bit. "Leave this with me."

He sniffed and looked up at me. "What are you going to do?" he asked.

"You don't need to know the details," I said. "But I'm going to sort this out for you, okay?"

He stared at me for a while, then nodded. I held out a hand and he took it. Firmly we shook hands.

"Oh, one more thing," I said. "The knitting thing. It's a bit of a secret for me. You know, some of the lads wouldn't understand. . . ." I left it hanging there.

He nodded seriously. "I get it," he said. "Not a word. It's our little secret, yeah?"

"Thanks," I said. Our little secret, along with Mum, the Hooper family, Jasmine Cook, Mrs. Frensham, Miss Swallow and half the people at Hampton Community College.

I am obviously delusional if I imagine I'm going to be able to keep this from the rest of the world.

It was only later, after I'd got out of the car and watched him drive off, that I wondered if Joe chose me to open up to not so much because I knew Miss Swallow, but because he knew I was a knitter. Like he saw me as the one man he could talk to about personal, sensitive matters, because I was obviously a bit of a drip who was in touch with his feminine side. The thought was irritating, yet at the same time understandable.

JANUARY 14TH

As it hasn't rained for a few days, I've been sanding down Mrs. Frensham's shed, ready to start painting. It's not unsatisfying work, but I find myself thinking and worrying a lot while I'm scrubbing. I keep thinking about Megan and Sean, and I'm worried I'm falling behind in maths. And I'm worried about Patt3rn and even more worried about what Dad will say when he finds out I've been lying to him, and so many other things that I don't even want to list them. Perhaps worst of all was when I pulled out the vest from the knitting cupboard and realized it had chocolate cookie crumbs woven all the way through it. I hadn't noticed last time, it had been so gloomy. I spent ten minutes picking them all out, and now the stitches look a bit fluffy. I'm thinking about scrapping the whole thing.

But after half an hour of this Mrs. Frensham came to my rescue. She came out with a tray. On it were two mugs of hot chocolate, a plate of custard creams and a tangled pile of yellow yarn with needles poking out. She dumped the lot down on the table inside the shed and beckoned me in.

"I need some help," she said. "Can you sort this out for me?"

I inspected it. She'd started on what looked like a scarf, but it had so many dropped stitches and misshaped purls that it was hard to distinguish it from the tangled ball of wool she was using.

"You'll need to sit down for this," I told her importantly. I took the other seat and began to untangle the yarn.

"Hold out your hands," I said. "This might take a while." I began winding the de-tangled wool onto her hands.

"Well, go on, then," Mrs. Frensham said after a while. "What are you so miserable about?"

I looked up. "Is it that obvious?"

She nodded.

So I began to tell her about everything. About Lloyd Manning, and Megan and Sean, and how I wanted to get away from my friends, but felt guilty about it, and not telling

Dad about knitting, and about the trouble with Patt3rn, and Joe breaking down and everything. She was a good listener; she grunted occasionally, but didn't jump in, she waited till I'd finished. I took the neat loops of yarn off her hands, tied it up properly and took a custard cream from the plate.

"So," I said, smiling expectantly. "Any advice?"

"About what?" she asked.

"About my troubles."

"Which one?"

"Any of them," I said.

She shook her head.

"I'm sure you'll sort it all out," she said. "You're a smart lad."

And with that she left, taking her knitting with her. I couldn't help feeling slightly shortchanged. Mrs. F was old, and wise in the ways of the world. She was supposed to guide me on the uncertain path through the fetid swamps of adolescence. I hadn't expected her to be quite so useless.

After I got home I realized I did feel a bit less worried. Maybe just having someone listen is all you need.

Along with a couple of Golden Oreos.

JANUARY 17TH

I got the results of the mocks back and found I'd dropped a few marks.

I've got to work harder on my revision, but it's hard because I am knitting like a demon every free moment I have. Also, I'm starting to get a bit obsessional again. I used to have this thing where both ends of the belt of the dressing gown on the back of my door had to dangle at the same height. I couldn't sleep for worrying if one hung lower than the other. I'm not saying it's OCD, but it must be on the spectrum.

JANUARY 18TH

Last night at knitting class Mrs. Hooper made an announcement.

"I'm pleased to tell you that the date and venue of the All-UK Knitting Championship have been confirmed. It will be held at the Knit Fair, at Olympia, on the seventeenth of February. As you all know, Ben will be representing Hampshire, in the junior category."

There was a small round of applause and I felt myself blushing.

"Well done, Ben," Mrs. Simpson said.

"Nice one, Ben," Amelia called.

Natasha high-fived me. I just felt more worried than ever.

After class, Mrs. Hooper handed me an application form in a manila envelope. It was surprisingly heavy and when I opened it a massive heap of documentation fell out. There was a sheet asking for any known medical conditions. Bedwetting, angina, senile dementia. There was a media waiver form, a PR questionnaire asking about hobbies (other than knitting), favorite films and foods. There were information sheets about how to get to the venue, how to get home again, where to eat, local hotels, etc. Then there was the application form itself, which ran to twelve pages. I glanced through it and noticed that it asked for confirmation that I had my basic proficiency certificate, which reminded me I haven't submitted my pattern.

"Will you be going?" I asked Mrs. Hooper.

"Oh yes," she said. "I always go to the Knit Fair anyway, but even if I didn't, I wouldn't miss your event for the world."

I took the lot home to look at properly tonight. Dad's out at pickup soccer thankfully so Mum and I looked at it together. The first thing Mum noticed was the date.

"Oh," she said. "I might not be able to go."

"What?" I replied. "Why not?"

"Edinburgh," she said.

I sat back in my chair and sighed. The Edinburgh Magic Festival. Of course, it always ran for a week in mid-February.

"I'm launching my new show," she explained. "With the floating coffin."

The floating coffin trick is actually pretty good. Mum demonstrated it for me in the garage, but she used a shoe box because there wasn't room for an actual coffin. She also used one of Molly's Bratz dolls instead of a real live person, which was just as well, as a real person would have been burned quite horribly when the shoe box got stuck against a light bulb and caught fire.

"Can't you leave a day early?" I asked.

"The last day is *Britain's Got Magic*," she explained. "I have to do a short slot there, judging."

She could tell I was disappointed though.

"Though it says here your actual event doesn't start until five thirty p.m.," she said. "My slot is at lunchtime. If I race down I might be able to get there in time to see the end."

"That'd be great," I said, smiling. I didn't really expect

she would make it but it would be nice if she tried. "I suppose I can go up with Mrs. Hooper."

She paused for a moment before speaking. "Or you could ask your father?"

I winced. "I'll think about it," I said.

"He'd be proud of you," she said.

"Hmm."

"Once he got over the shock. He's not a Neanderthal, you know."

"I know. It's just that I've left it so long now, I'm not sure how to tell him."

She nodded. "Yes. I know what you mean. He'll be cross with me too, for keeping the secret."

Oh, good. On top of everything else I will be the source of my parents' acrimonious and bitter divorce now too.

Or perhaps I am just a bit overanxious?

JANUARY 24TH

I told Mrs. Hooper that Mum wasn't going to be able to make it to the final. She looked concerned.

"And your father . . . ?"

"I haven't exactly told him about the knitting thing yet," I admitted.

Mrs. Hooper shook her head. "Ben! You really need to tell him."

"I know, I know," I said. "It's just not that simple really. . . ." I trailed off.

She regarded me for a moment.

"You're very welcome to drive up with us, you know," she said. "If you don't mind sitting next to Megan."

"Megan's coming?"

"Of course, she'll be there to cheer you on."

Well, that's nice at least. Maybe we could be friends after all. Maybe I can get away without telling Dad. I can say I'm off on a school trip to a museum or something. He never checks up on things like that. I do feel a bit guilty about the idea though. Lying to my father and going off with another family. I don't know. I'll have to think about this.

JANUARY 25TH

Dear Ben,

I hope you don't mind but I forwarded your lovely letter of support to the Home Office as an example of a successful probation. I've had a response back and they're very impressed by your case. It seems there are still some people at the Home Office who are determined to try to fight the cuts to the probation service. With your permission we'd like to make your case a highlight to go in the year-end report. This kind of good-news story is incredibly important to sway the mind of the ministers responsible. They like real stories about real people being helped by their policies.

So firstly, is it okay if I use the details of your case in this way? It will be for internal viewing only, not released to the papers or anything, so no question of confidences being breached.

If you're happy with it, we might arrange for a Home

Office representative and a photographer to visit you and get your story? What do you think about that idea?

I look forward to hearing from you.

Best wishes,

Claudia Gunter

West Meon Probation Services

Gee, thanks, Ms. Gunter. As if I don't have enough pressure on me these days. Now the very existence of West Meon Probation Services, not to mention the career of Claudia Gunter, rests on my unmanly shoulders.

JANUARY 30TH

Mum and Dad are shouting at each other downstairs and I can't concentrate. This is all my fault.

JANUARY 31ST

Dad's gone. He's taken the camper and broken for the Mexican border. Or Southsea, possibly.

"He'll be back, Ben," Mum said confidently this morning, but I could tell she was upset. This isn't the first time Dad has done a runner when he can't handle things. He's got form, according to my mother. She says it will all blow over, but it seems to me that my masculine dad is not being much of a man at the moment. Ironic much?

It's still nearly all my fault though.

This is how last night unraveled.

Mum and Dad went out as usual. They were going to Guildford for '80s School Disco. Mum has one of her old school uniforms she wears for such occasions. Personally I don't think it's an appropriate look for a woman in her forties, but Dad says she hasn't changed in twenty-five years, which makes me wonder what he saw in her in the first place. Can frizzy hair and torn tights really have been "The Look" back then?

Dad wears an untucked shirt and ties a stripy tie around his head. He looks like a giant version of the guy in that old rock-metal band AC/DC. I know he has all the albums. This must be his inspiration.

But what kind of school did my parents go to if that's their idea of a school uniform? Mum's skirt is almost obscenely short. It would definitely have got her suspended from Hampton Academy. And Dad would have been referred to a school for maladjusted children, surely?

Anyway, I'd pushed my sister off to bed quite early and had become heavily involved in Patt3rn. I'm trying out a few experimental stitches to see if I can pull off a kind of loopy effect on the sleeves. Very mathematical and complex. I lost track of time, to be honest.

It was 10:30 p.m. and I'd just completed an extensive section of one sleeve and was pulling it on over my top and admiring myself in my bedroom mirror when the door was flung open and Dad stood there, tie still around his head. It took him a second to register what was going on. It was like that scene in *Pulp Fiction* where John Travolta comes out of the bathroom to find Bruce Willis pointing a machine gun at him. We stood there like that, gauging the situation, waiting for the Pop Tart to go ping.

It was Dad who went ping.

"I knew you were up to something," he shouted. He began opening drawers, cupboards, then he looked under my bed and pulled out the Box of Shame.

He grabbed hold of a half-completed vest and a sheaf of patterns. He thrust one out at me.

"Classic Borgen!!" he yelled.

Mum appeared at the doorway, looking anguished.

Suddenly I snapped.

"So I knit!" I yelled. "So what?"

"So you lied to me!" he growled.

"I didn't think you'd understand . . ." I began.

"You saying I'm not understanding?!" he cried, incredulous. "I put up with you, don't I? Did I give you a hard time when you tried to kill that lollipop lady?"

"Oh yeah, throw that back in my face. . . ."

"You stole from Waitrose," he said, shaking his head in disbelief. "Waitrose!"

"David, calm down," Mum said.

"And you? You kept this a secret too," he said, rounding on her. "How long's this been going on?"

"Just since September," Mum said quietly.

"I just th—" Then Dad stopped and looked at me quizzically. "You're not really doing pottery, are you?"

I shook my head.

"You've been knitting," he said with a contemptuous tone. "All that stuff about you not being able to do my course, because of a conflict of interest. That was all lies too?"

I stared at Dad. "Yeah. Okay. I kind of lied. I did, in fact, lie."

Dad's expression was still thunderous.

"Dave . . ." Mum said.

"Enough," he said, holding up a hand to silence her.

"You can't stand to be around me, is that it?" he asked me. "You'd rather sit with a bunch of gossiping women than do anything with me?"

"No, Dad, that's not it," I replied, sighing. "It's not you."

"Then what?"

I took a deep breath and told him.

"I hate cars," I said. "I hate cars, and I don't like Jeremy Clarkson, and I think James May looks like a serial killer and I don't understand why Frank Lampard is still on the England squad."

He gasped, shocked.

"Take that back!" he hissed.

"He always boots it over the crossbar!" I cried. "Why does he do that?"

"He's aiming for the top corner!" Dad yelled back. "Where the keeper can't get it!"

"It's not working!" I yelled back.

"So you're a pansy?" Dad shot back, evidently stung by my attack on Frank Lampard. "A nancy boy? Don't like cars, don't understand Lampard. You like knitting, do you? What's next? Ballet? Flower arranging? Man-bags?"

"Dave!" Mum said, upset. "Stop it now!"

But then Molly woke up and started crying and Mum dragged Dad out of my room, giving me a sorry face, and Dad stomped downstairs and doors were slammed, peace talks broke down, and World War Mum and Dad broke out properly.

And when I woke up this morning, Dad was gone.

FEBRUARY 1ST

I stopped in to see Miss Swallow before knitting class last night. I pretended I needed more clay, but in truth I had more than enough. Most of it was sitting in the Box of Shame, going dry.

"How are you?" I asked.

She looked at me with a sideways smile. "I'll live," she said.

"I saw Joe last week," I said. "At the soccer game."

"Really?" she asked. "How . . . how did he seem?"

"He didn't score," I said.

"Makes a change," she sniffed.

"I spoke to him afterward," I said.

"You spoke to him?"

"He really misses you," I said.

"He's got a funny way of showing it," she said. "I thought he might at least make an effort, you know? Come around with flowers. Send me a letter?"

I shrugged. "He thinks there's no chance," I said. "He thinks you hate him."

"I do hate him," she said. "And I love him."

"He loves you too," I told her.

"Then he needs to show it," she said, and turned away.

Later on I told Mrs. Hooper that I'd like to take her up on her offer of a lift to London with them.

"Okay," she said. "You haven't spoken to your father, then?"

"Actually, I have," I said. "But he's . . . he's taking some time to come to terms with it."

"Oh," she said. Then, seeing my face, added, "Is everything okay?"

I nodded. Then shook my head.

"He didn't take it very well," I told her.

"At least the truth is out there now," she said.

"Yeah, that is a comfort," I said, unable to keep the sarcasm out of my voice.

I couldn't concentrate during the class. I didn't do any proper knitting. I asked Mrs. Hooper if I could work on Patt3rn and she agreed. But Patt3rn is not proceeding well. The loopy arm thing isn't working. I think it needs something else but I can't think what. Maybe I need to abandon it and move on to the Pattern Mk 4. Not sure what I'll call it yet but I need Pattern Mk 4 to be extremely good. I have a germ of an idea that Pattern Mk 4 could solve a number of my problems at one stroke.

FEBRUARY 2ND

Joz has given me another bit of *Fifty Shades of Graham*. Must be the comedy aspect, which I badly need right now, but I'm starting to enjoy it. Poor Daisy has had a rough time of it, but does Graham really offer her long-term happiness? After following him to New York, she caught him in a clinch with another woman and has decided she needs to confront him about it. Now read on. . . .

"I saw you with that girl last night," Daisy sobbed. She threw a vase at me and it smashed against the wall. I didn't even flinch.

"That was my sister," I said to her.

"So why did you have your tongue down her throat?" she screeched.

"What? Oh, you mean the other girl," I said. "Yes, but it was only because I thought you didn't love me. I was in shock, I was angry."

Why didn't she understand?

"You think I don't love you because I won't dress up as a milkmaid?"

"It's not just that," I sighed. "You never call me anymore. I feel like we're drifting apart."

She stared at me, eyes blazing, then without a word she tore off her clothes and leaped at me, wrestling me to the bed . . .

FEBRUARY 3RD

I hadn't forgotten about Joe and his problem. My idea to help him is taking shape, and it involves knitting.

As I mentioned, Patt3rn had been causing me sleepless nights and I think I've made a breakthrough. I sat up in my bed for an hour just now fiddling around with it, getting more and more frustrated, until the solution suddenly leaped out at me. I think the main problem was that I was trying to make it unisex, which ended up making it a bit middlesex, if you get my drift. It was then that it clicked.

Of course! There was absolutely no reason I should have to design something to be worn by men and women. Why not keep it simple? Just make something that might appeal only to women? And one woman in particular: my knitting muse, Miss Jessica Swallow.

I lay back on my bed and thought it through. I'd have to make it a little smaller, and not as long. Do you have to leave room for boobs? How big should the boob-room be? Is "boob-room" the correct technical term? My knitting muse. Jessica Swallow. I could close my eyes and visualize her body shape quite easily, I found. I remembered the loose-necked top she'd worn to the soccer game. I could visualize the loose-stitched top she'd worn at New Year's. There was a theme developing here. I could almost see Patt3rn on her then and there; why hadn't I thought of this before?

Was this all a bit creepy? Maybe a little. But all great artists have a muse. We creatives are allowed to be slightly sinister. The girls love it.

So the upshot is, I've abandoned Patt3rn, and the working title of the new design is now Patt.r.n.

Now I'm so excited about it that I can't sleep for another reason. I'm going to get down to Pullinger's early tomorrow to pick up some thicker needles and some untreated wool.

FEBRUARY 4TH

Dad's still not back. Mum got a brief text from him to let her know he was still alive, but he didn't say where he'd gone.

"Best to leave him alone for a while," she said. "Giving him a hard time won't do any good. He'll come back when he's ready."

"And then what?" I asked.

Toward the end of geography, just before the bell went for lunch, a note was delivered to our classroom. Mr. Grover read it, then looked up at me. My heart lurched. My first thought was something had happened to Dad.

"See me after class, please, Ben," Mr. Grover said. I nodded, my heart thumping.

I couldn't concentrate after that and was thankful when the bell went. I waited for everyone to move out. Megan shot me a curious look as she left and I winked to express a confidence I didn't feel.

"The principal wants to see you," Mr. Grover said. He didn't elaborate; he's not a man who says more than he needs to.

I made my way up to the office, trying to guess what this might be about. Halfway up the stairs I had to sit and take a few deep breaths. My nerves have been getting worse lately, I'm sure of it. The receptionist, Mrs. Lucie, smiled at me and told me to go straight in.

I knocked and Mrs. Tyler called me in. I quite like Mrs. Tyler. She always wears tops with complicated closures. Lots of buckles, loops and straps, that sort of thing, and I'm never convinced she's done them up properly. She sat behind her big wooden desk, smiling, which made me feel a little better. Then I noticed there was someone else in the room. A thin man in a suit. He looked like an accountant.

"Thanks for coming, Ben," Mrs. Tyler said. "This is Mr. Hollis from Virilia."

"Oh," I said as the man stood and stuck out a hand. I shook it, worrying that he'd find my palm a little clammy. "You're the people who put in the TV screens."

He smiled brightly at this. "That's right," he said. "We invest in people."

Mr. Hollis seemed a very neat sort of person. Everything about him spoke of quiet tidiness and organization. I liked him immediately.

"Virilia has done a lot more for us than just install screens," Mrs. Tyler said hastily. "Have a seat."

We all sat down and Mrs. Tyler started talking about the young entrepreneur award Virilia was sponsoring.

"We're very keen to find the next Lord Sugar," Mr. Hollis said.

I wasn't entirely sure he was looking in the right place, to be honest. I hate to be disloyal, but I don't think the student body at Hampton Academy is particularly enterprising. Apart from Holly Osman.

"Great," I said. "Good luck."

"This is why I've asked you to come and see me today," Mrs. Tyler went on. "It's come to our attention that you've recently established your own small business."

I froze. My expression must have betrayed my surprise as she continued.

"Miss Swallow showed me the vest you knitted for her young man. She says she has more orders for you."

"And there's your exciting eshop as well," Mr. Hollis added.

"How did you know about that?" I asked slowly.

"The World Wide Web is accessible to the wide world, lad," he pointed out, laughing. "I Googled you and that site came up immediately."

"That's great news," I said weakly. "Good old Google."

Mr. Hollis leaned across to me and lowered his voice as he spoke, as if imparting some secret wisdom. "Ecommerce is the future," he said. "The High Street is dead, I'm afraid, Ben. Soon all shopping will be done online. You're ahead of the game already."

I immediately thought of Pullinger's, stubbornly clinging to its apostrophe and capital *P*. How could you replicate the experience of yarn-browsing online? You can't feel fiber on your laptop, you can't twiddle a needle on an iPad. Nonetheless, I smiled and nodded, as you do when you meet someone so sure they know the future.

"Anyway, Ben," Mrs. Tyler said. "We hoped you might like to enter the Virilia Studentrepreneur Search."

"The what, sorry?" I asked.

"Student Entrepreneur," Mr. Hollis explained carefully. "Studentrepreneur for short."

"Oh, right, that's clever," I said, wishing I was somewhere else. I didn't like where this was headed.

"Great publicity for your enterprise," Mr. Hollis said, winking at me.

That was what I was worried about. Trying to sell vests to anonymous Americans on the internet was one thing. Displaying my knitting prowess to the entire school, not to mention my family, was something else.

Mrs. Tyler seemed to have identified my reluctance. "It would mean extra credit, Ben," she said. "And there's a cash prize."

I raised an eyebrow. I could frankly do with both of those things at the moment.

"And in my opinion, Ben," Mr. Hollis added, "you stand an excellent chance of winning."

"Oh, really?" I asked, flattered.

"There's not a great deal of competition."

"Oh. I see," I said, slightly deflated. "It's just this school then?"

"All Virilia schools," Mr. Hollis said.

"How many Virilia schools are there?"

"Three."

"The other two are in special measures," Mrs. Tyler

explained. Mr. Hollis looked glum at this. I wanted to help him, I really did. He seemed like an okay guy. And very neat.

"Can I think about it?" I asked.

"Think quickly," Mrs. Tyler said.

FEBRUARY 5TH

Dad made contact today. He and Mum had a brief conversation over the phone; I only heard Mum's side, of course.

"Where are you?"

-

"Really? Why did you go there?"

-

"You don't even like fish."

-

"Whatever. You know I'm away this weekend in Bristol?"

-

"No, they cannot go to my mother's. She's more gaga than ever. She thinks my name's Colin."

-

"Well, he could look after her, but he's supposed to be studying for AS levels this year. It's not fair on him."

-

"Oh, forget it. I'll sort everything out while you're off finding yourself."

-

She handed me the phone. "He wants to talk to you," she said.

I took the phone nervously and walked through into the kitchen.

"Hello?" I said.

"All right, Ben," he said. "Look, sorry about shouting at you."

"I'm sorry about lying," I said.

"I understand why you did," he said. "But let's not have any more secrets, okay?"

"Are you coming home soon?" I said.

"Soon," he said. "I'm in Cornwall, doing some fishing."

"Okay," I said. It must be nice to be able to run off like that, when things get a bit difficult. I wished I could do the same, but I didn't say that to him.

"Look," he said. "I've got us those tickets. Stamford Bridge. A week Sunday."

Typical Dad. Totally missing the point as usual. Still, he was trying, in his way.

"Great. I'll look forward to it," I lied.

It was only after I hung up that I remembered that that Sunday was the AUKKC final.

FEBRUARY 6TH

I got a text today from Joe:

Hi Ben. Just wondered if u'd tlkd to Jess yet?

I texted back:

All under control. Will see you after the game on Sat.

FEBRUARY 7TH

A wful day. Megan-related. I haven't seen her properly for ages, not since the brief encounter at Christmas, but I ran into her on the way home from school.

"Hi," I said.

"Hello," she said, and sniffed. "Haven't seen you around much."

"I've been busy." It was true. I'd had three orders off Etsy for my vests. I'd run out of yarn but was putting off a trip to Pullinger's to stock up because of the ongoing awkwardness with Natasha. Also, I'd reached a tricky bit with Patt.r.n and the ziggurat was taking up far more of my time than I'd anticipated. Because it was me doing it, and I can't just do anything in a simple, practical way, I'd decided to model it on that scene in *Apocalypto* when the captives are being sacrificed and thousands of screaming Mayans are dancing around down below. I had this idea of pouring red glaze over the top so it would look like it was all drenched in blood.

I should also mention that one of the bare-breasted female captives bears a striking resemblance to Miss Swallow. I'll have to squash it before showing it to her, or at least dress it in a modest tunic.

Anyway, with all that going on, I had to do my studying at school, so I was elbow deep in books in the common room over lunch and in the library for an hour after school most days. The only place I found I could get any studying done was where there wasn't anything knitting- or ziggurat-related.

"How's Natasha?" Megan said as we walked.

"Er, okay, I think." There was an awkward silence while I contemplated the subtext of her question.

"She's not my girlfriend," I added after a pause.

"Right," Megan mused. "But she likes you."

"See, I don't think she does," I said, though I had lately been wondering if maybe she did. "She's much too old for me."

"Ben," Megan said, stopping and turning to face me. "Believe me, she likes you."

Now, I don't really fancy Natasha, but it's nice to be liked. I was flattered by the thought. I was also embarrassed by it, and set off walking again so Megan wouldn't see my face go red.

"So you should go for it," Megan said, trotting after me. "You share common interests, after all."

I looked at her, slightly taken aback. "You mean knitting?"

"Yeah, isn't that nice?"

Now I'm sure she said this in a snarky, smirky kind of way, but she kept a straight face.

"Why are you being like this?" I asked. "I thought you were on my side."

"I am," she said, looking away. We'd nearly reached her house by this time.

"No, you're being sarcastic," I said. "Like it's a big joke."

She laughed. "Oh, don't be ridiculous."

"You think it's effeminate? Me knitting?"

"Ben," she said. "I don't want to argue about this. Enjoy your knitting, enjoy your older woman, I'll see you around, okay?"

And then she was gone.

Bloody women!

FEBRUARY 8TH

Something happened today that made me want to crawl under my duvet, whimpering, and not come out till Ricky Gervais becomes prime minister.

We were in assembly and I totally wasn't paying attention. Mrs. Tyler was waffling about the recession and green shoots of recovery and about leadership and entrepreneurial stuff, the usual things. I had my head full of Patt.r.n and was half a world away when I heard my name.

"Ben Fletcher will be representing Hampshire next Sunday in the junior division of the All-UK Knitting Championship at Olympia in London."

There was a collective intake of breath around the hall, and four hundred eyes turned to stare at me, agog.

What was she doing? Was this intended to flush me out of hiding? To make it more likely I'd agree to enter Mr. Hollis's competition? Would she stoop so low?

I tried to smile. All I wanted to do was stand and run, run for the exit, run for the hills, run under a bus. But I sat and soaked up the shame, the humiliation. I heard someone mutter something and someone else giggle. I heard whisperings of "knitting" clicking around the room like needles, or "Bellend" bobbing about like balls of yarn. I saw what was left of my reputation slide slowly, inexorably into the mud. I saw Lloyd Manning a few rows in front of me turn around and fix me with such a look of triumphant contempt it made me want to cry. I agreed with him. Right then, I was contemptuous of myself. He'd won. They'd all won. I was that loser. I was Bellend Ben.

"Ben is the only male knitter to have ever attended an

All-UK final," Mrs. Tyler continued, slicing another chunk off my masculinity. "I also understand that Ben has plans to turn his love of knitting into a business. Quite the entrepreneur. So let's all have a big round of applause for Ben to wish him luck in the final on the seventeenth."

The applause was huge, deafening and utterly, utterly sarcastic. There were cheers, wolf whistles, howls of encouragement. I was so red you could have been mistaken for thinking my skin was on inside out.

"Knitting?" Gex said later, shaking his head. We were under the oak on the far side of the soccer pitch, having taken refuge from the constant bombardment of knitting jokes and insults I'd been experiencing since assembly had finished.

"Yes, knitting," I sighed. "I had to take a course for my probation. It's a Waypoint."

"But . . . knitting?" Joz said.

"There wasn't much choice," I protested.

"Yeah, but . . . knitting?" Freddie added incredulously.

"Don't give me a hard time, guys," I said. "Sorry I didn't tell you, but I could really do with your support now."

"Knitting twat!" someone yelled at me from across the soccer field.

"Don't worry. We got your back," Gex said, patting me on the shoulder. Joz and Freddie murmured in agreement.

"Thanks," I said gratefully. We sat for a while, in silence. I took a deep breath. It was good to have friends around in my hour of need.

"Oh no," Freddie said after a while. "There's a hole in my sock. Ben, could you fix it with your knitting skills, please?"

"Very funny, Freddie," I replied. "But your darn holes, you don't knit them."

"Ben, I seem to have torn my underpants on a rusty

nail," Gex said after a pause. "Any chance you could knit the hole up for me?"

"Hilarious, Gex. But underpants are usually made of cotton, so a needle and thread would be more appropriate."

"Ben," Joz said a little later. "Could you please knit me a beanie with some writing on it? I want it to read 'Knitting Twat.' It's a gift for a friend."

I sighed and declined to respond to that one. I'm better than that.

"So can we come to this Crochet Smackdown?" Gex asked. "The principal said there was tickets available."

"I'm not sure it's really your thing," I replied hastily.

"Might be fun," Joz said. "Trip up to London and that."

"I don't know. . . ." I said, wondering how I could discourage them. I decided to change the subject.

"What am I going to do about my reputation?" I asked. "I'll never live this down."

"To be fair, mate, your reputation was pretty poor anyway," said Freddie unhelpfully.

"Nah. It'll be difficult, I reckon," Joz said. "What with all the constant needling."

I did a loud and long fake laugh in his face.

"You should be writing these down," I said. "They're comedy gold. How could Mrs. Tyler have done this to me?"

"Yep, she certainly stitched you up," Gex said. Priceless!

"Purl this, Bellend!" Lloyd Manning yelled at me across the mud. He was holding his crotch. I groaned.

"Seriously. Things will calm down eventually," Joz said. "Everyone will think it's hilarious for a few days and give you a hard time, then something else will come up and they'll move on to bullying the next loser."

"You really think so?" I asked, desperate for a crumb of comfort from my friend.

"Absolutely. These things always follow a pattern," he finished triumphantly. They all fell about, laughing.

"I can't do this anymore," I said, and walked off.

"Come on, Ben, we're only having a laugh," Gex called after me.

I spun, furious.

"You're always just having a laugh, Gex," I shouted. "You're supposed to be my friends. You're supposed to support me. But all you ever do is laugh at me, call me Bellend and get me into trouble. I've had enough."

I stormed off and hid away at the back of the library, staring at a chemistry textbook without taking anything in.

I've got nothing left but the competition now.

FEBRUARY 9TH

I've done it. I've snatched victory from the jaws of defeat. I got home last night, at the lowest ebb of my life. I shut myself away in my room with a bag of Doritos and stayed up till 3 a.m. finishing the Patt.r.n prototype. The first Hoopie. It looks amazing, and it is perfect for her. It's quite quick to knit as it happens, because the stitches are so big, and because the pattern is ingrained in my head.

I went to Hampton FC today. The first, and I anticipate last, time I ever go to a soccer match of my own volition. I caught the second half, one of around a dozen fans watching Hampton boot it around unconvincingly, like the semiprofessionals they are. Joe saw me in the crowds and waved a hand, earning me some curious glances from the other occupants of the grandstand. I'm no expert, of course, but I think Joe perked up after that and he scored Hampton's only goal in extra time. He came running over to the sidelines to meet me as soon as the final whistle blew. I handed him the parcel.

"What's this?" he asked.

"Valentine's Day present for Miss Swallow," I said, my teeth chattering in the arctic chill. "Leave it on her doorstep with a note telling her how much you love her. It can't hurt."

"What is it?" he asked, holding it as though it might be the Ark of the Covenant wrapped up in the pre-used brown paper I'd found in the recycling bin last night.

"It's something personal," I said enigmatically. "From the heart."

He grinned. "Thanks, Ben," he said.

"Good luck," I told him.

Hampton 1, Havant 3. This had better work. Joe seriously needs to get his spark back if Hampton are to avoid relegation.

Just read that back. When did I start caring about the fortunes of Hampton FC? I think I'm losing it.

FEBRUARY 10TH

I called Dad today to tell him I couldn't make it to the Chelsea game next week.

"Oh, that's a shame," he said, sounding gutted. "Has something come up?"

"It's the final of the All-UK Knitting Championship," I told him. "I'm representing Hampshire."

There was a long pause. "Right," he said.

"I'm sorry, Dad," I said.

"Okay," he said stiffly. "Maybe another time, eh?"

"Definitely," I lied.

When I'm really worried about something I get this weird fixation about pavement cracks. If I stand on a crack with my right foot, say, I have to stand on one with my left foot straight after. If there's not a crack nearby I have to hop on my right foot for a bit until I find one. Once it's "evened up" and I've stepped on a crack with both feet I can carry on. Unless one of the cracks is much bigger than the other, in which case I have to even it up again by finding a second, smaller crack to stand on with the "under-cracked" foot. Often, though, that second crack is just slightly too big, and I have to find a tiny crack with the first foot. And so on . . .

Anyway, I've got it at the moment. It takes me quite a long time to get anywhere doing this but I'm sure all the hopping must be good for my glutes and core stability, if not mental stability.

FEBRUARY 11TH

"They've organized a bloody minibus—" I stopped talking when half a cookie bounced off my head.

"What was that for?" I asked.

"Language," Mrs. Frensham snapped.

"Sorry. They've organized a minibus to take family and supporters up to London for the final. Mrs. Tyler said they have twelve tickets to give away to people who want to come up."

"That sounds wonderful," she said. "You must be excited."

"Over the moon," I said, monotone. I was excited when I thought I was going up with the girl I fancy and no one else. I'm not so enthusiastic now the whole school's coming and the girl I fancy is getting off with Sean.

Mrs. F looked sagely into my eyes.

"It'll be fine, lad," she said. "It'll work itself out in the end."

"You mean like a knotty ball of silk chenille?" I asked, nodding glumly.

"Er, yes. I suppose," she replied.

I've painted the inside of Mrs. Frensham's shed now but then it had started to rain and I couldn't do the outside. Mrs. F had brought out her knitting and we were going to get cracking once we'd finished the tea and cookies. I'd calmed down a bit since the Day from Hell. I don't know what I'd do without my weekly visits to Mrs. Frensham. I still enjoyed the Thursday-night knitting classes, but even those had their stresses now, what with the awkwardness with Natasha, the pressure over Patt.r.n and trying to avoid Miss Swallow. I don't want to talk to her after she shopped me; also she'll only ask me about the ziggurat, which is in a bad way after Molly went all conquistador on it last week and knocked it off my desk.

FEBRUARY 12TH

So today Psycho Manning finally caught up with me. I'd been quite careful to avoid him these last few days and had actually found Joz was right for the first time in his life in that the knitting twat comments had started to dry up.

People had mostly even stopped pointing at me or smirking as I passed them in the corridors. I think this might have had something to do with the fact that Otto Wilson was caught with Holly Osman in the sponsored toilet block receiving the thing that Freddie had told me cost fifteen pounds.

But just as I was starting to think I might have got off easy, Manning and his gang found me at the back of the library.

"Knitting tosser," Manning snarled, knocking my books off the desk. "Where are your mates?"

"They've abandoned him," Jermaine said. "Couldn't stand to be hanging out with a knitting pansy."

That was enough, I thought. I stood up and turned to Jermaine.

"What did you say?" I asked.

"I said, you're a knitting pansy."

"Gaylord," Manning added, in case there should be any doubt.

So I kicked him in the balls.

Jermaine leaped on me and wrestled me to the ground as Manning rolled around on the floor moaning in agony. The other one, I still don't know his name, held me down as Jermaine began pummeling me in the face. Then someone pulled him off and Carter the librarian was there and we all got sent to the principal's office.

I was mortified by what I'd done, but at the same time I felt quite pleased with myself. Not bad for someone suffering from a zinc overdose. Maybe I'm not quite the girly man some had me down as. Dad might even be impressed.

Mrs. Tyler saw us all separately. When I went in she asked me what had happened and I told her the whole story. She shook her head sadly.

"I believe you, Ben. I don't think you were responsible for what happened. But I will need to write an incident report, and I'm afraid this needs to be submitted to your probation officer."

I nodded, defeated. I'd expected this.

"But I will explain you were severely provoked and that your behavior has been otherwise excellent. That's as much as I can do for you."

"Thanks," I said.

"And Ben," she said as I stood. "Have you thought any more about the Studentrepreneur Award?"

I stopped and stared at her, my mouth open.

At least she had the decency to look guilty. "Please?" she said.

I never thought Mrs. Tyler would resort to blackmail. But she had me over a barrel, I knew. And anyway, now the secret was out a little more publicity wouldn't make any difference, and who knew, maybe I might make some money out of it. Then I could run off to Bermuda and change my name to Pedro.

"I'd be honored to represent the school," I sighed. "Please submit my name."

"Thank you, Ben," she said, clearly relieved. "I'll contact Mr. Hollis right away."

As I left her office, I walked past Lloyd Manning.

"Watch your step," he hissed as I walked past. "This isn't over."

You can say that again.

FEBRUARY 14TH

Got three Valentine's cards today. Three! One was from Mum. But who are the others from? Not Megan. Natasha? But I've hardly said a word to her since she kissed me at the regionals, as it were. I think she's probably embarrassed about it too. Who are the other women in my life? Ms. Gunter—unlikely. Miss Swallow? Not unless it was an act of pity. Some random girl from school? Unlikely, but possible.

Maybe all three are from Mum? Maybe she's trying to cheer me up?

It kind of has.

FEBRUARY 15TH

Dear Ben,

As we discussed recently we need to arrange a visit at your home or some other suitable location. This forms part of the official assessment of your probation. We have also been discussing the possibility of a civil servant from the Home Office visiting you, along with a photographer, to put together a favorable report on your success story.

It strikes me that we would be missing a golden opportunity for a great story if we didn't combine the two and cover your participation in the All-UK Knitting Championship finals in London. I hope it's okay with you, but I have purchased some tickets to the event and will be attending, along with Mrs. Barker—a junior undersecretary from the Home Office, as well as a staff photographer. We can have a brief meeting there to discuss your progress, which frankly is just a formality. Then the Home Office official will ask you a few easy questions which the camera operator will film. We will then film the results announcements in the hope that you win!

So we'll be there Sunday to cheer you on and hopefully get a great, feel-good story with accompanying pictures. This is precisely the sort of thing we need to get a sympathetic hearing from the minister. We need to make continuing funding of the probation service a real vote winner. I hope you don't feel this increases the pressure on you. I wouldn't ask if I didn't have complete confidence in you.

Could you please let me have your permission to proceed with this?

Thanks so much in advance.

Yours,

Claudia Gunter

West Meon Probation Services

"You say this now, Ms. Gunter," I muttered to myself. "But will you be so enthusiastic when you find out I kicked Lloyd Manning in the balls? That's not going to play well with the minister, is it?" I can't say no, though. I just have to hope Mrs. Tyler takes her time submitting the incident report, or that Ms. Gunter decides to bury it at the bottom of my file.

Fat chance.

FEBRUARY 16TH

I'm home alone this weekend. Molly's been sent off to our cousins in Southampton. Mum just left for Edinburgh. Dad's still in Cornwall. Our family couldn't be more separated at the moment. I helped Mum pack the car. The dove cage is the hardest thing to fit in and I'm worried I might have squashed the top hat a bit.

"Stop worrying," she said. "You'll be brilliant."

"So will you," I said.

"I'll try and be there," she said. "But I won't promise. I'm not happy with your father. He should be here."

"It's okay," I said. "I let him down."

"Hmm," said Mum. "It's a game of two halves, if you ask me."

"Very true." I gave her a grateful smile. She was on my side, she just couldn't bring herself to totally slag Dad off in front of me.

"Oh, Ben," she said. "Sometimes it seems you think you need to carry the world on your shoulders."

"I have a lot of things to think about," I replied. "It's not just Dad, it's the final, it's school, it's . . . a lot of things."

"Everyone worries, Ben," she said, looking me in the eye. "It's natural, but you try to worry about too many things at once. Just pick one thing to worry about and leave the rest for later."

"That's not how my mind works, Mum," I said. "I take a holistic approach to worrying."

"Then learn that there's another way," she said. "Concentrate on one thing at a time. Shut everything else out. That's the only way you can do something properly. And once you've done it properly, then you can stop worrying about that, and move on to something else."

She's right. And this is what happens when I'm knitting. I stop worrying about everything else; only the next stitch matters. And yet, even then I need to have that complete pattern at the back of my mind. I need to know there is a pattern.

FEBRUARY 17TH

8:27 a.m.

This is it. The big day. I feel sick to my stomach. Last night was horrible. The house felt so cold and empty. I watched *MasterChef* for a bit, just to have some company, and Mum called to see how I was getting on, which was nice of her. But I'm not good on my own when I'm this anxious. I went to bed early, thinking about how important it was that I got a good night's sleep, and the more I told myself that, the further from sleep I found myself.

My mind was literally buzzing with all the things I'm stressing about. So I got up and wrote them all down, hoping it would help. This is the list, in no particular order:

Will Dad ever come home and if he doesn't is it my fault for being effeminate?

Will Ms. Gunter find out about the incident report and be cross with me?

Will the Home Office lady find out about the incident report and throw me in jail?

Will Mr. Hollis, the man from Virilia, be so disappointed

with my lack of entrepreneurial skills that he'll stop funding the school?

Will Miss Swallow find out I've been lying to her about the ziggurat?

Will my friends turn up as threatened and wreak havoc on the Knit Fair?

Will Lloyd Manning catch up with me and cut off my testicles?

Will I fail all my AS exams through lack of study?

Will I ever get a girlfriend?

Writing them down didn't help at all, as it happens. The only thing that did help was knitting. I worked on a vest. Something easy and repetitive. Eventually I grew tired and got to sleep around 3:30 a.m. I dreamed that I was playing for Chelsea in a cup tie. I kept trying to explain that I wasn't any good but people would just laugh like I was joking. And on the pitch I couldn't move my legs. The ball came to me and I had a perfect opportunity to pass to Frank Lampard, who was in a great scoring position and begging for the ball.

My dad was in the crowd, screaming at me.

"Pass it! Pass it to Frank."

There was a defender coming my way to take the ball, and with horror I realized it was John Terry, who'd switched shirts and was playing for the opposition like the traitor he is, and I couldn't move my feet at all.

"I've got an open goal!" Frank Lampard screamed.

"Pass it to Frank!" Dad bellowed.

But it was no good. John Terry shot past, taking the ball with him and sneering at me. "You were right, you really can't play," he shouted.

It was bad enough not being able to pass to Lampard,

horrible to let down my dad, but having John Terry look down his nose at me? That was the worst.

I'll show him, I thought. I'll show him.

9:31 a.m.

I'm on the bus. Which is almost completely full. I can't believe it. I turned up first and introduced myself to the bus driver, Rob. He seems like a nice guy.

"You're the knitter, then?" he said, giving me the look everyone gives me when they find out I knit. I'm used to it.

"Yes," I said. "I'm the knitter."

"Well, good luck today, mate," he said genuinely.

"Thanks, Rob," I replied. "I appreciate it."

After a bit Joz turned up, shuffling along with his trainers unlaced. I was really pleased to see him.

"All right," he said.

"Thanks for coming."

He sniffed. "Ah, y'know. Nothing on TV."

Next to arrive was Mrs. Frensham. She glared at Joz, who hid behind me, then she winked at me and went to sit on the bus, where she got out her knitting and started clicking away without saying a word. Mrs. Simpson and Mrs. Grissome from the knitting class arrived after that, giddy with excitement, carrying huge bags of hard candy.

Then Natasha and Amelia arrived. Natasha gave me a kiss on the cheek. "Feel I haven't seen you for ages," she said. "Not properly."

"Yeah," I said awkwardly.

"Who's your friend?" Amelia said. Joz looked alarmed.

"This is Joz," I said. "He's an author."

We waited around after that, chatting about books, until it was nearly time to go. I was beginning to think this might be it, when who should turn up but Gex and Freddie. I was less pleased to see them than Joz but I thanked them for coming.

"S'all right, the school gave away free tickets, we got the last three," Gex said, looking at the ground. "Sorry about making jokes."

"Yeah, sorry," Freddie said.

"Oh yeah, sorry," Joz said from behind me. "I forgot."

They'd obviously talked this through and decided they were going to make a group apology. I was moved.

"Thanks," I said gruffly.

We all stood around for a while, inspecting one another's shoes, not saying anything.

We got on the bus then and we were about to leave when two more people came running up. Rob opened the door and Miss Swallow got on, looking flushed but beautiful. She was wearing the Hoopie. Joe clambered on behind her, ducking his head. He caught my eye and grinned at me. Miss Swallow stopped at my seat and leaned down. I could see Joz looking down her top, wide-eyed.

"Thank you," she whispered.

"No, thank you," Joz replied.

"You're welcome, Miss Swallow," I said, elbowing Joz in the ribs. Joe slapped me on the shoulder as they walked past to grab two seats at the back.

Maybe this wouldn't be so bad, after all.

11:44 a.m.
In a café in Olympia. Writing stuff down before it all kicks off.

The journey took forever. Getting to London was quick

but as soon as we got into the city everything slowed down to a crawl. Why is there so much traffic in London on a Sunday? Where is everyone going? I suppose some of them must be going to the Chelsea game. I wondered where Dad was. Was he even now trying to park the camper van somewhere on the King's Road? Surely not.

I felt a bit of a pang about Dad.

I've been trying to work out who took all the tickets. There's Joz, Gex and Freddie. Miss Swallow and Joe. Mrs. Tyler is coming, along with Mr. Hollis. Rob the bus driver has one, I have the ninth. The knit class crowd got their own tickets, I know. Gex said all twelve tickets that the school had were taken, so who else is there? This sort of detail worries me.

I'm also slightly concerned that Gex, Freddie and Joz immediately disappeared as soon as we arrived. I've got a feeling they're up to no good. They must have had an ulterior motive for coming along today, but what it is I couldn't say. Mrs. Frensham had leaned over and tapped me on the shoulder while we were on the bus.

"This lot," she'd said, tilting her head toward Gex, Freddie and Joz, still sitting beside me. "Are they going to cause trouble?"

"Probably," I said, earning myself a wounded look from Joz and a nod of confirmation from Gex.

"Don't worry," she said, glaring at each of them in turn. "I'll keep an eye on them."

Even Gex looked a little scared.

Anyway, the big news is that the *Knitwits!* podcast girls are here! I'm starstruck. I saw them interviewing someone at a stand earlier. Must try and work up the courage to go and introduce myself. Maybe they'll interview me!

12:16 p.m.

Just seen Megan. I'm writing this in a restaurant on the mezzanine level. Mrs. Hooper thought it would be nice to get out of the mayhem for a bit and have a quiet lunch. Just me, Megan and her. I went to meet Mrs. Hooper, who was going to introduce me to the event organizers and get my details registered or whatever. And Megan was just there, hanging around.

"I'm surprised to see you here," I said.

"Thought I'd come up and do a bit of shopping," she said coolly.

"Oh," I said.

"I'll be back later on to watch the final, though," she said. She was picking at a loose seam on the handle of her bag, not looking at me.

"Only if you have time, don't bust a gut," I said, which may have come over a touch sarcastic. Oh well.

Mrs. Hooper called me over at that point and I saw that Mrs. Tyler had turned up, along with neat Mr. Hollis, who shook my hand and told me he would be cheering me on from the stands. Mrs. Tyler looked nervous and pulled me aside as soon as she had a chance.

"Ben," she began. "Um, how do you rate your chances here today?"

I swallowed. What was she getting at?

"Er. I'm in with a chance, I suppose."

"Good, good," she said, glancing over to where Mr. Hollis was chatting with Mrs. Hooper. "It would be excellent if you won, of course. It would certainly be a huge benefit for the school, and for Mr. Hollis."

"How?" I asked, trying to ignore the threatening tone to her voice.

She sighed and gave me an intense look. "Look, Ben, I really shouldn't be discussing this with you, but Virilia is in a bit of trouble. There's talk of them being bought out; the share price is suffering."

"Okay," I said.

"They're considering selling the school," she said.

"Is that bad?"

"It could be very bad," she said. "We need a great deal of investment, and we need it right now. We can't afford to be waiting around for a new owner."

I waited for her to go on. She licked her lips nervously and dropped her voice.

"If you win this thing, you're virtually guaranteed to be nominated for the short list of the Young Entrepreneur Awards. If that happens, there's no way they will be able to sell the school. It would be a PR disaster for them. Mr. Hollis is very much on our side, but he needs your help."

"I see," I said as my stomach slowly filled with cement. "I'll do my best."

"Thanks, Ben," she said. "I know you will." And then she was off in the direction of the lecture theaters, collecting Mr. Hollis on the way.

No pressure, then. Thanks a bunch, Mrs. Tyler.

Mrs. Hooper introduced me to Julie, a potato-faced lady who was organizing the junior final. Behind her was a tiny, frightened-looking woman with enormous eyes who reminded me a bit of the bush babies in Madagascar.

Then there were forms to fill in and IDs to be checked and fingerprints to be taken and irises to be scanned. Honestly, what a palaver. As I was writing my name on one list, I had a quick look down the page and a name jumped out at me.

Jeanette Fairbanks (Surrey)

Miss Angular! Knitting for Surrey! Could she do that, after registering in Hampshire? The scheming little . . . But hey, I'd beaten her once. I could beat her again. No problem.

Better go, Mrs. Hooper and Megan keep clearing their throats.

1:57 p.m.—Café

Megan's gone shopping in nearby Kensington High Street. So, after lunch Mrs. Hooper and I went back down to have a wander around. The first thing we noticed was a huge kerfuffle around the Singer stand. I hurried over to check it out, only to find an outraged Gex being questioned by a suspicious security guard. Gex was wearing half a sweater. Strands of wool coiled everywhere and some harassed Singer employees were tidying up, shooting black looks at Gex.

"What's going on?" I asked Freddie, who was standing to one side, grinning with delight.

"They've got this amazing machine in there, it knits an entire sweater in fifteen minutes," Freddie said. "Gex decided he couldn't wait that long and tried to put the sweater on before the machine was finished. It got messy."

"For crying out loud! You'd better not get me thrown out," I said, hoping neat Mr. Hollis wasn't around to witness this. "It'll look bad for me. And for the school."

"Since when do you care about the school?" Freddie asked.

"Just try not to get arrested, okay?" I said, ignoring the question.

"Okay, Miss," he said in a high-pitched voice. "Sorry, Miss."

"Where's Joz, anyway?" I said, exasperated.

"Saw a girl, went after her."

"Fantastic," I muttered. "Let's hope he doesn't try to do anything illegal with her."

Gex managed to get away from the security guard and he and Freddie headed off to cause more chaos.

I turned around, wondering what to look at first. I saw potato-faced Julie talking with two girls wearing *Knitwits!* T-shirts. I sidled over, my heart pounding. This could be my chance, I thought.

"Excuse me," Julie said to the girls, noticing me standing there. "This is Ben Fletcher, one of the finalists of the junior category of the AUKKC."

"Wow!" Alana cried in her sexy Midwest accent. I recognized her voice immediately. "It's so great to have a guy who loves knitting. And so cute too."

I nearly collapsed then and there. Alana is actually quite pretty, in a big-boned, big-haired American way.

"I'msuchahugefan," I mumbled, shaking their hands.

"We're so overwhelmed by the reception we've had here," Alana gushed. "We knew we had listeners in Britain, but we never expected everyone to be so nice."

"And your teeth aren't nearly so bad as we expected," Marie added.

"Cheers," I told them.

"Ben is representing Hampshire," Julie said.

"Is that near Edinburgh?" Alana said.

"Near Basingstoke?" I suggested. Alana shrugged.

"Well, good luck today, Ben," Alana said. "Maybe we could get a quick interview with you?"

"Right now?"

"Sure, why not?"

Alana pulled out a microphone attached to her ereader. "I'd be lost without this," she said. Then she held the mic up to her mouth. "I'm here with Ben Fletcher, finalist in the junior category of the All-UK Knitting Championship. Hi, Ben. Good to have you with us."

"Thanks," I said. Then, realizing something else was needed, added, "I love your podcast."

"Thank you, your accent is so cute. So tell me, how long have you been knitting?"

"Oh, not very long at all," I replied. "Less than six months."

"Really? And you're already in the final of the All-UK Knitting Championship?"

"Junior category," I said. "And I don't expect to win, there's some really tough competition out there. I hear Marian Joyce is a bit of a demon, and Harriet Evans won the Welsh championship at fifteen."

"I'm sure you'll do great," Alana said. "Now, sorry to have to ask you this, but why do you think it is that so few men decide to involve themselves . . ."

But I'd lost track of her question. I'd seen something which made my blood run cold and my bile run dry. A dozen yards away, walking along through the crowds with his dumb gang, was Lloyd Manning.

Oh Jesus, I thought. Just when I thought my life couldn't be any more stressful, along comes Psycho Manning to show me just how wrong I could be. This explained who'd taken the other three tickets.

"Ben?" Alana was saying. "Why is it, do you think, that boys don't knit?" I looked at her, panicked. I wanted to run. Suddenly, the pressure was just too much. On top of everything, I couldn't deal with Manning and his gang.

My vision swam and I felt hot and cold at the same time. Please don't faint, I told myself, please don't faint.

I couldn't run. I'm not my father. I had an interview to finish. Out of the corner of my eye, I saw Manning point me out to his gang and they swaggered toward us, laughing.

I took a deep breath and turned back to Alana.

"I don't know why boys don't knit," I said loudly. "Perhaps they think it's effeminate. Perhaps they think that it's women's work, beneath them."

I was aware of Manning and his gang standing close now, listening to me.

"But to me knitting is many things. A creative outlet, a mental challenge. I can knit on my own, losing myself in the work, in the pattern. Or I can knit with friends, chatting and putting the world to rights. I don't think it makes me less of a man. It's no different from carpentry or being a painter or an architect or a chef. It's using your hands with skill and creativity. It just needs some better PR," I told her.

"Well said," Alana responded.

I looked up to see Manning take a step forward, a nasty smirk on his face. He wouldn't assault me here, while I was being interviewed for a knitcast, would he? But I never found out, because someone stepped in between him and me. Three people, in fact. Gex, Joz and Freddie, to be precise. I'd never been so glad to see them before. In fact I'm not sure I'd ever been glad to see them at all. The cavalry had arrived.

"So, Ben, what are you working on at the moment?" Alana was saying. I dragged my eyes away from the standoff and concentrated on the interview again.

"I've recently completed quite a complex sweater, inspired by the Ocean Spray design," I told her. "I have a small business selling garments on Etsy, mostly vests, so that keeps me quite busy, and I've developed a new style of loose hoodie, which I call the Hoopie."

We carried on for a bit. I talked more about my page on Etsy and the pictures of star striker Joe Boyle. She asked me for the address, which I think I got right. I was just about able to ignore the scuffling and raised voices offstage as the confrontation continued. Hold them off, lads, I thought. Just a few minutes more.

And then it was over. Alana thanked me for my time and promised they'd be watching the final later on. Then she was gone. I spun quickly, just in time to see Manning lunge at Gex and knock him flying into the Australian Wool Marketing Board stand.

"Watch it, mate!" someone yelled from inside.

Then it properly kicked off, with Jermaine punching Joz and Freddie leaping, screaming, onto the other one's back. I stepped forward to help, but Gex, now covered by a sheepskin, had just managed to extricate himself from the melee.

"Go," he told me. "You can't get involved. You've got to get to that fin—oof!"

The last word was cut off as Manning slammed into him and they went rolling across the aisle into the stand of the South-West Wool Dyers Association. I watched a large pot tumble lazily off a shelf, flip over and liberally douse both Gex and Manning in a bright green liquid. Joz was still on the ground, rubbing his jaw, and I saw Jermaine stepping toward me menacingly. He has this ridiculous bowlegged walk because his trousers hang so low and it makes him look like he's just got off a horse. Behind him, three fat security guards were rushing toward the scene.

Gex was right. I had to go. It was time to run after all.

3:43 p.m.—The Cauldron

Things have quieted down out there.

Gex texted me to tell me they'd got away from the security guards, but that both he and Manning had been covered in a green dye, which was making him cough. It also made them readily identifiable to security so he was keeping a low profile and assumed Manning would be as well. It worries me that Manning and his gang are still out there somewhere, but I'm safe here, for now.

I've taken refuge in the Cauldron and have had a good look at it for the first time. Just by the entrance is a huge fake plastic yarn ball and two giant needles. The arena is surrounded by partitions and beyond those, raised grandstands for the audience. The finalists sit in a ring in posh black leather seats like on *Mastermind*. There is a little table beside each one for the needles and yarns.

Mrs. Hooper explained there are two sections to the final. First we have to knit to a pattern; marks will be given for accuracy, speed and technique. Extra points if we manage to improve on the pattern, marks taken away for dropped stitches or other mistakes.

Round two is free knitting. We can knit anything we like. The temptation is to do something complex, something that will wow the judges. But that's a risky option, I think. Complex patterns can go very wrong very quickly. I might be better off sticking to something simple, but doing it well and quickly. My advantage is my speed. In an hour, I could complete a sock, or a small cushion cover. That would impress them. Having to keep just a simple pattern in my head will decrease the chances of me being distracted by Angular Jeanette, as well.

Hold on, someone's coming.

4:16 p.m.—Café

It was Megan.

"Hello," she said.

"Hello," I said.

"I just came to . . . wish you luck, for later."

"Thanks," I said.

There was a pause.

"Did you know your friend Gex is covered in camouflage paint?"

"It's dye," I said.

"He looks like he's in the military."

"He's here to protect me from Lloyd Manning," I told her, without shame.

She came and sat next to me. I could hear the hubbub of the fair outside and smell the sheep pen. Megan looked beautiful, I thought. She had a little makeup on and her hair was tied up in a sort of double-purl stitch.

"They're quite protective of you really, your friends."

I shrugged. "I suppose so."

"We're all fond of you, Ben," she said.

Fond. She's fond of me. Like my gran is fond of Quality Street toffees.

"Thanks," I said stiffly.

"You know what I like about you most?" she asked.

"My cabling technique?"

"No. It's that you don't know how great you are," she said, smiling shyly.

"Great in an effeminate way?" I suggested.

"I don't think you're effeminate!"

"So why did you run off after I won the heat? How come you've hardly spoken to me since you found out I like to knit?"

She stared at me, squinting in confusion.

"That had nothing to do with your knitting. I think it's amazing how talented you are."

"So why did . . . why did you go cold on me?"

"It was you who started kissing other girls." She sniffed.

"Natasha kissed me, I didn't want her to. And anyway, what about you and Sean?" I said quickly before I could stop myself.

She frowned sadly. "Sean was just there," she said. "And you didn't seem interested."

But I barely heard her.

"Is he your boyfriend?"

"Is Natasha your girlfriend?"

I was just about to say no, when Megan's mum turned up.

"It's all happening out there," she said. "The goats have escaped and there are security guards running all over the place."

Megan and I looked at each other, both thinking the same thing, I expect—that Lloyd Manning was responsible for releasing the goats. He was trying to sabotage the final, ruin everyone's day. The only thing that could save us now was Gex.

So basically we were doomed.

We had a quick look around the fair after that, occasionally being bowled over by a rampant goat or a sprinting security guard.

"I expect the security guards thought this might be quite an easy gig," I said.

"Just goes to show," Megan replied as we watched a sweating guard wrestling with an enormous billy goat, which was chewing on his walkie-talkie.

We inspected the rabbits, who were very sweet, and we looked with interest at a display of looms through history. I wanted to carry on my "talk" with Megan but there wasn't the chance.

As the time for the final approached I began to grow more nervous. I kept looking back toward the Cauldron, worrying about what the fixed pattern was to be.

We ran into Miss Swallow, who seemed to be having a lovely time, and Joe, who looked as if he'd rather be anywhere but here. I didn't see Gex, or Joz, Freddie or Lloyd either, though I thought I spotted Jermaine at one point, skulking behind a potted plant between two stands.

We had a lemon Fanta each at the café where I'm writing this, scribbling quickly. I'll go back over it tomorrow and write it all out properly. I can't really manage much to eat. I've had half a muffin and a few sips of my drink. My tummy is churning. So much depends on this.

Mrs. Hooper's just told me to put away the notebook. It's time.

FEBRUARY 23RD

I feel bad that it's taken me so long to write this next entry. It's been a strange week. This is the first time I've really felt able to write about what happened. I felt I needed to do it justice so I've been going over everything in my mind. Writing the story, rereading my notes. Creating the 3D pattern in my head.

Just before we left the café to go back to the Cauldron, I got a text from Ms. Gunter:

We're here. Sorry we're late. Do you have time for a quick interview?

I'd totally forgotten about Ms. Gunter, what with everything else going on.

Mrs. Hooper said there was time, as long as I was quick, and soon Ms. Gunter turned up at the table with a cameraman and the lady from the Home Office.

My head was whirling with so many things as I was talking to the Home Office lady that I have no idea what I said. I was stressing about the final, about Lloyd Manning, about the incident report, about Megan, about whether Mum was going to make it. I tried to talk about how helpful I'd found the probation period, about meeting Mrs. Frensham and Giving Something Back. I told her that I'd started my own business and had found a potential career in knitting.

She asked me if I'd been tempted to go back to a life in crime and I shook my head firmly, which Ms. Gunter seemed to appreciate.

After it was over they all thanked me, and Ms. Gunter and Mrs. Hooper gave me warm smiles, which I took as a good sign.

Then it was down to the Cauldron for the final. I checked my phone again on the way. A text from Mum!

Have left the venue. On the road now.

She'd sent that at 4:12 p.m. There was no way she was going to get here in time. But at least she'd be back tonight. There was no text from Dad. But there was one from Gex.

Manning's gone to ground. I've diverted security by releasing animals. Joz with girl but has said will be in grandstand keeping look out. Freddie AWOL, but don't worry, we've got your back.

Was I reassured? Hmm, on the one hand it was good to know they were around, keeping an eye out for Manning and his gang, but I was a bit concerned to hear that it was Gex who'd released the goats. I just needed everything quiet for two hours. After that, they could pull the place apart for all I cared.

I met up with the other contestants in a side area, blocked off by partitions. There were twenty-two of us. I spotted Jeanette Fairbanks, looking cool as a cucumber. I nodded briefly to her and she totally ignored me.

Julie stood up on a chair to address us. I was too nervous to really hear much of what she said, but the gist was that we were to go in one by one, our names being read out as we entered the Cauldron. As if I wasn't petrified enough without having to endure that. I saw Bush Baby peeping out from behind a partition, looking even more terrified than I felt.

The pattern we had to follow for the first section wouldn't be revealed until we were all seated. We'd have five minutes to choose needles and yarn and to plan our approach. We had one hour to work on the fixed pattern. Then there'd be a ten-minute break before we'd go back in for the freestyle section. I was still uncertain what I was going to do in the freestyle. To a certain extent it depended how I went with the pattern. If I was feeling confident, I might do something more complex. If the first section had been a disaster, I would probably just stick with a sock. Or scarf. That's if I hadn't slit my wrists in the bathroom during the break.

I don't remember much about the next few minutes. Just noise, the smell of the goats, the bright lights overhead hurting my eyes, the sweat rolling down my back. I was not confident.

Then I heard my name being called and Mrs. Hooper said, "You're on," and pushed me gently toward the entrance to the Cauldron. I walked in to a blaze of light and a smattering of applause. Camera flashes were going off, presumably from the Home Office photographer, and I heard a few whoops of support from my posse. I stumbled toward an empty seat, my mind a muddle, my vision blurred.

I sat and scanned the stands. At first I couldn't see anyone I knew. I blinked to clear my vision and saw Ms. Gunter, with the Home Office lady, who was gazing at me intently. The cameraman was at the back filming everything. I carried on looking and saw Megan, waving at me. I waved back. Then I saw Miss Swallow, looking ravishing; Joe was next to her playing on his phone. She waved, elbowing Joe to make sure he did the same. He gave me the thumbs-up and went back to his phone. Then I saw Joz, and next to him was Amelia and next to her Natasha and there was Mrs. Frensham, right at the front, arms folded, looking grumpy. Even Rob the bus driver had turned up to watch, and had sat himself next to Mrs. Frensham.

I suddenly felt much better. Everyone was here. I turned to my neighbor to wish her luck, and it was only then that I realized it was Jeanette Fairbanks. The Lance Armstrong of the knitting world. She eyed me coldly, perhaps wondering why I'd chosen to sit next to her. My heart skipped a beat and I considered moving seats, but it was too late. The last of the contestants had taken her seat now and the circle was complete. Oh well, what did it matter? She wouldn't try anything here, I told myself, not with so many people watching.

"You may turn over your patterns now," Julie called out. Taking a deep breath, I flipped my paper over and my heart sank.

It was a tea cozy. With stranded colorwork—a green tea leaf. The worst possible combination. My bête noire. I sat staring straight ahead, feeling the color drain from my face. A tea cozy? A bloody tea cozy?

Everyone else had begun rummaging through their boxes of yarn, inspecting needles, flipping them like drummers flip sticks. I sat there, slowly, gently panicking.

But then I looked up into the stands and saw Mrs. Hooper working her way along the aisle toward Megan. Farther back, at the top of the stand, in the dark, I saw a merino sheep sitting texting. It coughed. That had to be Gex. Then I saw Mrs. Frensham give me the thumbs-up. I couldn't let them down, I thought to myself. I could do this. I just had to visualize the pattern, get it fixed in my head. Handle hole, spout hole, base hole, lid hole, green wool for the leaf. This was not impossible. I had to smash the mental block. Get over myself.

"You may begin knitting . . . now!" Julie called. Everyone else sprang into action, needles clicking like a monkey on a typewriter. I didn't move.

I closed my eyes and tried to imagine against-the-odds success. Frank Lampard wandered through my consciousness. I moved him gently aside and replaced him with Mo Farah. Then I thought of the pattern. I didn't need to look at the sheet again. I had taken what I needed from it. I just had to knit it in my head first.

I cut everything out, the noise of the clicking needles, the more distant hubbub of the fair. I cut out the lights and the smell and focused on nothing but the pattern.

And slowly it came, weaving itself together. The tea cozy formed itself, spinning slowly, growing inside my mind. I could see the rows, the columns, the stitches. I could see where I needed to increase and where to decrease. I saw where I needed to change wool, where to add in the holes. I knew what yarn I needed, what needles. I had it. I had it!

I grabbed the needles and yarn, cast on and I was away, lost in my own world, content, sure of myself. Calm and relaxed for the first time in weeks.

That lasted about ten minutes, at which point I became aware of something in front of me and a rippling of laughter from the crowd. My concentration was broken immediately. I tutted and looked up to see a goat staring at me. I stared back, hypnotized. Then the goat trotted forward and began to eat my yarn.

"Get off," I yelled, kicking at it just as a security guard arrived and crash-tackled the beast. It went down with a thump and a truncated bleat.

"Sorry about that," Julie said, rushing up. "I'll get you some more yarn."

By the time she came back the tea cozy had disappeared from my mind. I risked a quick glance at Jeanette, who was still knitting as if nothing had happened, but did I notice a tiny smile on her angular features?

I sighed, closed my eyes again and tried to recapture the vision. It took longer to come this time. I was unsettled and angry. But come it did, and after a few minutes I was back into it. A deathly silence had fallen across the audience; they were engrossed in this, watching twenty-two people sitting in a circle, knitting.

Then someone's mobile phone went off. An N-Dubz song played at top volume.

I looked up in annoyance.

"Sorry!" the merino sheep called, fumbling with his phone.

Jeanette tutted.

"Please turn off your mobile phone," Julie shouted out.

"S'off, s'off now," Gex yelled back.

"Give me strength," I muttered.

Again I had to recapture the vision. I tried breathing exercises to calm myself and after a while found myself back in it, knitting furiously. After fifteen minutes I was going at a fair rate, and didn't think I'd made many mistakes so far. If only I could get through the next half hour uninterrupted, then maybe . . .

Crash!

We all leaped a mile as a partition wall fell inward, revealing the scaffolding that supported the grandstands. Also revealed were three figures who'd been crouching behind it. One of them was covered in green dye. The other contestants stared in alarm at the intrusion.

"Oh crap," I muttered, standing. "Not now."

"KNITTING TOSSER!" Manning's gang screeched in unison and rushed toward me. I heard a yelp of terror from Bush Baby and a gasp from Jeanette.

Time slowed. Julie stood watching, openmouthed, apparently at a loss for what to do. The security guard had disappeared, wrestling the goat back to its pen, no doubt. I stood alone as the gang rushed toward me, Lloyd's face turning with twisted malevolence.

I braced myself, ready to meet the charge, my sword an 8mm acrylic needle, my shield a half-finished tea cozy. There was no way I was backing down. It was time to face the bullies.

But the charge of the shit brigade never reached me, for over the sides of the Cauldron came the cavalry. Joz was there first, followed by Freddie, who'd apparently sprung from nowhere. Then finally came the merino, landing heavily and nearly tripping over his ill-fitting fleece. They came roaring, cheered on by the crowd, and Manning's gang stopped in surprise.

And so battle was joined. The details are hazy in my mind, but I remember Joz performing an extraordinary barrel roll to knock Jermaine's legs out from under him. Freddie grabbed the other one around the neck and hung on, being flipped from side to side like a puppy biting a walrus. Manning and Gex went mano a mano. Chief vs. Chief. It turned out neither of them was very good at fighting. Lots of slaps and face protection.

"Stop this, stop this!" Julie was yelling, to no effect. Bush Baby had disappeared.

"Where's security?" someone else called. I stood, clutching my knitting, wondering if I should get involved, but conscious there was a cameraman and a lady from the Home Office in the audience. Unfortunately, it looked like Manning's gang were getting the better of the good guys. Gex was by now on the ground, with Manning on top of him, banging his head into the Astroturf flooring. Freddie was walking unsteadily, dazed, having been thrown from the other one's shoulders. The other one was approaching him now to finish the job, growling. And Joz? Well, he hadn't actually recovered from the initial spectacular roll into Jermaine's legs. He was writhing on the floor, clutching his shoulder and looking pale.

Jermaine looked up at me and grinned. I was next, clearly. He took a couple of steps toward me.

But then there was the sound of someone clearing their throat behind me and Jermaine stopped, looking over my shoulder with an expression of horror. I turned, expecting to see the security guard had returned.

It wasn't security. It was someone better. Mrs. Frensham, in full warrior-queen mode, ready for battle. She walked over to the giant knitting display and seized her weapon, one of the eight-foot-high needles. Lifting her lance, she pointed it toward Jermaine and roared like St. George.

"You go, girl," Alana cried from the audience.

Jermaine's eyes bugged and his jaw dropped. Manning was still banging Gex's head on the Astroturf and hadn't registered this new development, or the fact that Mrs. Frensham had by now received backup. Joe stood beside her, and on her other side was Rob the bus driver, looking mean.

"It's the lollipop lady!" Jermaine cried, finding his voice, which sounded like an eight-year-old's. "It's Mrs. crapping Frensham!"

Manning looked up, alarmed. He got to his feet. Suddenly, his gang didn't look so hard. They huddled together in the center of the arena, like Christians surrounded by lions.

Then Mrs. Frensham charged.

Manning's gang stood for half a second, momentarily frozen in terror before they were able to get their legs moving. They turned and sprinted for the gap in the partition wall, Mrs. Frensham and her two brave knights following.

Once they'd gone, the Cauldron was suddenly quiet, as everyone tried to get their heads around what had just happened. Except it wasn't entirely quiet. To my left I could hear the unmistakable sound of needles clicking. I turned to see Angular Jeanette knitting away, as if nothing had happened. She glanced up at me and smirked as her eyes flicked over to the giant clock.

I knew she was low, but to do this? To take advantage of a pitch invasion to get an advantage over the rest of us? Katniss would never have done that. As the rest of the contestants realized what was going on, they too began to resume their knitting. Julie looked surprised at first, but then she called, "The clock is still running, please carry on."

I sat back in my seat heavily, closed my eyes and tried to revisualize.

FEBRUARY 24TH

Somehow I got through the first session. I completed more of the tea cozy than I expected to. But Jeanette finished hers completely. She rested it on her knee as she waited for it to be collected, displaying it so I could see. Showing off. I could see a couple of dropped stitches, but apart from that it looked amazing. I was still a dozen rows short, but the stranded colorwork was neater on mine, and I thought maybe my leaf was a little more lifelike than hers.

Either way, I was definitely behind the eight ball on this. Even at a distance I could see some of the others had made a much better job of things than I had.

During the break Mrs. Hooper came rushing up to me to see if I was okay.

"Not really," I said. "Mrs. Frensham was amazing, though."

"You're amazing, Ben," she replied, warming my cockles. "That's why you have such supportive friends."

I felt myself blushing and looked at my feet. "I'm sorry I couldn't win the trophy for them."

"It's not over yet," she said. "Your cozy was wonderful, so neat."

"I didn't finish it."

"That's not the only consideration," she said. "Anyway, there's another session yet. Have you decided what you're going to knit?"

"I think I'd better just play it safe," I said. "I can't afford any mistakes, and if my concentration is broken again . . ."

"Up to you," she said. "But you have a talent, Ben. Now's your chance to display it." She turned around and I saw that Megan stood behind her.

"I'll give you two a moment," Mrs. Hooper said, and walked away.

"Are you okay?" Megan asked.

"Well, let's see," I said. "My parents have abandoned me, the school is counting on me to pull off the impossible and win this final, as is the entire UK Probation Service. I haven't done any studying for three weeks, my life is in danger from Lloyd Manning and I have no idea what I'm going to knit in the next session."

I stopped talking then as Megan leaned close and kissed me.

She pulled back a little and looked me in the eye. "You can't worry about everything at once," she said.

"You sound like my mother," I told her.

"I hope I don't kiss you like your mother."

"No. It's different with her," I admitted.

"Stitch by stitch," she said. "You can't do everything at once."

"What should I do first?" I asked.

"Kiss me, obvs."

I did as she suggested, then pulled back and smiled at her. She smiled back.

"Stitch by stitch?" I said.

"Stitch by stitch," she repeated.

"Thanks," I said.

"Any time," she said. Then she was gone.

So as I reentered the Cauldron, this time to a huge round of applause, I still hadn't decided what to knit. The crowd seemed to have grown. Maybe word had got out that this was the place to come for that new extreme sport, Combat-knit. I scanned the crowd as I sat down, looking for my friends. I waved at Alana and Marie, who whooped loudly as though this were a college basketball game. I sat well away from Miss Angular this time.

And then I saw Dad. In the back row, watching me. He raised a hand. I waved back, smiling. He should be at the game. At Stamford Street, or wherever, watching Lampard score a hat trick. He'd given up the chance to see his beloved Chelsea for me. For this. I felt a huge surge of confidence. I felt I could do anything. If I was going to win this thing I needed to do something amazing.

And that's when I decided it was time to bring out Patt.r.n.

I knew I might not be able to get the whole thing completed. But if I used huge needles and made massive stitches

I could do a lot of it. I had another advantage too. There was someone modeling the Hoopie for me in the audience. My muse.

I grabbed the biggest needles they had, wooden ones, huge fat things, like candles. I selected the heaviest wool available, dark blue with hints of silver glitter, and decided to double it up. I could see Jeanette watching me curiously from across the circle.

I looked back at her, raised an eyebrow and curled my lip slightly. Like a more vulnerable and slightly built Clint Eastwood. She sneered right back.

"Ladies and gentleman," Julie called. "You may knit."

There were no more interruptions after that. Even Jeanette was playing fair from then on. We all put our heads down and got stuck in. I quickly entered the zone. I don't remember much about the next hour, but Joz filmed some of it on his camera phone and I watched it later, gobsmacked by how fast I was. I'd never watched myself knit before, of course. My face takes on this weird, trancelike look. Making me look a bit dopey, to be honest. But it's my hands that the eye is drawn to. So fast. I'm like a robot: under, lift, over, off, under, lift, over, off. I got through six balls of yarn during the hour-long session and successfully completed Patt.r.n. An entire hooded top in an hour. Admittedly, the stitches were huge, there were only thirty rows. But the hood is tricky, as is the neckline.

I could see the other contestants looking at it, astonished. Jeanette had made a cushion cover with a bow-and-arrow motif. It was good, but she'd only completed one side. And it was just a cushion cover.

Marian Joyce had done a baby's wooly hat. Pretty and complete it may have been, but it was just a hat. The Scottish girl, Kirsty Thingummy, had kept it really simple and done three squares of a patchwork quilt.

I was happy. I was sure the disaster over the tea cozy had taken me out of the contest, but I'd pulled off a real achievement. I looked up at my supporters in the crowd, who were all grinning and giving me the thumbs-up. I looked for Dad, who nodded at me, smiled and pointed toward the Cauldron entrance. I turned around and saw Mum standing there, waving at me. She was wearing full magician regalia, clearly not having waited to change on the way down.

All was right with the world.

7:22 p.m.

We had to clear out quickly to let them get prepared for the senior competition, which was due to start at eight. The results would be announced just before that. We went back to the café while we waited. I was ravenous and ate two sandwiches, a packet of crisps and a muffin. We took over about six tables, there were so many of us. Everyone kept clapping me on the back and congratulating me.

Joz was still looking pale. He was worried he'd broken his shoulder.

"You're a goddamn hero!" Gex told him.

"Shove off," Joz replied, looking green.

Mrs. Frensham told me they'd chased Manning's gang all the way down Kensington High Street, where they escaped by jumping on one of the new Boris Buses. They wouldn't be bothering us again tonight.

Soon it was time to go back for the results. We all crowded into the Cauldron, the contestants standing in the middle, surrounded by our supporters and knitfans. Julie stood on a chair.

"I have here the results from the judges," she cried, holding up an envelope, to raucous applause. "Firstly, can I just say how impressed we all were with the extremely high quality of the knitting here this evening. I think I can quite honestly say that the junior category has never before produced so many excellent contestants, including some who have only been knitting for a few months."

Someone slapped me on the shoulder at that point. I looked for Jeanette, but didn't see her.

"Now, we don't have much time," Julie said. "So I'll move on. The name of the third-placed contestant is . . ."

She held it for a few seconds and everyone went quiet, except for Gex, who was talking on his phone and ignoring everyone shushing him.

"Marian Joyce!" called Julie. There were cheers and a red-faced Marian was ushered up to the front to receive her prize.

"Marian wins a fifty-pound voucher from Royal Yarns, Kaffe Fassett's new book *Knit to Win* and a bottle of Veuve Clicquot champagne."

I felt a little bit of disappointment. I hadn't really expected I might win, but I thought third might be an outside possibility. There was no way I could have beaten Jeanette, and in Kirsty Whatsit there was at least one other contestant I was sure had out-knitted me.

"And now, the name of the contestant in second place," Julie went on, when Marian had disappeared back into the crowd. "Is . . ." Again there was a long pause. Surely it couldn't be . . .

"Ben Fletcher!"

I was properly amazed. I thought there must have been a mistake. I was swamped by my friends and family. They were all slapping me on the back. Natasha picked me up in a great bear hug and swung me around. I saw Megan eyeing her coolly.

"Brilliant, Ben!" I heard Dad cry from somewhere.

"Nice one!" Gex yelled, breaking off his phone call for a second.

"Though Ben's tea cozy was only ranked fourteenth out of twenty-two," Julie called over the din, "his extraordinary achievement in finishing an entire hooded top during the second session without dropping one stitch ensured he finished a strong second."

Someone pushed me up to the front, where I was handed a bag of goodies.

"Ben wins a hundred-pound voucher from Royal Yarns, a signed copy of Kaffe Fassett's book, a bottle of champagne and a meal for two at any Yolo Japanese restaurant."

There was another round of applause as I came back with my winnings. Mrs. Frensham ruffled my hair and Megan practically shoved Natasha over so she could kiss me on the cheek.

"Finally, the name you're all waiting for," Julie said. "The winner of the All-UK Knitting Championship junior category is . . ."

"Jeanette Fairbanks," I mouthed as the seconds ticked off.

"Jeanette Fairbanks!" Julie yelled.

"Boo," Megan murmured.

"Yes!" Jeanette screamed. She rushed up to the front and turned to look at me with an expression of such smugness I wanted to murder her. I had intended to congratulate her on her win. It had been fair and square after all, unlike the regional heats. But after that, I decided not to bother.

"Congratulations, Jeanette," Julie said. "Your tea cozy

was almost perfect, and your cushion cover both neat and attractive. The judges admired your classic technique and your refusal to allow distractions to get in your way."

She then handed Jeanette a trophy. "This will have your name inscribed on it. You also win a two-hundred-and-fifty-pound voucher from Royal Yarns, a signed copy of Kaffe Fassett's book, a bottle of champagne, and perhaps best of all, two all-inclusive tickets to the New York Knit Fair, including air fares, hotel accommodation and spending money."

Not bad, I thought. Maybe next year that could be me.

And then something odd happened. Julie's wide-eyed assistant came running up and tugged on her trousers. Julie bent down so Bush Baby could whisper in her ear.

"You were fantastic, son," Dad said, elbowing his way through the crowd to chuck me on the shoulder.

"Thanks, Dad," I replied. "Sorry you had to miss your game."

"Oh, don't worry about it," he said. "They were probably going to lose anyway."

"It's nice to see you," I said. I could see Mum waiting behind him, still wearing her top hat.

"Yeah, well, sorry about running off like that," he said. "Shouldn't have done it. . . ."

But our reunion was cut short at that point.

"Ladies and gentlemen," Julie shouted out. "Ladies and gentlemen, if I could have your attention, please." Some people had started to leave, but stopped to listen.

She went on. "I'm afraid to say there's an irregularity in the results. It turns out that our winner, Jeanette Fairbanks, actually registered twice for the regional heats. Once for Hampshire, and then again for Surrey."

I subtly scanned the crowd, looking for my adversary, but she was nowhere to be seen. Had she run off already, clutching her trophy?

"Though I'm sure this was just an oversight on Ms. Fairbanks's part," Julie went on, "rules are rules, and this does, unfortunately, mean she has been disqualified. Therefore, the winner of the All-UK Knitting Championship junior category . . . is Ben Fletcher."

There was a stunned silence for half a second, then the place just went mental. Whether it was because my posse was so big, or because of the dramatic circumstances, or maybe because the entire crowd had taken a dislike to Jeanette, I don't know, but it seemed the whole world was there screaming and cheering. Gex and Freddie lifted me up onto their shoulders, Mrs. Frensham was waving her giant knitting needle around dangerously, Dad hugged Mum, Mum kissed Dad. Joz kissed Amelia, Natasha kissed Freddie. Gex ended his phone conversation. The lady from the Home Office grinned in delight while the cameraman filmed everything. I saw neat Mr. Hollis hugging Mrs. Tyler at the back. Megan leaped up and down, grinning ear to ear and clapping her hands together.

Even Julie looked pleased, though Bush Baby had disappeared again, perhaps terrified by the noise.

Someone must have wrestled the trophy back off Jeanette, because it was thrust into my hands. I lifted it high, and it glinted in the overhead lights.

I'd won.

FEBRUARY 25TH

I'm at Mrs. Frensham's. It's raining again and she's gone to make a fresh pot of tea.

Must finish writing the account of the final. I suppose there's not that much more to tell. We all decided to get back to Hampton and have a late pizza together. Most of us managed to squeeze onto the minibus, though not Mum and Dad, who came back in Mum's car. It turned out Dad hadn't been able to find anywhere to park the camper van, so he had just left it out at the front of the venue. It got clamped. Poor old Dad, he didn't have the most comfortable of journeys home apparently, squashed between the swords and the cage with the surviving dove, which kept pecking him. Mrs. Hooper drove her own car back with Mrs. Tyler and Mr. Hollis.

Joz was still in pain, but Amelia sat with him and plied him with some strong painkillers she happened to have. He began to feel better once we were on the highway and they snogged the rest of the way back.

As the bus pulled out of the parking lot onto the main road, I saw, through the window, Jeanette Fairbanks standing by a bus stop, looking absolutely furious. I'm not proud of myself for this, but I couldn't resist sticking my head out of the window.

"I'M KATNISSSSSS!" I screamed at her as we shot by. She looked up in confusion, then flipped me the bird when she realized who it was.

I sat back down next to Megan, grinning, and felt my phone buzz. A text from Mum.

Just heard on the radio that Chelsea won a nail-biter. Lampard scored the winner. Your dad's being philosophical about it.

Good old Lampard. The one time I didn't want him to score.

"How did you do it?" Megan asked. "You managed your distractions. It was chaos in there."

"Sometimes chaos is okay," I replied. "Sometimes, to make something beautiful you need a little disorder. You can't always control everything, sometimes you need to let things flap free."

"It's not just knitting you're talking about, is it?" Megan said.

"No," I replied. "You were right in there. I can't hold everything in my head all at the same time. Sometimes I just need to concentrate on one thing at a time. Mum said the same thing."

"Exactly," she said. "This is how normal people think."

"It's like a patchwork quilt," I said. "You don't do it all at once. You can only work on one square at a time. At the end you sew them all together to finish the piece."

"I'm not sure why everything has to have a knitting analogy," she said. "But yes, you're right."

I sighed and looked out of the window at Londoners going about their chaotic business. A whole world was out there that I couldn't control. And that was okay, as long as my little bit of it was fine. And it was, just for the moment.

"So what now?" Megan asked.

"Pizza," I said after a pause. "Let's just have pizza for now. We'll take care of everything else tomorrow."

MARCH 1ST

Just putting the finishing touches to Megan's birthday present. She's invited me around to her house for dinner. Her parents are going out and she's cooking for me.

I would have liked to have bought her something, but I'm a bit strapped at the moment. I've had a pile of orders for the Hoopie via Etsy, thanks to Miss Swallow modeling it for me and managing to look sweet and sexy at the same time. My site got hundreds of hits after I put that up. I have a sneaking suspicion a fair number of them might have been boys at my school but clearly not all since I got so many orders. I bought loads of wool using the voucher; just enough, I think. I calculate I stand to make nearly a thousand pounds though if I manage to fulfill all the orders, so it's just a temporary cash-flow problem.

So in the meantime, Megan had to put up with a sweater, using the wool she'd bought me for Christmas and inspired by the Ocean Spray, in dark blue. I was going to make her a Hoopie, but I thought it might seem weird if she had the same top as Miss Swallow.

Oh, nearly forgot. Neat Mr. Hollis, the man from Virilia, sent me an email today.

Dear Ben,
Congratulations on your triumph at the AUKKC-JC! It was a remarkable day and the goat bite is healing nicely. I just wanted to give you advance "warning" that you've been shortlisted for the Virilia Young Entrepreneur of the Year Award. Congratulations on that too. I'll be in contact soon with details of the awards ceremony but just wanted to

check in now and make sure you are willing to accept the nomination, so could you please confirm by return?

Finally, regardless of that, we'd be interested in meeting with you here at the Virilia head office to discuss your business going forward. I meant what I said when I told you Virilia invests in people, and in you we can see some exciting opportunities.

Best wishes,

Mark Hollis

Head of Investment, Virilia

Oh crapping hell. I'm supposed to be taking AS levels this year. And I have six Hoopies to knit, not to mention five outstanding vest orders. Then there's keeping Gex, Joz and Freddie out of trouble, and soccer to watch with Dad. And the last fifteen pages of *Fifty Shades of Graham* to edit.

Bright side. I don't need to finish that bloody ziggurat. And I've got Megan. Most importantly, I've got Megan.

I'll tackle the rest later.

One stitch at a time.